Praise

ADMIRAL

D0401197

"A fast-paced and engaging intrigue with characters the reader will be attached to and root for despite their flaws and faults. . . . *The Martian* meets *The Bourne Identity* by way of *Alien*."   —Marko Kloos, author of *Chains of Command*

"This story reminded me of a cross between the action-filled suspense of *The Martian* and the tricky mental maneuverings of *The Stainless Steel Rat*. *Admiral* is a satisfying military adventure filled with plenty of science fiction mystery wrapped in layers of caper-style suspense . . . and if it was food, I'd be demanding seconds."
> —Jean Johnson, national bestselling author of
> the First Salik War series

"A seductive mix of mystery and action! A riveting space mystery. Pure entertainment!"
> —William C. Dietz, national bestselling author of
> the Legion of the Damned novels

"A wild, page-turning ride through a locked-room mystery on a wrecked starship where nothing and no one is what it seems. I can't wait to see what this great bunch of characters does next."   —Mike Shepherd, author of *Kris Longknife: Bold*

"*Admiral* could be the most entertaining military science fiction novel I read all year. . . . Delivering an enticing combination of mystery and suspense, Sean Danker's debut is an intensely action-packed and fast-paced survival adventure that's sure to appeal to both sci-fi veterans and newcomers to the genre alike."   —The BiblioSanctum

continued . . .

OTHER NOVELS BY SEAN DANKER

Admiral

FREE SPACE

AN ADMIRAL NOVEL

SEAN DANKER

ACE
NEW YORK

ACE
Published by Berkley
An imprint of Penguin Random House LLC
375 Hudson Street, New York, New York 10014

Copyright © 2017 by Sean Danker-Smith
Penguin Random House supports copyright. Copyright fuels creativity,
encourages diverse voices, promotes free speech, and creates a vibrant culture.
Thank you for buying an authorized edition of this book and for complying
with copyright laws by not reproducing, scanning, or distributing any part of
it in any form without permission. You are supporting writers and allowing
Penguin Random House to continue to publish books for every reader.

ACE is a registered trademark and the A colophon is a trademark of
Penguin Random House LLC.

Library of Congress Cataloging-in-Publication Data

Names: Danker, Sean, author.
Title: Free space: an Admiral novel/Sean Danker.
Description: First Edition. | New York: Ace, 2017.
Identifiers: LCCN 2016038201 (print) | LCCN 2016043700 (ebook) |
ISBN 9780451475800 (paperback) | ISBN 9780698197268 (ebook)
Subjects: LCSH: Space warfare—Fiction. | BISAC: FICTION/Science Fiction/
Military. | FICTION/Science Fiction/Adventure. | FICTION/
Science Fiction/Space Opera. | GSAFD: Science fiction
Classification: LCC PS3604.A537 F74 2017 (print) |
LCC PS3604.A537 (ebook) | DDC 813/.6—dc23
LC record available at https://lccn.loc.gov/2016038201

First Edition: May 2017

Printed in the United States of America
1   3   5   7   9   10   8   6   4   2

Cover photo of figure © Collaboration JS / Arcangel Images; background
images courtesy of Shutterstock Images
Cover design by Adam Auerbach
Book design by Kelly Lipovich

FOR THE COPY EDITORS OF THE WORLD

FREE SPACE

PROLOGUE

I'VE made a lot of mistakes.

"Is everything all right?"

"I'm having trouble with the clasp," I replied, fumbling with it.

"They're tricky. Would you like help?"

"Please," I said.

The hostess slipped into the dressing booth. She deftly helped me fasten my cuffs.

I pushed the curtain aside and stepped into the open.

It was quiet, and there wasn't anyone else shopping. All the movement in the boutique came from holographic displays and animated mannequins. The smell of flowers and perfume was a little much, and it was starting to get to me.

I gazed at the entrance for a moment, then turned back to the hostess and spread my arms.

She patted me down and checked my tunic's fastenings. She

walked a circle around me, arms folded, one finger resting on her chin. She stopped and looked me up and down.

"I'm going to recommend some alterations," she said. "You have such a good waistline, so we should tweak the hem so it has a bit more flare, and I want to go a little more snug on the trousers, show off your legs a bit. Another possibility with your physique would be to add an extra taper here"—she touched my shoulder—"to emphasize the shape." She moved her hands in the shape of a V.

"Will it take long?"

"Thirty seconds."

"Be my guest."

She snapped her fingers and an android stepped forward.

"Please hold still, sir."

I obediently put my arms out and held the pose. It took only moments for the android to tailor the outfit I was wearing under the hostess' direction. He finished with the trousers and removed his hands from my calves. His sewing tools folded back into his palms, and the hostess took his place in front of me.

"I'll remind you that it's not in vogue to go monochrome with this cut," she said. It was about the fourth time she'd reminded me. "Particularly not in black. Has someone died?"

"Not yet," I replied.

"It's also not traditional to wear gloves with this ensemble," she said.

I turned to look at myself in the display. This was something I hadn't seen for a very long time.

"What's the matter?" the hostess asked.

"In the Empire they issue you a set of formal wear when you graduate from compulsory schooling. Those outfits look a little like this. Not the color, just the style. They're called blanks."

"Blanks?" The hostess looked puzzled.

"Because they're very plain. Always gray or blue. I remember when I got fitted for mine." I adjusted my collar, watching the display closely. "I was with a friend. He didn't like the idea of blanks much. He didn't even want to take them."

"Why not?"

"He thought they were patronizing. A sort of handout. It was a pride thing."

The hostess shrugged. "It was my understanding that a lot of Evagardian life is subsidized by the Imperium."

"It is. I never said my friend was rational."

"It suits you, sir. Actually, you look a little familiar. I think you have a bit of a resemblance to Prince Dalton." I checked myself one last time in the display. The robotic tailor had vanished, but the android lingering near the exit was still there. I smiled at the hostess.

"I get that a lot," I said.

The android bumped into me as I left the boutique. I ignored it and kept walking.

I hadn't felt the puncture. No tickle, no itch. No touch, really. I felt nothing. No, that wasn't true—I did feel a little insulted.

I wasn't in the station's main gallery; this was just a wide hallway, lined with shops and businesses offering minor conveniences for travelers. The lights were bright. Underfoot, I saw myself reflected as nothing but a vague black shape in the polished marble—but that wasn't right. My vision had blurred.

I hadn't felt the puncture, but I knew it was there. And even if I hadn't noticed the delivery, I could feel the poison in my bloodstream. It was acting fast. There was a subtle wrongness—about what I'd expected. I took out a physical holo and touched the screen, bringing up my contact list. There was only one entry. I touched it, sending a prepared message.

I tried not to give myself away by speeding up, but it was hard not to feel a certain sense of urgency. Evagardian poison wouldn't take long to kill me; this wasn't the time to drag my feet.

There was a flight schedule on the wall nearby. I had a shuttle to catch, but death wouldn't wait.

My heart gave a twitch that was difficult to ignore. To make matters worse, a Prince Dalton song was playing over the station's audio feed. A real Dalton song, not one of mine. In fact, it was one of the last ones the real prince had written and performed before I killed him.

I stumbled and caught myself, making my way to a bench and collapsing onto it.

People were looking at me curiously as they passed. Maybe it was my behavior. Maybe it was my outfit. The sounds of the tunnel came and went.

I listened to Prince Dalton singing about broken hearts.

A second twitch. I silently chided my heart. It had never gotten what it wanted before; why would things be different now? At the very least my heart could take this like a man and not be a whiner. Did it hear *me* complaining, after all? No. Death was just a part of life. Plenty of people had done it before, including me. It was an inevitability.

Now, later, or probably both.

But it wouldn't do to let it happen here. Not where people could see.

I forced myself to my feet, faltering. For most of my life I'd taken good health for granted. That was an easy trap to fall into, particularly on Evagardian worlds. Withdrawal and poison had taught me the truth: if you haven't got your health, you haven't got anything.

The holo in my wrist sensed my condition and asked if I wanted to signal for medical attention. I ignored it. There was an emergency station ahead, but that wasn't where I was going.

I staggered to the side of the tunnel, and several people had to dodge me. I wasn't at my most considerate.

I hit the wall and leaned against a feed advertising holo software promising to streamline day-to-day life for the busy galactic. Ahead was a hologram indicating the presence of a restroom. It wasn't ideal, but privacy was privacy. I staggered to it and got inside, falling on the taps and wondering if my heart was going to literally explode. That was the sort of thing that sounded terribly romantic, but in practice it would just be messy. There were a lot of things in my life like that.

I would have liked to get a little cold water and throw it on my face, which was very hot, but I didn't get the chance.

I tried to look at my chrono. Death notwithstanding, I had an appointment to keep.

I

THE shuttle rocked gently, and I reached up for a safety handle. The carpet was blue; the seats were blue. Even the viewports were tinted blue. Like, if you didn't have the color blue burned into your retinas, you might fly with another service next time. Galactic branding sensibilities. Subtlety was an alien concept to these people. Primitive, really.

A serving android was making her way down the aisle, a tray of glasses in her hands. I stepped aside to let her pass, and moved up to take the seat beside Salmagard.

From the way she looked up so quickly, it was clear she was full of nerves. The smile she offered was a reflexive one, one she'd used a million times before. There was nothing real about it.

After that automatic smile, she looked back down at her hands in her lap for a moment, then slowly looked up at me a second time. I didn't look *that* different. If she hadn't recognized me, she was even more preoccupied than she looked.

"It's me," I said, settling in. The last time I'd seen Tessa Salmagard, she'd been dead and I'd been trying to get her body into stasis so she could be revived. That had been almost three weeks ago. A part of me expected her to be different here in civilization—and she was. Back on that planet, with things like oxygen and hostile xenos to think about, Salmagard had had use only for the soldierly parts of herself.

In a place like this, there was no need for any of that.

"You're different." Her voice was just as musical as I remembered.

"This is closer to my real face. I still look a lot like him, though, don't I?"

She nodded.

I sighed. "But at least we're not perfect twins anymore. I didn't think you'd show." It was risky for her to meet me, after all.

"You saved my life." She said it as if it was obvious. Like the risk meant nothing.

Maybe it didn't. Salmagard was nothing if not bold. In part because she was an aristocrat and had been brought up to look down on everyone and everything to include danger—all in the interests of her bloodline. And in part because of her military training, which had taught her essentially the same things, except, rather than her own line, the Service compelled her to bring glory to the Empress.

She didn't see danger the way most people did. For many in the gentry, danger and risk were things that happened to other people. Salmagard had actually been killed in action—so she knew better. Maybe that was what had emboldened her. She'd already died, so what was the worst that could happen? Dying again? That wasn't likely. Meeting me was dangerous to her career, not to her physical safety.

Maybe that was her thinking. Such was the life of an aristocrat.

"Don't tell me you're here out of obligation," I said.

Salmagard shook her head. Did she mean it? I'd never know. It was obvious that she hadn't been sure I'd actually show up. That didn't particularly hurt my feelings. She didn't seem disappointed I was there, though. That was a good sign.

She was wearing an extremely becoming red dress in an Isakan cut, with a beautiful sash. Her dark hair was especially elaborate, with lots of jeweled clips. She'd clearly gone to some effort. I was flattered. Of course, I'd gotten all dolled up too— but my new black outfit was already a bit rumpled. That was a pity; I'd bought it only an hour ago.

"How, though?" she asked. "How is this safe?"

"It's not." I shrugged. "But it's doable because there's some bad news," I told her. "The threat level's up. There's not as much Imperial Security presence out here, and I'm not at the top of their list anymore. 'Safe' isn't the word I'd use, but I'm not hung up on details."

"What's going on?"

"Apparently there's credible intelligence that New Unity's up to something. Imperial Security and Evagardian Intelligence are extra twitchy with the peace talks so close. All the imperial agents in Free Trade space are on alert status—they think something's going to happen. So the people that might be on the lookout for me— Well, they're not looking for me at the moment."

Salmagard didn't look surprised. The war wasn't really over; there was only a cease-fire—and it was tenuous. The Empress wanted real peace, and Salmagard knew what every Evagardian was brought up to know: if the Empress wanted something, New Unity wanted the opposite.

It stood to reason that Evagardian forces would be more interested in preventing terrorist attacks than hunting for me.

But I didn't want to talk about terrorists, and I especially didn't want to talk about New Unity.

"Lucky timing, I guess," I said.

"What about automated security?" She meant facial recognition and DNA scans.

"That won't work on me anymore," I said. "My face is different enough not to trip any searches looking for Dalton. And there aren't any records left. Of who I used to be."

"You have a fake ID?" She said it very quietly, looking around as if someone might hear. I was taken aback, but it was no surprise she'd find that scandalous. In Salmagard's world—at least before she'd joined the Service—lawbreaking had probably been an alien concept to her.

But there were dampeners around our seats to give us privacy, and the other passengers on the shuttle had their own lives to live. A few were talking; most were absorbed in their holos. One woman I'd seen had actually put on a VR collar and completely checked out for the flight.

"I can't walk into the Evagardian consulate, but I can walk around a Free Trade station. I'd have to change my DNA if I wanted to take a trip to imperial space, though."

"Then you're free," she said, gazing up at me.

"I could move around before, just not in the most comfortable ways," I told her. The serving android came by, and I accepted a small cup of tea. "So what have I missed?"

"Lieutenant Deilani's been reassigned."

I recalled the tall physician. I'd met Deilani when I'd met Salmagard, and she'd been instrumental in our escape from

Nidaros. Normally I liked to travel, but that was a planet I didn't feel a powerful desire to visit again.

Salmagard had recognized me as Prince Dalton right off. Deilani hadn't.

"What'd she get?" I put the cup aside and gave Salmagard my full attention. The shuttle's overhead chime sounded and the vessel shuddered again—but only for a moment. Perfectly normal, but it got my attention every time.

"Demenis Affairs," she said, troubled. "I don't know the details. Something must have happened. I saw her before I came here, but it seemed like she couldn't talk about it."

I winced. "That's probably my fault," I said. "Well, no. It's her fault. But it's because of me."

"What happened?"

"She confronted me on Payne Station right after we got off Nidaros. It was in a public space, so while there probably wasn't audio, it's on the record that she saw me. She didn't try to stop me, and that probably put her under suspicion. Remember, everyone that matters thinks I'm one of the bad guys—so being seen with me isn't a good career move. It's not too late to back out," I added.

Salmagard shook her head. If she'd taken the plunge to come this far, she wouldn't break it off now. And she wouldn't be turned from the topic at hand. "Why the reassignment, though? Why not investigate her? Clear her?"

What was this? Was Salmagard concerned for Deilani? Of course she was. That was how she'd died, after all—buying time for the lieutenant. That was her duty, I supposed, but still. Deilani had been awfully abrasive during that crisis, but Salmagard had no trouble looking past that. She had a big heart.

"I'm sure they're investigating her. But she doesn't know anything. She'll be all right."

"She wasn't happy. At least, not when they reassigned her. When I saw her just a little while ago, I don't know. She seemed different."

"It was vain of her to come out and gloat at me," I said. "I'll take my share of the guilt. She gets the rest. She's not stupid. She knew that wasn't a brilliant thing to do."

Salmagard smiled slightly. "That does sound like her." She really was worried.

"What about Nils? How's he doing?"

The ensign had been almost as bad off as Salmagard by the time we got off Nidaros. I'd been about done in by my withdrawal by that point; Deilani had been the only one of us still on her feet.

"He's almost out of treatment. He's on Mikkelgard. A university hospital in the provincial capital. I can't pronounce it."

"Sounds fancy. I hope he gets out soon."

Salmagard nodded. My chrono chirped. Grimacing, I took a hypo from my jacket and injected. Salmagard watched, but didn't say anything. Obviously someone like her could never let anything as vulgar as judgment or disdain show on her face.

I hesitated, then held up the empty hypo. "It's an antidote. Look for yourself."

"To what?"

"I'm told it's called Cleyane Strychnine."

"What is it?"

"Some kind of poison."

Her eyes widened.

I put the hypo away. "Don't look at me like that. This is part of the reason I can move around freely. I let EI get me."

It had actually taken Evagardian Intelligence a little longer than expected to catch up to me.

"And they poisoned you?"

"Actually, they had an android do it remotely, kind of sloppy, but they didn't actually have any people on-site, so they didn't have a lot of options. If I pop up, they pretty much have to go at me with whatever they've got." I shrugged. "I had to let my vitals go so they'd be absolutely sure I was dead. They have to confirm these things. I had a guy on tap to revive me. You can buy anything out here. It went pretty smoothly, I think. Since I'm here." I worked my neck and shoulders. "Now I know how it feels. I guess you do too."

She swallowed, then leaned back in her seat. "What if they'd shot you instead of poisoning you?"

"I like to think I know what to expect from these guys. Now they'll think I'm out of the picture for a little while."

"Why didn't you tell me straightaway?"

"I didn't think the negotiator in you would approve." Salmagard was a security specialist. Protecting things was her particular area of expertise, so a plan allowing myself to be killed probably wouldn't strike her as ideal. It was deeply contrary to the worldview the Service had worked hard to indoctrinate her with.

She licked her lips. "It's bold."

"That's who you're spending your leave with," I said.

"It's mandatory downtime. I've only just finished my evaluation for Nidaros."

"Really? It took this long?" I arched an eyebrow.

"I died."

"I guess they take that pretty seriously. I take it you're coming through it all right."

"More or less. You?"

I waved a hand. "I've had worse."

There was a pause. She stared up at me. I kept my eyes on her, though it was making her uncomfortable. She fidgeted a little, looking expectant. "Where are we going?" she asked finally.

"Why are you asking me? You're in charge. I'm just a poor kid from Cohengard that you picked up on Nidaros. Because you're a fan of Prince Dalton and I happen to look like him, I assume."

She smiled. "Is that the story?"

"How else could anyone read it?" I leaned back. "We're on the way to Imperial Pointe, so I was thinking Red Yonder. But you're leading. I wouldn't dream of going against the proper way of things. That would be un-Evagardian."

It wasn't even a flicker. There was surprise on her face—I *thought* I'd seen it—but it was gone so quickly that I couldn't be sure.

"I think I've heard of that," she said slowly.

"I went there a few times as Dalton. It's a good time." I couldn't help but notice the way she was staring at me. "What? I had to. It was expected of me."

"Not that. I suppose I shouldn't be surprised. If there's one thing you've got, it's nerve." There was a slight coolness there. I actually preferred this side of her, but I hadn't expected to see it here and now. What had I done wrong?

"Thanks, I think. Wait," I said, narrowing my eyes. "You— you're—I bet you've heard all the wrong things about Red Yonder. There's a little more to it than what you're thinking about. Yes, there *is* that, but there's a lot more."

"I've heard about the tower."

Of course she had. There was nothing imperials loved more than to be appalled by the perceived depravity of galactics. Naturally, when Evagardians heard about Red Yonder, the part they'd remember would be the tower, notorious for its attractions for couples that were, admittedly, a bit over-the-top, but all in good fun.

I hadn't actually been planning to take Salmagard *there*.

I swallowed. "Like I said—there *is* that. There's also more."

She wasn't buying it, though what I was saying was absolutely true.

"We can go somewhere else."

"No." Her face had become that placid mask again. "Let's go to Red Yonder."

I watched her turn to look out the viewport. I'd already known about Tessa Salmagard's poise and courage; she had plenty of that.

But when we'd met on Nidaros, I hadn't really gotten to see her pride.

"You're sure?" I asked with a straight face.

"Oh, yes," she replied. "You certainly bring more surprises to the table than my other suitors," she murmured.

"You have other suitors?"

Being asked about it directly seemed to take her aback. She cleared her throat. "Well, yes."

"I mean—on the *Julian*, obviously you do. Do you guys cruise with implants on?"

"Always."

I winced. Being in the Service was already a cloyingly structured environment. Having to deal with that environment while having one's hormones and reproductive urges suppressed—to me, that just sounded cruel.

"Oh. Where's the fun in that?"

"That's the actual Service," she said, a bit sternly.

"I wouldn't know anything about that. But spies are people too; we just don't have any of those rules. So if there's no fun allowed on the ship, where are the suitors coming from?"

She sighed. "It's an issue now because, technically, I've been in action. My family's trying to make the most of it."

"Does that increase your value?"

"Considerably."

"So the fact that you're in the Service *and* you've seen action gives you the edge over the first daughter from the next district, because she's just spending her time looking gorgeous."

Salmagard nodded slowly. "There's a bit more to it," she said.

"I'm sure. Do your suitors know about me? Because I am, technically, an assassin. What if I don't like competition?"

She covered her mouth, then rolled her eyes. "I've gotten quite a few applications since my revival."

"They have to apply to marry you?" These things differed from province to province, planet to planet. No one could know *all* the customs, and I was curious. "I thought you had to be the one to propose to them."

"I do. But they have to petition my family to get invited to functions where they would have the opportunity to meet me," she said, clearly finding it all distasteful. "There are traditionally some gifts involved."

"So they buy their way into these parties. Then they have to find a way to get you interested. Then you go after them."

"That's succinct. More or less. Yes."

"You know, normal Evagardian women have the opposite

problem. They have to do all the work. You've got them lining up."

"Yes," Salmagard said bitterly.

"Anyone good?"

She gave me an odd look, as though trying to determine if I was joking.

"Some new prospects are potentially more advantageous than my previous outlook," she said slowly, choosing her words carefully. "So you might say that my experiences on Nidaros are proving beneficial to me in that sense. But as I've told you before, I've never been disposed to those sensibilities."

"I don't think you put it quite that way," I said.

"It's so strange to be sitting here talking to you," she said.

"Why? My fifteen minutes are up. You'll never see me onstage again. I'm just another terrorist now." That wasn't what she meant, of course.

"It all happened so quickly," she said, staring up at me. "Less than a day. The memories don't feel real. But you're really here."

"You *are* a Dalton fan. I knew it."

Salmagard went a bit stiff.

On Nidaros there had been too much going on, too much uncertainty—but here there was no mistaking the way she was looking at me. She wasn't just surprised to be seeing me, that man she'd met on Nidaros, again; she was coming to grips with sitting next to a galactic celebrity.

Did she really think she could hide it from me? Or did she want to keep it a secret on principle? Was it supposed to be beneath her to like a galactic entertainer? Not ordinarily, but during wartime, perhaps. And Evagard had recently been at war with the Ganraen Commonwealth, so for the daughter of a family with a tiered bloodline to openly enjoy the music of a Ganraen prince—that might be unfashionable.

"Yes," she replied.

I wasn't going to press her on it. Better to let it go and change the subject, but I wondered if the detail that she was a fan of Dalton's had influenced her decision to defend me from Deilani on Nidaros. At the time she'd thought I was really him; she hadn't known I was a double.

I smiled. "Where are you from exactly? You're making me curious when you talk about these suitors. I remember you're from Old Earth."

She gave me a look. "My family's land is in Morocco. A place called Casablanca."

"Where's that?"

"Africa."

"So you're ninth tier, first daughter—is that land considered desirable?"

"Very, actually. No estate, though."

"So are these guys serious about marrying you, or are they just networking?"

There had been a time when I'd wished I could be like Salmagard—to come from that kind of family. Many years ago.

"Some of each. The more prestigious ones just want to establish the connection." Salmagard was being modest. Or was she? To the boys from her circles, was she anything special?

"Have they seen your picture?" I asked.

She cocked her head. "Of course. The data-gathering services would provide that as a matter of course."

"Can't hurt."

She gave me a stern look, then turned to look out the window. I picked up my tea and took a sip. I'd gotten glimpses of her bashful side on Nidaros. It wasn't my favorite side of her, but I didn't mind it.

"How long before your mother passes the bloodline to you?"

"Traditionally after the birth of my first child. But I may not be getting it."

"Why?"

"My sister could be the better choice. I've said and done things that have probably jeopardized my candidacy."

"Such as?"

"Such as choosing to be here, rather than going home to meet these suitors and remind everyone how committed I am to the responsibilities of taking the Salmagard name into the next tier."

I drew back a little. Salmagard spoke softly, as always, but for a moment her voice had gotten terribly cold. No one could hear us, but I wondered if the other passengers hadn't felt a little chill there.

"The last time we talked you weren't quite this militant," I said.

"That was before I saw the *Julian* from the inside."

"Not impressed by the best of the best?"

She shrugged. "I can manage it at home, but if I do become mistress of the bloodline—if I *do* elevate it—all of this is only going to get worse."

Her calm demeanor was so convincing that, until that moment, I hadn't seen how conflicted she was. It looked like I'd reached out to her at a troubled time. I wondered if that had anything to do with why she was doing something as foolish as accepting my invitation.

Salmagard was wrestling with a serious personal crisis. It wasn't my place to weigh in on something like that. Whether she chose to follow her family's path or strike out on her own—that was up to her.

But I could take her mind off things for a little while. Perhaps that was what she really needed.

"You're out here on your first tour. Your folks have to expect you to want to have some fun."

"Some fun," she repeated. "That's a bit vague. Yes, to a degree—perhaps. But they know I'm leaving Evagardian space." She patted her armrest. "What does that look like?"

"Perfectly ordinary curiosity? Or a sheltered girl running wild for irresponsible excess and debauchery?"

She glanced at me, then went back to looking out the window. "That *is* how they'll see it."

"Sorry. I didn't realize it was quite that serious."

"They won't pass me over for just this."

"You sure you aren't *trying* to get your responsibilities pushed on your sister?"

It took most of the shuttle ride for me to understand that Salmagard was desperately using anything and everything she could think of to hide her nerves. She was daring enough to agree to Red Yonder, and probably to see it through—but just because she was agreeing to everything didn't mean she wasn't feeling anxiety about it.

I'd assumed she was nervous about leaving imperial space, or doing so with someone in my complicated situation, but maybe it was something a little simpler. Maybe she was just shy about being alone with me. After all, we weren't in any danger this time.

It was just us.

Dealing with a crisis came easily to her because she had the best training and good genes, but was she equally well prepared for a romantic getaway? There was more than one kind of self-confidence, after all.

I was just speculating. She wasn't an easy read, and, all told, we'd known each other less than a day.

Imperial Pointe was the first destination in the Free Trade sector that could be reached easily from the Tressgard system, where Salmagard had disembarked from the *Julian* for her leave. In terms of distance, we were actually traveling a very long way, but the jump route from Tressgard to Free Trade space was so narrow that only special shuttles could make the trip in good time. Any larger ships had to take another route or fly the old-fashioned way, with passengers in sleepers for the three-week journey.

Our flight lasted a little over an hour.

Salmagard and I emerged into the Free Trade Tourism Guild's spacious lobby. The only times I'd ever been to Imperial Pointe had been as Dalton, to visit Red Yonder—one of the late Ganraen prince's favorite destinations.

By Free Trade standards, Imperial Pointe was not a large station, but it was still crowded. There were four or five million permanent residents, and another million people passing through at any given time. Its main claim to fame was that it housed one of the larger imperial immigration offices, and was the primary jump point for people who wanted to get from Free Trade space into Evagardian systems quickly. On top of the tourists, there were a lot of wealthy galactic professionals with fresh visas, anxious to charter jump shuttles to imperial destinations.

The public areas were spacious, vividly decorated, and generally festive. There were plenty of people around, though Imperial Pointe had not yet reached the level of occupancy that made it feel choked—though it would soon, now that hostilities had ceased, and galactic commerce was quickly getting back to normal.

I watched Salmagard as she strolled beside me. I should've been on the lookout for imperials, but she was more important at the moment. It was immediately clear to me that she didn't have a lot of experience with large stations, which made sense. Obviously her ardently proper family wouldn't want her in this kind of environment, and she'd spent most of the time between Nidaros and this moment in medical treatment, or aboard the *Julian*.

Maybe she hadn't gotten much shore leave, if any. Maybe, apart from whatever stops she made in assignment travel, this was her first time on a galactic station.

She had her calm face on, but she was looking around with interest, and not hiding it as well as she wanted to.

Imperial Pointe was a clean, and in my opinion relatively classy, example of the Free Trade business model. All the same, there were people and things on display that Salmagard wasn't used to.

Things you probably didn't see often on Old Earth. Exotic fashion sense. Personal aesthetic choices that defied imperial ideals. Loud music, bright lights. There was no aura of institutionalized sensibilities. That was something only found in imperial space. It was uniquely Evagardian.

On Free Trade stations, decorations tended to be digital and holographic. Projected light was easier to work with and more flexible than a physical object. On Old Earth, decorations were overwhelmingly physical. That wasn't very practical, but the Old Earth fixation on the memories and ways of the Earth before the Unification had never struck me as being very practical in general.

The Empire was diverse; depending on which city in which province under which Tetrad on which continent on which planet of which imperial system you were dealing with, there was no telling what kinds of culture and values you'd have on your hands. The general precepts of the Grand Duchess' ideology and imperial law would always be there, but Evagardian culture left plenty of room for local improvisation.

I'd never heard of this Morocco place, Salmagard's homeland, but the way she was reacting to the station inclined me to think the people there tended toward the more conservative, stodgy end of the spectrum.

I knew I had a rose-tinted view of aristocratic life, but I couldn't help it. It was because of those aspirations that I'd done what I had.

It just hadn't worked out.

Salmagard would've been content to wander the station all night. She was completely distracted by a ten-meter-tall advertisement for glowing body paint, equal parts fascinated and aghast. She couldn't get enough of the sights and sounds—the endless rows, tiers, multilevel domes of businesses, cafés, and restaurants—but we had a schedule to keep.

The most expensive restaurant on Imperial Pointe was actually at the bottom of the station, completely enclosed, and very exclusive because of things that I knew would not appeal to Salmagard. And now that I wasn't a prince anymore, I couldn't afford it anyway.

Instead of that place, I took her to the Red Yonder Ballroom: the officially licensed Red Yonder restaurant that was at the top of the station, occupying a sizable dome with a breathtaking view of Red Yonder itself.

The dining room was gently tiered, making the most of the

space so that every table had a view of the dome and everything outside it. Dampening fields kept it all quiet, despite the fact that there were no physical barriers between the tables. It was spacious, and that appealed to me. I'd eaten there only once before, but I'd found it quite relaxing.

It was a popular place, but I had reservations. If we were doing this properly, Salmagard would've been the one making all the plans, but we weren't.

We followed an animated line on the floor to a table at the far end of one of the upper tiers, an especially good spot because we could look down on the whole of the restaurant as well as all of space.

We sat down and the table glowed to life.

"Would you like to hear tonight's live music?" it asked with an exaggerated Marragardian accent.

I looked down at the very bottom of the tiers. The band's costumes left no doubt that they were Martian. That wasn't my kind of music. I glanced at Salmagard, whose expression told me she felt the same way.

"No, thanks," I said, keying up the table's menu and setting it to play something quiet and ambient. "I forgot how strong these places come on."

But we did have a good view.

Red Yonder itself was apart from the station, which was arranged in a sort of crescent around it. Tonight it was lit up with red and gold, and soon there would be a light show as the station's day cycle wound down.

Bright white lines shot out from Red Yonder, the tracks connecting it to a dozen different ports on Imperial Pointe, where visitors could board special shuttles that would carry them slowly to the park itself. Getting there was part of the experience. I'd enjoyed it the first time, but after that it became a little tedious.

Tonight it would make for a few quiet moments alone with Salmagard.

A robotic chef done up to look like something from the twentieth century unfolded from the table, eyes flashing yellow.

"Howdy," it said with a bizarre accent I wasn't familiar with. "I'm y'all's cooking friend for tonight, so let's get friendly. What y'all wanna eat? Come on, lay it on me—you know I'm the best in the galaxy. Ain't nothing I can't make. Might stop your heart but that's what stasis is for. Come on now, come on. Don't be shy. I know you're hungry. I can read y'all's vitals."

The robot spoke very quickly. Salmagard stared at it. She definitely wasn't used to galactic stations.

"Okonomiyaki," I said, and the robot's head turned toward me.

"Now yer talking, pardner. Everybody knows about my pans from here to Isaka. Now how about your pretty little date, then? Where y'all from?"

"Luna," I replied.

"Luna. I tell y'all I make the best Luna deep-dish proteins this side of the Commonwealth—let me tempt you. Still thinking, darling? How 'bout a drink?" it asked me.

"Wine," I said.

"What kind, amigo?"

"Commonwealth."

"Which system?"

"Frontier."

"Which planet?"

"New Earth."

"Which region?"

"South Indies."

"Red, white, or pink?"

"Pink."

"Price range?"

"High end."

"How about a Neo Jersey Grapefruit, ten years old."

"That'll work."

"Coming your way, pardner. Make up your mind yet, sweetheart?" The chef turned back to Salmagard.

She cleared her throat, almost looking flustered. "Have you got anything unique or exotic? Something I can't get anywhere else?"

"Anything you can dream up, honeybunch."

She was looking to me for help, but she was on her own. I didn't know what Salmagard liked to eat. If she could beat out all the other trainees to become a negotiator, she was more than qualified to order her own food.

"May I have this Free Trade platter?"

"Oh, you know your book learnin', pardner. I'm on it—don't you two go nowheres."

Laughing uproariously, the chef folded back into the table, and it was suddenly very quiet.

"What did I just order?" Salmagard asked me.

"It's a big dish that's basically a history lesson." I shrugged. "I hope you're interested in Free Trade culture. I think usually people get it to share. One of my bodyguards ordered one when I was here as Dalton. It was fun. Good tourist choice."

She looked intrigued.

"I do like Nipponese food," she said, looking at the holographic representation of the dish I'd ordered. "But you didn't tell him to make it Earth or Kakugo."

"He didn't ask."

The table opened and our wine rose into view. I picked up the bottle and the corkscrew, and Salmagard turned over the glasses.

"It's pretty," she said, looking out at Red Yonder again.

"It's even better when you're over there." I could see her eyes lingering on the infamous tower.

"Isn't it quite exclusive?"

"You have to get your spot ahead of time," I said, getting the wine open and pouring.

She turned to me, one eyebrow raised. "When did you make these plans?"

"On Payne Station," I replied. "I was stuck in a crawl space waiting out an imperial patrol. I used the time to take care of some things."

"They were searching for you and you were thinking about me?"

"I never stop thinking about you."

That wasn't exactly true, and she knew it. But where was the harm?

Salmagard sat back and swallowed, clamming up. I politely poured the wine and placed her glass, pretending not to notice how awkward she was being. I'd never seen someone work so hard at not blushing. What had happened to make the imperial gentry think that being honest about your feelings was uncouth?

I lifted my glass, and she took the cue, clearing her throat. I understood now that the throat clearing was her tell.

"Let's say this one's for Deilani," I said.

That sobered her a little. "Indeed," she said, and we both drank. The wine was exceptional. And it had better be; being a fugitive didn't pay very well.

The robot chef erupted from the table with a cry, and we both choked.

"Well, howdy! I bet you missed me—you look like you missed me. Good wine? You know it is. I recommended it. I got y'all's food here—let's do this. Let's do it big like we do in Texas. All right now."

With six arms, the robot began to shovel raw ingredients onto the table, which divided itself into sections with cooking surfaces, bowls of ice, and everything he would need.

The arms worked furiously. Raw vegetables were tossed into a wok, batter was being stirred, and slices of protein were being laid out in attractive patterns on Salmagard's platter. Holograms leapt into the air over each of her morsels, explaining what they were and why they were historically significant.

Martian Brie: Served when the Trigan Aerospace-Station Conglomerate CEO and noted entrepreneur Tenbrook discussed the plans for PERDITA.

Salmagard tried to read everything, but at the same time she was trying to watch our chef. That wasn't her fault; it was distracting. Overwhelming, even.

Our meal took shape rapidly. My okonomiyaki was sizzling nicely, and two of the arms were drizzling sauce onto the griddle.

Traditional Old Earth Grilled Cheese Sandwich (Extra-Sharp Cheddar): Served when Prince Mugambo met with the Order of Clerics to found the Lumbley Trade Council. HC 2101.

It took the chef all of five minutes to prepare and lay out the feast, and he immediately vanished back into our table. ("Holler if y'all need me!")

"So," Salmagard asked, breaking the jarring quiet that followed the chef's departure. She sipped her wine and gazed at Red Yonder. "Where *did* you book us?"

"Hmm? Oh. In the hotel."

"Not the tower?"

"No." I couldn't tell if she was being shy or just herself. "We're in the same place as the people who come here with their kids. Nothing your family could possibly object to."

"So you do know how to be a gentleman," she murmured.

I raised an eyebrow. "I was a *prince*."

"And I know all your songs."

She had me there. Yes, Prince Dalton's lyrics were well-known to be very forthright and intimate. "Do you? You don't know which songs were mine and which were his before I replaced him. I had to copy his style. So is any of it really mine?"

"There's also that you lie for a living. And you did destroy the Ganraen capital."

"Yeah," I said, looking down at my glass. "Yeah, I did do that, didn't I?"

2

"WE'RE a little ahead of schedule," I said, looking at my chrono. I'd expected to spend more time in the restaurant.

"We can't just go?" Salmagard seemed puzzled.

"They're always at capacity. For us to get over there, someone has to leave. We'll have to wait."

The disembarkation atrium was dim and quiet; only people scheduled to depart could get in, and we were the only ones at this particular dock. I followed Salmagard to the panoramic viewport. The light track curled down and away from the station, forming a smooth curve leading to Red Yonder. That was the path we would follow when it was our turn. I could see a carriage leaving one of the other ports, heading for the park.

Our carriage arrived. It was the size of a large room, and completely transparent, though from the outside it looked reflective, like a drop of mercury. There were a lavish bar and deep, comfortable seats. There were no controls, no pilot. It was all automated.

I lit up my holo to show our reservation, and we boarded. The doors closed behind us, and I sank onto the sofa, where Salmagard joined me.

"You ask a lot of questions about Earth," she said. "What about Cohengard?"

"What about it?"

"What's it like?"

"I don't know if I can tell you anything you don't already know." I shrugged. "You know history. We have a lot of immigrants. A lot of people under sustenance. There's a pretty thriving counter-Empress culture, of course. New Unity. Lots of recruiting for them." I leaned back and thought about it. "It's not the most attractive city. Some big buildings were destroyed and never rebuilt, so it looks a little spotty. I feel like a lot of people don't really want to be there. There's an increased IS and EI presence. A couple military bases. One of the adjuncts for Second Fleet command is there. There's also a really big shipyard."

"A shipyard? Planetside?"

"Colony ships. Lots of very heavy, very deep colony recruiting too. It's a good place for it. Everybody wants out. They want a new start."

"Oh."

I could see Salmagard eyeing the bar curiously, but she made no move toward it. At dinner she'd reluctantly stopped after only a single glass of wine. Propriety. It wasn't that she wasn't allowed to enjoy herself, but in her circles there was so much emphasis on appearances that she wouldn't risk anything that might even slightly compromise her control.

"What about you?" she asked. "What sort of place did you grow up in?"

"I was raised by the district." Might as well admit it. "A pretty big institution."

"You're an orphan? How did you end up in the Service?"

"I didn't. Well, not the same Service you're in. I was recruited." I leaned back. "I went into sustenance when I was pretty young. That's common," I added. "For people in my area, not just people without family. I graduated. I had a . . . couple friends, but we didn't have anything. We were all in sustenance. I'm not going to say we didn't have opportunities, but they weren't great. No one was going to hand us anything."

I saw the way she was looking at me. "I wasn't sure what I wanted to do. One of my friends was trying to do something that they honestly didn't have a good chance at. And my other friend didn't want to apply himself, because . . . You know, by the time we graduated, New Unity already had its hooks in him. Anti-Empress people don't get very many apprenticeships."

"What about you?"

"I didn't care about any of that, but I let him drag me along for some of it. I was actually thinking about trying to get an apprenticeship in . . . Well, I shouldn't say."

"What? Tell me."

"No, it's embarrassing." I shook my head. "Doesn't matter— it didn't happen. They came for me, and I thought it was a good opportunity. Me and my friends—we didn't have a future. We knew war was coming. The government knew it too. They were checking aptitudes and recruiting. My friends didn't have good chances. I thought I could do it for the three of us. That's why I went for it."

That was the truth. Salmagard said nothing.

"Things didn't go like I thought they would." That was true as well.

"How old were you?"

"Pretty young."

"So you were in place before the war even started," she said, looking impressed.

"At that point war was inevitable."

She looked at me curiously. "Are you all right?"

"I'm fine. Free Trade space has been a problem for a long time. Back then the Empress called for a summit to discuss laying some ground rules for all the annexation that was going on; without getting into specifics, that was all the Royals needed. The war was going to happen either way, so it might as well happen before they lost a massive part of their expansion prospects." I took a deep breath. "They all knew. They had all known for a long time."

"Is it really all just a race to see who can snatch up as much of Free Trade space as they can first? Was that really what was happening?" Salmagard asked, looking grim.

"The Empire was being classy about it; Ganrae, not so much. There was some hostile action. That wasn't the only problem, but it pushed us into open fighting faster. Free Trade shot callers knew which way the wind was blowing, and they were starting to favor imperial interests. That didn't sit well with the Commonwealth. They didn't teach you all this?"

"More or less. The Service paints the Commonwealth as being a bit more malicious."

"Naturally."

"Why didn't Kakugo sit it out? They're supposed to be neutral."

"They're still technically a part of the Commonwealth. There's plenty of leverage there, but I don't know. Dalton didn't have a lot of exposure to that side of things."

"Why haven't we annexed Imperial Pointe?" she asked, leaning over to look up at the station. "The war was the perfect opportunity."

"No reason to. It's not about real estate; it's about jump paths. Guidance rings are expensive to build. Evagard's starting to shake off the expansion freeze it's had for the past couple decades, and when it comes to expansion . . ."

"Nothing's more important than roads."

"Exactly. That's why the Empress is probably going to come out of this race in front of the Ganraen Royals."

"Aren't we already in front of them? We won the war."

"Nobody's won anything yet. Until the peace talks are settled, everything's up in the air. It's only a cease-fire, but they lost their capital, not their fighting capability. It's not over. The Empress still has to close it out. And she has to do it in a way that no one really loses, or we'll just do all this again in five years." I caught myself there. "But that's not really the most romantic topic." I moved closer to her and glanced around the carriage. "I didn't ask for a private ride. Someone must've canceled."

"It's a busy place out here."

"No busier than imperial stations. Just louder."

She smiled.

"And full of opportunity," I went on. "I mean, I've got lots of transferable job skills. I've probably got a bright future here."

"What sorts of job skills? You can't sing—you'll give yourself away."

"I did deep-cover work—I can act. Can't you see me in some holo dramas? The dashing hero? I'm tall enough now."

"Now?" she asked curiously.

"I had to have my height augmented to be Dalton. I used to be . . . not quite as tall."

Her brows lifted. "Hard to picture that. You *are* quite the performer."

"But just because you're good at something doesn't mean you like it. I'd rather stay offstage, and instead of acting, I'd rather be up-front with people. What do you think?" I wasn't being subtle; there was no percentage in that here.

"I agree," she said.

I kissed her. Too much time in the Commonwealth had put me woefully out of touch with how things were done in the Empire. For a man with my lack of status to take the lead this way with the first daughter of a good Evagardian family was way out of line. Just being alone with Salmagard could be seen as problematic, given that we barely knew each other.

And even if we were social equals, the privilege of initiating these things was supposed to be hers.

But those were Evagardian rules. I'd just spent several years being a Ganraen prince. A Ganraen prince who wasn't interested in women—but still immersed in a culture where it was more socially acceptable for men to be aggressive.

I could blame that for my behavior, but it wouldn't be true. The truth was, I just wasn't impressed by rules the way I'd once been. It would have been nice to go about this the right way, but that wasn't going to happen.

Salmagard hadn't been able to stop herself from blushing as I got closer to her. Her lips were soft, and she smelled like caramel. Her shyness vanished immediately, of course. There was no hesitation at all. Her assertiveness didn't surprise me; contraceptive implants and hormone control might make for a more professional work environment aboard a ship, but no-body *liked* it.

I pushed her down on the sofa, and Salmagard put her arms around my neck.

The doors to the carriage hissed open.

I reluctantly looked up to see two people staring at me and Salmagard, who, lying beneath me, was very red in the face.

I smiled and looked apologetic, helping her up and leaning back with my arm around her.

"Sorry," I said. "We were about to leave. I didn't think anyone else was coming."

It was a young couple, and the man seemed winded, as though he'd been running. He held up a hand.

"Our fault," he said. "We're late. Sorry. Sorry to interrupt, very sorry." He gasped for breath as they stepped into the carriage. The woman wasn't breathing hard at all.

Salmagard's poise was perfect, or it would've been if her face wasn't exactly the same color as her dress. She was checking her hair and giving the two newcomers her best, perfect, aristocratic smile. I pulled her a little closer, and I didn't laugh. She covered her mouth with her sleeve and looked away.

The young man was leaning against the bar. He was a little shorter than I was, slender, and improbably—indeed, unfairly—handsome. He wore sensible, becoming galactic casual clothes.

But I knew an imperial when I saw one. It looked like he came from Earth Asian blood.

The girl was another matter; her skin was perfectly white. So jarringly, unnaturally white that it had to be an aesthetic augmentation. Her eyes were so red that they appeared to glow. She wore a black dress with a lot of frills and lace, and her glossy black hair fell in generous ringlets. Maybe she'd been pretty before she'd started messing with her skin and eye color, but now she was just bizarre.

She was still staring at us. I tried to turn up my smile a little, and made sure it wasn't my Dalton smile.

She burst into tears.

That took me off guard. I turned questioningly to the guy, who looked up in panic.

"Come on," he said. "It's all right. We made it. Let's have a drink."

The girl pushed him away and went to the bar, snatching a bottle of Evagardian Ale and snapping off the top effortlessly. That got my attention. You were supposed to need a special tool for that. Evagardian Ale always came with sealed tops that had to be clipped, then peeled back. There was no practical reason for it; it was just tradition.

But she'd just twisted it off like it was nothing.

The pale girl put her head back and began to drink straight from the bottle. Salmagard and I watched as the bright blue liquid disappeared in a truly frightening amount of time. Seven hundred fifty milliliters of Evagardian Ale contained enough ethanol to kill a human being. She should've passed out after the first quarter of the bottle.

She didn't *move* like someone with an artificial body, but there had to be an explanation for this.

She finished the bottle, tears still shining on her face, a face that was not a prosthetic. I was genuinely baffled.

"That's not good for you," her companion said. That was an understatement.

"It's like water," she muttered, and for a moment I thought

she might smash the bottle. This was the kind of awkwardness you usually only saw on galactic dramas about young people. It was perfect; these two were ridiculous, and Salmagard had enough manners for the both of us. Now there was balance.

The carriage began to move—we were on our way to Red Yonder—but Salmagard and I were more interested in this strange couple. Actually, I was beginning to suspect they weren't a couple.

The guy led his companion to the other sofa and sat her down. She put her head on his shoulder and closed her eyes, still crying softly. He stroked her hair, giving us a look that begged for understanding.

Salmagard and I both tried to look understanding.

"This is Diana; I'm Sei. We're imperials. Where are you guys from?"

"Same," I replied. "Is everything all right?"

"It's fine," Sei said, looking down at Diana. "We're both just—you know. Dealing with heartbreak." His eyes flicked toward Red Yonder. "Hoping some mindless debauchery will help."

"That's the spirit," I said.

"She's an *immigrant*." Diana sniffed into Sei's chest.

"I think that's her parents. She's not so bad," Sei chided her, but she gave him a fierce look, and he started to stroke her hair again. "We're in the Service—well, Diana's former now. We had a rough tour. The guy she had her eye on got poached, and I lost someone too. We're kind of a mess. Sorry to make a scene."

"No worries," I told him.

"But he was *my* support," Diana went on, then hiccupped. Even with an augmented metabolism, which she had to have, an entire bottle of Evagardian Ale wasn't something you could shake off.

She was wasted—but that was impressive, because she should've been in a coma. She had to have some artificial parts inside. It was the only explanation. Rough tour? Maybe she'd been wounded; that would explain some of this, though not all of it. It probably wasn't relevant to my life, but I was intrigued.

Sei looked up, surprised. So did I.

"What's the matter?" Salmagard asked.

"We aren't moving." I turned to look back over the sofa, out the rear of the carriage. Imperial Pointe loomed behind us. Ahead, Red Yonder. Far out to our left, I could see another carriage moving sedately toward the park.

Seconds ticked by. It wasn't clear to me why we'd stopped.

"Is this you?" Salmagard asked quietly.

"I don't think so. If imperials made me, they wouldn't telegraph a takedown like this," I murmured. "They'd just be waiting for us on the other side. They know better than to put me on my guard. I think we've just malfunctioned."

"What happens now?" Salmagard asked, more curious than concerned.

I looked at Sei. "Any ideas?"

He shook his head. "I'm just a pilot. Sorry."

I thought it over. If we were dealing with a hardware issue, repair bots would take care of it. Or they'd fly a work team out here. If it was a system issue, it would be fixed shortly. I couldn't think of anything else.

"Could be our spot isn't open," Sei said, pointing at Red Yonder. "If someone's gotten held up leaving, or there's something wrong with our welcome, they could be buying a couple minutes."

"In that case I'd expect them to say something," I said. "At least, they should. Right?" I leaned down to Salmagard. "If it *is* me, I apologize in advance."

Salmagard swallowed. "What will happen to you?"

"Don't worry about that. I've made my bed and I'll sleep in it. You have to worry about yourself."

"I'll end up like Deilani."

That was if she was lucky. I wasn't going to say it, but if she was actually found with me, her career would be over. She wouldn't have the luxury of being reassigned. "Would that be so bad?"

"No. Demenis Affairs doesn't sound so bad to me at all." She smiled wistfully. "You're *sure* this isn't you?"

"If it is, whoever's coming isn't very good at their job."

We began to move again.

I let out my breath. "Trust me," I said. "If imperials ever get another line on me, I'll never see them coming."

"That's comforting," Salmagard said, snuggling up to me a bit.

"Hold on," Sei said, disengaging himself from Diana and getting up. "We're off course." He pointed, and I turned to see the white line of the track leading to Red Yonder shrinking behind us.

"Can we do that?" Salmagard asked, puzzled.

"We shouldn't be able to," I said. "This has to be something else. Maybe a gravity tether. Maybe we're broken down bad enough that they want to put us in dry dock."

Sei snorted. "Great first impression."

"Even Red Yonder's going to have a problem here and there." I shrugged. "They'll probably upgrade our rooms to make up for it."

"That'd be nice," Diana muttered.

"Odd they haven't said anything," I said, frowning. "It's not good business to leave us in suspense."

"Even for maintenance," Salmagard said, pointing, "why would we be moving away from the park?"

"Their dry dock could be on the station," Sei told her, going to the wall of the carriage and looking out. "But this is weird."

Salmagard was looking at me, and I didn't know what to tell her. I was growing increasingly confident that whatever this was, it wasn't about me—but I was also getting worried.

All my instincts were on their feet, making themselves heard, but I still didn't have an answer.

Even Diana was sitting up and paying attention. She looked serious, and with those red eyes, that was a little intimidating. Why would a girl like her go out of her way to make herself look scary? It had to be some kind of personal, cultural thing— but hadn't Sei said the two of them were in the Service? There was no way Diana's look was in regs.

Salmagard was still looking up at me intently. Maybe she didn't believe me when I told her Evagard wouldn't come after me this way. I was telling the truth.

"What's the worst-case scenario?" she asked.

"The worst?" I raised an eyebrow and thought about it, looking back toward Red Yonder. Then I turned and gazed toward Imperial Pointe. We were still approaching, though we were moving toward a part of it that I didn't know anything about. Maybe that lent credence to the theory that Red Yonder's emergency dry dock was our destination. There was probably a mixture of computer and hardware errors that could produce this bizarre situation, but what were the odds?

"The worst case would be that we're about to be the victims of a terrorist attack," I said finally. "Imperials are softer targets in neutral space. I guess this is a good place to take a shot at a couple of us unprotected."

"So where's the attack?" Sei asked. "And who's this? Is that a supply ferry?"

A dark shape had emerged from beneath the station, and it was moving toward us.

"Looks like it. He shouldn't be out here where people can see him."

"They can't see him," Diana pointed out. "We're way down here. Everyone up there is looking at Red Yonder."

"Is anyone else off course?" Sei asked, crossing the carriage to have a look. "Are we in trouble?"

I shook my head. "I'm going to feel ridiculous if we end up in some bay with a work team and a park rep bowing and apologizing."

"We're going to collide with this guy," Sei said suddenly, backing away from the side of the carriage. "He doesn't see us. I don't know how, but he doesn't."

That got my attention. I reluctantly let go of Salmagard and got to my feet. These carriages didn't have much in the way of safety measures. Depressurization sealant, oxygen masks—and that would be it. If we actually hit something, that would be the end.

And Sei was right. The ship was coming right at us. Salmagard and Diana joined us, watching the freight hauler come closer.

The forward doors opened, and my heart sank.

"Oh," I said as comprehension dawned. "Somebody's kidnapping us."

I saw the way they were all looking at me.

"I'm serious," I said. "If they were picking us up, they'd send a real shuttle, and they'd communicate. And this guy shouldn't be here. Do the math."

Sei stared at me for a second, then lit up his holo.

"Don't bother," I said. "We're already cut off."

Salmagard abruptly moved her hand to her hip.

"What is it?"

"My implant just died," she said, looking troubled.

I blinked. "You can feel that?"

She gave me a look. I turned to Diana. "Do you feel any-thing?"

"I don't have one," she said.

That seemed to surprise Sei. "Really?"

"But I do have a tracker. If someone *did* kidnap me, they wouldn't get far." Diana folded her arms, looking unimpressed.

"If they're jamming our network access, they have some idea what they're doing. Don't hold your breath." I looked back at Red Yonder, which now appeared quite distant.

"Why us?" Sei asked.

I shrugged, then took Salmagard's hand and pulled her close.

"You should stay away from guys like me," I told her quietly.

"Let's not panic yet," she murmured as we drifted into the hauler's bay. At least she didn't think I was behind this.

It was time to think about business. If we really were being kidnapped, that was bad enough. If possible, I didn't want anyone to make things worse.

"Let's be cooperative," I said. "Don't try anything."

Sei shrugged, then looked at Diana, who just looked faintly disgusted.

"They're on their honeymoon," she grumbled. "And this is me. This is my life."

"There isn't even a date for the wedding yet," Sei told her, visibly exasperated. "How could they be on their honey-moon?"

Diana didn't reply to that. She just folded her arms.

Sei sighed.

The doors closed, and our carriage locked into place.

The bay was dirty, but not neglected. It had seen a lot of use. I tried to take in as much as I could. Did our bad guys own this hauler? Did they regularly snatch people from Red Yonder carriages? Was Red Yonder in on it? What were they up to?

This bay had been cared for. Not scrubbed to shine, but maintained. That meant it was owned by people who wanted to use it for its intended purpose.

Stolen, then. Borrowed for this specific job. The specific job of redirecting and capturing a Red Yonder transport with passengers aboard.

That would take some fancy computer work, both to get the carriage off course and to keep anyone from noticing.

Pictures and scenarios were beginning to form in my mind. This *wasn't* about me. That meant there was hope. There were plenty of people who wanted me, but none of them would go about getting me this way.

The doors finished sealing, and our carriage sat alone in the dim bay. I went to the bar and poured myself a drink as the others watched the bay warily.

A hatch opened, and a woman entered, lugging a heavy case. She was around thirty, and a little taller than Salmagard. She had bright red hair that was tied back in twin braids. Her coveralls were stained and worn. She wore thick gloves and heavy boots.

She walked right up to the carriage and put her case on the ground, kneeling to open it.

"We should sit down," I said, guiding Salmagard to the sofa.

"Why?" Sei asked. He didn't look happy, but he was calm. I was glad he and Diana were in the Service, or former Service, or whatever. A couple of panicky civilians would only have made things worse.

"She's going to knock us out."

The carriage was reflective from the outside; the woman couldn't see us watching her.

Sei looked thoughtful as he took a seat. Diana looked dangerous.

"Then they're not going to hurt us?" Salmagard asked, watching the woman pull a round device from the case.

"Not yet."

The woman fixed the device to the side of the carriage. It began to glow. It would eat through the carbon shielding and release a pulse that would render us all unconscious. We didn't have long.

"I wanted an exciting getaway," I said to Salmagard, leaning in a little. "But I had some different things in mind."

"Me too," she replied.

I offered her my drink, and she took a sip, looking grateful.

"You're not afraid?" she asked.

No. I wasn't. Just annoyed.

"Why would I be?" I said. "My date's a professional bodyguard."

3

I woke up on carpet.

I couldn't feel my hands, and that meant control cuffs. It should've been gratifying that the conclusions I'd drawn were turning out correct, but it wasn't. My head hurt from the disabling pulse, but the pain was nothing compared to my rising temper. I groaned, but there was no sound. I could feel the mute strip attached to my throat keeping me silent.

My arms were behind my back, my hands enveloped by full-profile shackles that numbed them. Shackles like these could also administer an electric shock to keep a prisoner in line.

Mute strips and control cuffs were a good indication that these people had done this sort of thing before.

I opened my eyes. I was in a bedroom and Sei was lying in front of me. It looked like he hadn't come around yet. I sat up, spotting Salmagard and Diana as well.

We weren't alone.

The woman we'd seen in the freight hauler was there,

though she'd taken off her protective jumpsuit to reveal leggings and a utility vest. Her arms were heavily tattooed, and she had a pair of large goggles hanging around her neck. Her pupils were unnaturally dark and flat, probably the result of modifications to protect her vision in extreme light conditions.

That was telling. It was something you'd see on poor workers in the belt, or even on indentured servants. People who worked in dangerous conditions and didn't have the money for a more sophisticated operation.

"Stay," she said, pointing at me. I didn't try to get up. Salmagard was stirring. The others were all bound and muted, just like me.

Our captor was sitting on the bed, fidgeting. Waiting for something.

I turned my attention to my surroundings. The wall behind me was a single massive feed that was serving as a mirror display. There were assorted light fixtures overhead that could probably create a variety of moods. At the moment the room was bathed in blues and purples.

The carpet was deep and lustrous. The space seemed cramped, but that was because there were four of us on the floor. There was a pleasant artificial scent in the air that I couldn't identify.

Two doors. One was an exit, and the other probably led to a bathroom.

I closed my eyes and concentrated on the gravity, the feel of the ground beneath me. I listened.

We weren't on a ship, but it wasn't a planet either. A station, then? The air was recycled. The gravity wasn't quite right. I couldn't have been out for long. A disabling pulse was a flexible tool, but the longer the knockout, the worse the hangover. My head hurt, but the pain wasn't unreasonable. I hadn't been unconscious for more than an hour or two, and that limited the number of places we could be.

Imperial Pointe? No, Imperial Pointe had better gravity, gravity that could almost pass for the real thing.

I discreetly watched the woman. Her twin braids were what I'd call a Free Trade hairstyle. That didn't narrow it down much.

She had a large gun in a shoulder holster, which she didn't seem terribly conscious of. It was a big model, intended for utility. Rather than bullets in a detachable magazine, it had chambers that could be loaded with different types of cartridges for different purposes. The rubber grip was battered and scuffed, and the gun was missing a rear sight. It might be loaded with benign stun rounds, or they might be explosive bullets that could turn a person into liquid. No way to tell.

The woman looked as tired as I felt.

Her boots were a style that was common in Trigan systems, but that didn't mean anything.

I needed more to work with.

The door opened and two men entered the room.

One was a head taller than I was and almost twice as wide. He was wearing casual galactic clothes. Not exactly trendy, but they suited him, giving him a slightly genteel aura. A massive guy like that should've had the presence of a barbarian, but he dressed to come off as someone a little more cosmopolitan. I could smell his cologne. He was only a little older than I was, and he had the look of someone who'd been through his share of things.

I wasn't interested in him, though—it was the other man who had my attention.

He was in his early forties, trim, and with a neat beard. He wore trousers in an outdated Old Earth style and an expensive hooded shirt beneath an Isakan blazer. Casual, expensive, relatively tasteful galactic clothes. The big man had taste, but the smaller one had taste and money.

We were on a station. Not Imperial Pointe. This guy was in charge—or at least in charge of something. We were still in Free Trade space.

I listened with interest. The woman's name was Willis, and the big guy was Freeber. They were obviously partners. Willis called the older man Idris.

He sank onto the bed with a groan and considered the four of us.

"I think your radiation shield must have failed," he said to Willis. "Because you're out of your mind."

"This isn't a selection," she said. "You came to us, not the other way around. Lump sum."

"No one ever said anything about a lump sum," Idris replied, not taking his eyes off Salmagard. I knew she was awake; no one else did. Sei had come around as well, and I had a feeling Diana had been awake all along. If she could metabolize ethanol fast enough to survive a full bottle of Evagardian Ale, then a stun pulse probably wouldn't keep her down for long.

I was doing a good job looking scared, but my performance was wasted. They weren't paying attention to me.

"Whether you want all of them or none, we have the same amount of risk," Willis said. "Pay what you owe."

"I *will* pay what I owe," Idris confirmed, rubbing his shoulder. "But I decide what I owe. Where did you find them?"

"Imperial Pointe."

"Gutsy. I guess nobody'd expect to get pulled there. How did you even know they were imperials?"

"We checked their reservations."

"For what?"

"Red Yonder. We took the carriage that had all imperials in it."

"Any record of that?"

Willis shook her head. That didn't sound quite right to me—she must've paid someone off. I doubted it was possible to just lift a Red Yonder transport without some kind of help on the inside. It was still a neat little maneuver, however they'd done it. There would be consequences for someone—but probably not in time to do us any good.

"I'm not taking these two," Idris said, motioning at me and Sei. "Obviously."

"Why not?" Freeber asked, getting to his feet.

"Not my market. I stick to what I know. So let's talk about these two. What's wrong with this one? Is she synthetic?" Idris asked, jerking his chin at Diana.

"No." Freeber knelt beside her and pulled her up by the arm. Diana did a good impression of coming suddenly awake and glared at him. "She's flesh. It's not a cosmetic. Whatever it is, it's permanent."

"A freak." Idris scowled at her, then looked thoughtful. "But that might not be all bad. Definitely a curiosity. Exotic flavor. Maybe she's rich. Getting changes like this can't be cheap, even in the Empire." He leaned forward and took Diana by the chin, examining her face. "Actually, not bad. We could cap an image, make some edits, put her best foot forward. I wish we could do something about the eyes. Hmm. She started out pretty, at least."

He let her go and leaned back, turning to Willis. "Was this the best you could do?"

"Getting imperials is hard," she said, shrugging.

"This one's good," Idris said, pointing at Salmagard. "I'll take her for sure. I've seen better, but she's what I need more of."

"What about the guys? That one looks a little like Prince Dalton. Can't you sell that?"

"I told you, I don't want guys. Still not sure about this one." He stared intently at Diana, who returned his stare with more hostility than I thought was prudent. "She doesn't look very cooperative, but we might still be able to do something with that. Let's have a look."

Willis nodded to Freeber, who yanked Diana to her feet. He grabbed a handful of her hair, pulling back hard to force her to arch her back, keeping her from moving. Willis got up and produced a knife. She grabbed the collar of Diana's dress and began to saw in a businesslike fashion. She split the dress down the middle and pushed it over Diana's shoulders so that it gathered behind her; then she cut it free of her wrists and tossed it aside.

Diana wore simple, almost boyish undergarments in a very dull gray. Every inch of her body was as white as her face, and her skin was flawless—but it wasn't her skin that had everyone in the room staring. It was her physique and muscle tone.

In a dress, she was obviously slender—but with it off, everyone could see that she was positively skeletal. There was no body fat to speak of, but it wasn't the emaciation of malnourishment. Or at least, it wasn't *just* malnourishment.

Diana had muscles. She wasn't big or bulky, but every muscle on her body was visible in razor-sharp definition.

I'd done some traveling and encountered some interesting physiques—but I'd never seen anyone like this before. There were plenty of women who had their metabolisms tweaked to stay slim, but they didn't want their bodies to be rock hard— they usually wanted to keep some curves.

Diana didn't have curves. She had angles. Now I understood the frills and the gloves and the boots she'd been wearing. With her body on display, she went from a little scary to downright terrifying. She was only as tall as my shoulder, and probably thirty kilograms lighter than I was.

But I didn't want to be on her bad side.

I saw Idris swallow. He'd never seen anyone like her either.

"Interesting," he said, looking her over. He lowered his gaze, looking thoughtful. "Make sure she's normal," he said to Freeber.

The big man let go of Diana and reached for her shorts.

She crushed him with a head butt so savage and abrupt that even I flinched. I was twice Diana's weight. Freeber was more like four times.

Blood exploding from his nose, the big man crashed backward like a rag doll, slamming into the wall and crumpling to the floor, stunned.

Willis immediately triggered the electricity, and I don't think she noticed it, but I did: Diana hesitated for just a moment before she fell to her knees, putting on an expression of pain.

A split second. Less than a heartbeat. Electricity moved fast. Faster than that.

Diana was acting. Maybe the shock from the cuffs didn't even bother her.

Idris let out a sudden bark of laughter, staring at Freeber's fallen body. He put his head back and laughed louder.

Willis gave him an irritated look, then turned to Freeber, scowling.

"Pussy," she said, and spat on him. He moaned several vile swearwords.

Idris was getting himself under control.

"Okay. I'll take her too. I'll even take her at full price. You ought to give me a discount for bringing me a problem child. How'd he ever get out of New Brittia alive with a glass jaw like that?" Idris asked, looking at Freeber.

"I'm not sure," Willis said, looking taken aback. "I've seen him walk away from worse. She must've gotten lucky."

Idris got to his feet, still looking down at Diana. He nudged her head with the toe of his shoe. "Don't look at me like that. You'll be on your way soon enough, but until then getting upset's not going to do you any good. You better just start getting in the right state of mind now, Princess." He looked at Willis. "Cover her up. I feel like a deviant."

Exasperated, Willis straightened Diana's underwear, then tossed the remains of her dress over her.

"You better get him up," Idris said, hooking a finger through his belt and eyeing Freeber. "He has to get these two out of here. Because you're not leaving them with me." He glanced at me and Sei again, expressionless.

"Can't you do anything with them?"

"How many of my customers are women?"

"Almost half," Willis said, indignant.

"How many of them would pay for this instead of just putting on a VR collar?"

"I don't know. Maybe some."

"I'm not spending money on 'maybe some.' I'll stick to what I'm good at. They're imperial, so it's not like you can't get something for them. And if you can't, don't just toss them out an airlock. Make sure to put the bodies back where you found them."

"Get up," Willis snapped, kicking Freeber. He groaned, and his eyes opened. His nose was still gushing. His shirt was ruined. His face looked terrifying. Diana hadn't just broken his nose—she'd annihilated it.

Obviously these were rough people. I could tell they'd both seen action, but Freeber was actually going to need some real treatment if he ever wanted to go back to looking the way he was supposed to. From the look on Willis' face, she was coming to that conclusion as well.

She glanced at Diana, shook her head, and glared at Idris.

The well-dressed man took a pair of crystal bonds from his jacket pocket and held them out. Willis snatched them, then gave him the code for the control cuffs.

Now Idris had the power to shock us at will.

Freeber was getting to his feet. Willis pushed him toward me, and Salmagard caught my eye as Freeber effortlessly pulled me and Sei to our feet. I didn't react; staying docile and cooperative was key here.

I held Salmagard's gaze for as long as I could, trying to look apologetic—but this was *not* my fault. Then we were in the corridor, Diana and Salmagard were still in the room, and the door was closing.

4

TRUTHS about the Empress of Evagard were often subject to debate.

Few specifics of the Unification were considered fact. Some of the Grand Duchess' deeds were canonical. But when it came to details about her life, particularly her life prior to the Unification itself, little was known for certain. There was plenty of information, but no one knew exactly which stories were true.

But it was believed that the Duchess' philosophies and worldview were shaped largely by two things, one of which was her mentor.

No one knew much *about* the Empress' mentor—or, if they did, the government was keeping it secret. But historians tended to agree that she'd had one.

No one knew where it started, but it was common knowledge all the same.

That was the root of what would become an imperial tradition of mentorship for the first daughters of tiered families. It was considered by many to be a sacred duty: more of a privilege than a chore. The word "mentor" itself had been forcibly shifted from a rather broad term to one reserved for this particular duty.

Anyone could be tapped as a mentor, though it was typically an honor reserved for men and women who were considered extraordinarily accomplished. There were those who formalized it, who made it official. People who brought money into it, making it a business—but at the end of the day, all a proper family had to do was find someone suitable and ask.

Salmagard's mentor had been a historian named Alice Everly. She was from England. After a decorated tour in the Service, Alice wrote several notable books, held a few public offices, and at the age of forty retired with her three husbands to Casablanca.

There, she met Jane Salmagard, whose ten-year-old daughter was deemed ready for a proper imperial influence from outside the family.

Alice Everly's children were all away at prestigious academies. All she was doing at the time was publicly writing scathing columns about the Commonwealth and privately writing racy scenarios for virtual reality simulations.

She was honored by the request. Though she herself was seventh tier, she wasn't the sort to look down on those with blood valued less highly than her own.

It was the duty of a mentor to provide perspective to a young aristocrat. Alice had seen a bit of the galaxy, which made that easy. Life skills, communication techniques, manipulation strategies—a good mentor offered it all. Companionship. An objective ear. An exclusive camaraderie.

A good mentor would help with a youth's studies and give

guidance to navigating the frequently choppy waters of gentrified Earth life. The mentor would be the one to teach her charge about sensitive things like politics, sex, and religion.

Salmagard had always believed that, in all the Empire, there was nowhere a finer mentor than Alice Everly. And she believed it now. One conversation in particular was fixed in her mind.

She had been fourteen at the time.

They had been sitting on Salmagard's balcony at sunset. Alice had promised some VR time with access to her private collection of scenarios in exchange for a perfect score on Salmagard's upcoming essay on Imperial Law and Skaarvold Interpretation.

"Tessa, Imperial Law is fundamentally simple. Everything is based on what the Grand Duchess believed to be right. In turn, her views on morality and ethics were influenced by her own life, the lives of those she read about, and the laws and sensibilities that had been laid down before her. There are some universal laws, or pseudo-universal ones. Cannibalism. Incest. Even without being taught to do so, we discourage these things. Here on Earth, before the Unification, there was a time when all cultures were entirely separate. It's remarkable that they had so much in common during that time. People don't agree on everything, but there are certain concepts of basic decency that we all rally behind, regardless of who we are. And the Grand Duchess' philosophy is, for the most part, built on what she regarded as decency. Proper treatment of other human beings was her core value. There's no perfect philosophy, and the Grand Duchess was never arrogant enough to believe she could change that. She just set out to do the best she could. It's something we should be grateful for. Totalitarian rule wasn't always a good thing, Tessa. And

indeed, there are parts of the universe now where it isn't. But you've grown up here. Not only in the Empire, but on Earth. Not only on Earth, but in a privileged house. You're not going to truly understand this until you see it up close, but there are people out there who don't believe what the Duchess believed. People with different values. When you do see them—and if you do enter the Service, as you plan to, it is likely that you will—you must be ready. Yes, yes—you've been exposed to entertainment, and you understand the concept of people doing . . . unseemly things. But when you see it, Tessa—when it's right in front of you—it's different. You'll never be ready. It will shock you, but you may not have the luxury of time to be shocked. When that day comes, don't spend any time thinking about how different those people are. Don't pity them, don't resent them; just be thankful, and do what you must. Never hesitate. Hesitation has never brought glory to the Empress. Hesitation has no place, no value in the lives of the gentry. The burden of action is our responsibility as those who lead, Tessa. We are held to a higher standard."

"Ladies," Idris said. "Ladies, pay attention. I know you're awake, and if you're not, you should be." He clicked the controller several times, sending brief shocks through both Salmagard and Diana. "Come on. Up. Get up." He reached down and pulled Salmagard to her feet, then pushed her toward the bed. "Sit. I don't have all night." He prodded Diana into place beside her.

They watched as he backed up to the opposite side of the room and leaned against the feed, folding his arms.

"The first thing you need to do is relax. You need to pay close attention and remember everything I tell you—but the *most* important thing to remember is that I'm not going to kill you. I have no desire to kill you. There's nothing in it for me if I kill you. Secondly, you will get out of here. You will. You really will—and probably sooner than you think. So if you're upset, and you probably should be, then you should concentrate on those two things. You get me? Go ahead and nod—I like it when you nod. Makes me feel like I'm being heard."

Salmagard and Diana nodded.

"You came from Imperial Pointe. You won't show up at Red Yonder. Forty-eight hours after you don't show, they're going to try to contact you. When they fail to reach you, they'll make a note. Forty-eight hours after that they'll contact the Evagardian consulate—and probably twelve hours later Imperial Security will start to look for you. So if you're doing your math, I've got you for a little less than a week before I have to get rid of you. If anyone's expecting you, don't hold out much hope: they might get the search started a little sooner, but nobody's going to show up here—not as long as I get you back safe in a timely manner. Are you following me so far?"

They nodded.

"Good. You have to trust me. You have to trust in the fact that I don't want a *serious* Evagardian investigation. You're never going to know where this place is. You're never going to know who I am. You were asleep when you came here, and you'll be asleep when you leave. You can tell the authorities anything you want when you're back out there—none of it's going to hurt me. You will never see or hear from me again. Sound good?"

They nodded.

"See? We're working together already. You probably have an idea what I want from you. You're real imperials. You're attractive—well, *you* are," he said, looking at Salmagard.

"And you're interesting," he added, glancing at Diana. "I'm sure you already know this, but you people aren't very popular out here. There are people who don't like imperials very much. Guys who need a safe, controlled environment to express that. I'm not going to lie to you. They aren't allowed to really hurt you, but they're not going to be gentle. That's the point. That's what they're paying for; they have . . . desires and resentment, and you're going to help them. You don't have to act. The fact that you're not here by choice is part of the point. Are you following me?"

They nodded.

He pointed at Diana. "You're not a team player. You're going to be tied down the whole time, so you don't have to worry about anything. Probably blindfolded too; I don't want anyone seeing those eyes. I know they turn *me* off. I'll get you some painkillers or something, make it a little easier for you. You, on the other hand," Idris said, turning to Salmagard, "are going to have your hands free so you can use them. I've got you for less than a week. I don't have time to train you, and I don't need to. You know exactly what to do. You're going to play your role—you're both going to play your roles— or you're going to have a hard time. You think I haven't done this before? You think people haven't tried things?" He raised an eyebrow. "I'm still here. They aren't. Don't try anything. You'll get through this. It's less than a week. Are we clear?"

They nodded.

"Good. You imperials are smart. You're tough—tougher than people give you credit for. Sometimes you have to just bite it. Just put your head down and go forward. Be smart—it's worth it. When your life's on the line, anything is worth it. Don't give me any trouble, and I'll look out for you. These guys are paying to have you sober, but if we're on good terms, I can probably slip you something that's going to make all of this that much easier. So you've got something to aim for."

When Salmagard's mentor had told her about unseemly behavior from galactics, this probably wasn't what she'd had in mind. But Alice Everly hadn't been wrong. She'd called it.

Though her military career had left her no shortage of war stories to share with a young Tessa Salmagard, one experience was missing from Alice Everly's impressive history: that of being a prisoner. She'd had a full career and never been captured.

Salmagard had less than two weeks of operational time, and she was wearing control cuffs.

Idris pointed at the ceiling. "Follow instructions. Anything we bring you to wear, you wear. Anything your client tells you to do, you do. Don't worry—they don't expect you to be experts. If you are, that's fine. If you aren't, that's fine too. They know you aren't pros." He looked at Salmagard. "This is your room. Your friend's going to be next door. As soon as I move you, you're on the clock. You're going to get cleaned up and changed; then you're on the job. I'll give you a little extra time," he said, pointing at Diana. "For grooming. Relax. We've been doing this a while. Lots of girls have been where you are now. The vast—*vast*—majority of them are out there living their lives. I know what I'm doing. This is a delicate business, but I've got it down to a science. Do you understand what I've told you?"

They nodded.

"Do you have any questions?"

Salmagard nodded.

"I'm going to let you ask. But don't waste my time—no insults, none of that. Anything you do that you know I don't want you to do—that's just going to get you into trouble. I said I wouldn't kill you. I didn't say I wouldn't hurt you. We clear?"

Salmagard nodded.

He crossed the room and peeled the mute strip from her throat.

"What will happen to the men that were with us?"

"I have no idea. It's very unlikely that you will see them again. Don't worry about them. They were your dates, weren't they? Well, if they care about you, then they want you to live. To live, you obey me for a couple days." He tapped his chrono. "It's the only thing you can do for them—minimize your own suffering. And it's the only thing you can do for yourselves."

5

I looked as hard as I could, but there wasn't much to see.

Freeber and Willis led us through a dull corridor into a dull stairwell. An actual stairwell. That struck me as a strange architectural choice. Then they hurried us through another corridor and into a cramped bay where a small tugboat waited.

All the way, Freeber clutched at his face and groaned. Willis said nothing. She had a firm grip on the back of my neck, and her nails dug into my skin. She was furious. Not about Freeber—his injury didn't seem to bother her much—but about still having me and Sei on her hands. It looked like she'd been hoping to sell us all and be done with it.

The tug's freight doors were standing open to reveal its bay, the old-fashioned sealing flaps hanging loose.

It wasn't much of a cargo compartment, but it was obviously what Willis and Freeber called home. There were a table, a lot of trash, a pair of armchairs, and a large sofa that appeared to serve as their bed.

The idea of turning the cargo compartment of a little tug like this into a cozy nest for a couple in business together struck me as terribly romantic. I was a little jealous. In a different life, something like this wouldn't have been the worst thing I could think of.

"Kneel," Willis told us, and we obeyed.

Freeber went to the counter, rummaging through cabinets for first aid supplies. I thought Willis ought to at least offer to help him with his nose, but she just stared at me and Sei for a moment, then began to pace, viciously kicking a bottle that was sitting on the floor. It clattered into the bulkhead, then rolled down the ramp and into the dock.

Freeber cleaned the blood off his face, probing tenderly at his nose and wincing. He was tough. Diana had dealt him a blow that probably would've put a lesser man in a coma.

He groaned, and his voice came out sounding quite different from when his face had been intact. He coughed. "Christ." It was refreshing to hear someone swear at an actual deity instead of the Empress.

"What was that?" Willis asked. "She was my size."

"Strong." He gasped, knocking back painkillers. "What do I even do with this?"

"Is it broken?"

He nodded, wiping away blood.

Willis seemed to soften a little. "Clean it up. We'll get it looked at."

I watched Freeber apply a clear plastic brace to his nose. It sealed in place, immediately frosting over to reduce the swelling.

"That's a little better," he said, his voice sounding closer to the way it had before. He looked ridiculous, but a funny nose was better than an openly mashed one. He pulled off his bloody shirt. It wasn't the tattoos or the muscles that bothered me; it was the scars. They looked brutal. Someone back there had mentioned New Brittia. Freeber certainly looked like the type of guy you'd see in there. And if he was here, that meant he'd gotten out alive. That was rare.

Still shirtless, Freeber took a bottle from a cooler and opened it with a clipper set in the counter. He leaned back and took a long drink. Willis joined him and grabbed the bottle, taking a pull herself.

Together, they stared at us.

Wordlessly, Willis passed the bottle back to Freeber, who pressed it to his eye.

"Your type?" he asked finally.

"Maybe that one," Willis said, eyeing Sei. "We're not taking them back. It was too much hassle to get the hauler. I won't take a loss on this."

"How? Who'll take them?"

"I want to try Heimer."

"What's he going to do with them?"

She shrugged. "Remember what his wife did at the Bazaar?"

Freeber looked thoughtful. Then he saw her look and sighed.

Willis drove her heel into his foot. Freeber was wearing such massive boots that he probably didn't even feel it, but he politely pretended to wince. Willis turned and marched into the cockpit. "Let's just do it," she called back. "I hate imperials." Freeber touched the shield over his nose gently, letting out a long breath. He glanced down the passage to the cockpit, looked at us, then moved past us to the doors. The decor in the bay was too eclectic; it was impossible to guess precisely where these two were from.

Sei and I watched Freeber lean on a lever, and the cargo doors began to close, the tracks grinding loudly. We could hear Willis speaking in the cockpit. She was telling someone they were about to take off.

My eyes fixed on the hatch we'd come through, willing it to open, for Salmagard to come charging through—but no such luck.

The cargo doors closed and the pressure in the bay changed. Freeber checked the seal, knocked on the metal, then started to pick up some of the mess. Willis had just tossed aside the bottle after she drained it. I wondered what this place would look like without Freeber to tidy it up.

"Let's go," Willis called.

Freeber stopped cleaning and pulled us both to our feet, dragging us into the cramped cockpit. He shoved us into the seats behind the pilot and copilot's chairs and strapped us in.

Because we had our hands behind our backs, it was not an escapable arrangement. We couldn't make a play because of the control cuffs; it was that simple. It was frustrating, but there was nothing for it.

I didn't have time for this.

Heimer. The name didn't ring any bells with me, but it was a big universe, and the Free Trade sectors were hardly my area of expertise.

At least Sei and I wouldn't be bored during the trip; there was almost too much to look at in the cockpit. This was an old ship, and though Willis and Freeber clearly didn't baby it, it seemed to be functioning remarkably well. These two knew what they were doing.

There were knickknacks and mementos, plastic sheets advertising musical concerts—the entire cockpit was like a scrapbook to their travels. There was the preserved head of an animal I'd never seen before mounted on the ceiling, and a holographic AI dancing and twirling across the controls.

I didn't see any Prince Dalton paraphernalia, but there was a large scattergun wedged between the seats.

Trying not to make too much noise, I tested my restraints. I could lean a little in either direction, but that was all the movement I had. Sei wasn't much better off.

Willis handed Freeber his headset as he strapped in. Together, they powered up the ship, and I listened to the engine struggle. A little plastic dancing girl in a grass skirt jiggled enthusiastically on the console as the holographic one cartwheeled past it.

The front viewport digitized, and I leaned over to look at the readouts. Fuel, maintenance stats. None of that would help me. How about a starscape? I couldn't see that screen.

I kept still as Willis glanced back at us.

Freeber turned on some music, which I was grateful for.

Ahead of us, the bay doors were opening. Willis touched her headset briefly, then finished strapping in and deployed her controls.

Several red warning lights appeared on the heads-up display at the top of the viewport. Freeber absently started flipping switches to erase them.

Maybe these two *didn't* know what they were doing.

We began to drift forward. Freeber was doing the flying. Willis slouched down in her seat and put her boots on the console, applying a hypo to her neck. She promptly closed her eyes and lay back.

I was only a little jealous.

We left the bay, and I looked ahead with interest, but I didn't know what I was seeing. Open space, but no recognizable formations. There was a beacon out there, and a light line, so we were at least near civilization. A moving light was probably a shuttle.

The motion was smooth. Freeber had that look as he piloted the ship: that look that this was all muscle memory. He was good at this. This wasn't a huge ship, but it wasn't some tiny skiff either. It wasn't meant to handle like a shuttle, but Freeber was treating it like one. That took experience and expertise. New Brittia survivor. Skilled with manual piloting. Where had Freeber gone wrong?

If I really craned my neck, the feed from the tug's rear camera was visible.

I could see the bay doors closing behind us. As we got farther away, the place we were leaving took shape.

It was an asteroid. An asteroid with a brightly lit structure on it and dozens of instantly recognizable ships clustered around it. Lights, signs, and advertisements flashed madly. Figures moved inside an atmosphere bubble.

A fuel post.

It was coming into focus. It was a tiny business for refueling ships. Specifically, long-range cargo haulers. There were also a restaurant and some comfort-related amenities.

There would be a VR parlor and probably some kind of gambling opportunity. The men and women who piloted those long-distance haulers made a lot of money and usually didn't have much to spend it on. They spent the majority of their time flying. Not even flying, just being in their ships, which mostly flew themselves—but galactic law demanded a pilot be present regardless. It wasn't a very exciting career.

So that was who Idris was: the proprietor of this facility. But why kidnap people? It was because a lot of these pilots had implants and augmentations that made it difficult, or impossible, for them to safely use full-immersion VR, which meant they needed real, physical outlets for their personal comfort needs—but this was Free Trade space, so there was no shortage of perfectly willing sex workers. On top of that, a proper fuel stop ought to have some comfort androids as well.

Kidnapped women had to have a more specific purpose. The Empire wasn't popular with everyone, but I doubted that random pilots wanted to pay money to mistreat unwilling Evagardian girls. Idris had to have a more specialized business on the side.

Charming.

Maybe his trade in people was part of the service he offered with his business, but more likely it was the real business, and the fuel, food, and other distractions offered by his establishment were just camouflage.

I was starting to get a feel for it. I could hardly imagine anything more upsetting, but getting upset wouldn't be constructive.

Light and movement caught my eye. There was a tablet-style holo in a webbed holder on the back of Willis' seat. Sei had managed to activate it with his feet. On the screen was footage of Freeber and Willis. I couldn't tell what they were doing; it was dark. Sei determinedly prodded at the commands with his shoe, oblivious to the panicked looks I was giving him. Maybe he thought he could somehow use it to call for help.

Freeber's music covered up any noise he was making, but that wasn't the point—our captors weren't going to take kindly to this kind of invasion of their privacy. Maybe Sei didn't fully appreciate how dangerous these people were. They didn't want to hurt us—they wanted to sell us—but that didn't mean it was a good idea to provoke them.

Now Sei was looking at footage from a space race at Isaka, a fairly prestigious one. These two certainly got around.

His eyes flicked to Freeber, who was busy flying the ship. It looked like the big man was plotting a course, not a jump. The ship was accelerating. Wherever we were going, it couldn't be very far away.

Now Sei was watching video of a hermaphroditic figure covered in pink fur, with a tail and two large catlike ears. Willis and Freeber were both there as well, and I doubted that they wanted strangers to see this footage. In fact, it looked like it had taken place in the pleasure tower at Red Yonder.

I wasn't sure if the pink thing was an android or not, but people didn't usually record things they did with androids. Probably a human specialist with a lot of modification.

While that sort of thing wasn't really my cup of tea, it reminded me of the time with Salmagard that I wasn't going to get, of the disruption these two had brought to my life, which was in a fragile place.

I kicked Sei savagely in the knee, and he glared at me, then reluctantly turned the reader off.

Freeber looked back at us, then at Willis, who had begun to tremble and shiver. He pulled a blanket from the floor and tossed it over her sleeping form, reaching over to arrange it better, then to wipe a little drool from her mouth and fondly stroke her hair for a moment.

She was completely gone.

It would've been a sweet gesture if the blanket had been a little cleaner.

The scene ahead of us was changing. It took me a moment to realize what I was looking at.

It was a truly gargantuan shape, looking like it was composed entirely of cubes of all sizes, all mashed together into a space station.

It certainly wasn't traditional station design, and though I'd never been inside, I knew it by sight.

This was the Bazaar.

Any decent-sized space station offered a lot of shopping, but the Bazaar was different. It was the only establishment of its kind. Free Trade space wasn't exactly lawless, but it was far from safe—big-ticket vendors and merchants needed protection. The Bazaar, in exchange for a steep price, offered that, along with a fixed location and the simple prestige of being part of the Bazaar. Which was a big deal.

Once a very utilitarian mercantile fixture, the Bazaar had become its own brand over time, and one of the most fascinating destinations in Free Trade space. In addition to the massive amount of business it received, there was also a thriving tourist trade. It was almost as large a draw as Baykara City.

Shopping in person for physical goods wasn't very efficient, but it was the only option if those goods were sensitive enough. Out in the galaxy, shopping for certain things would draw attention. In the Bazaar, at least in theory, you could shop without leaving records that could be accessed by any major galactic authorities.

The Bazaar's interior was considered sovereign space, and it wasn't accountable to the Free Trade Charter. That meant it was legal to buy anything, but it also meant the Bazaar itself could treat you however it liked. There were no laws against trafficking controlled commodities, but there were also no consumer protection laws.

Stealing in there could get you executed; the Bazaar offered security for its vendors, and it meant business. Murder might go unpunished, though. I didn't know the details; I just knew the Bazaar was very much its own world, and that there was nothing there that you couldn't get. Commerce wasn't exactly the law there; it was more like the religion.

It was the sort of place Prince Dalton would have wanted to visit—not that his personal security would have let him.

Even if they weren't governed by it, most of the businesses in there still operated under the Free Trade Charter because their customers would have to leave at some point and didn't want to become criminals the moment they walked out the door—but not all of them.

There were whole industries built around smuggling illegal things out of the Bazaar. Every intelligence service in the galaxy knew that weapons of mass destruction were being sold in there—and they were all waiting to pounce on anyone who came out with them, so wares like that had to be moved discreetly.

The fuel stop made sense. The cargo pilots were bringing wares for the vendors in the bazaar, but the pilots weren't going to pay the exorbitant entry fees to get themselves into the Bazaar. They would deliver their goods, then take their leisure at places like the one we'd just come from, or the various smaller stations clustered around the Bazaar, before they moved on to their next contracts.

Between the entry fees and rent and commissions from the actual merchants, I'd heard the Bazaar was staggeringly profitable. The station was little more than a shell with life support.

It was massive—so massive that it couldn't be cheap to run, but compared with more lavish facilities, it had to be pennies on the Commonwealth dollar.

And I knew exactly where it was. We were deep in Free Trade space, near the Trigan curvature, but even nearer to the frontier.

Imperial Pointe was considered genteel by Free Trade standards, thanks to its close proximity to Evagardian space. But I remembered how easily we'd been kidnapped there.

Out *here*, things were probably pretty rough. My time as Prince Dalton hadn't been all easy, but it *had* been luxurious. I didn't have a lot of hours clocked in this kind of environment, and my dealings with people like Willis and Freeber were limited.

But it made sense for them to bring us here. People were sensitive cargo. I didn't know exactly where Free Trade law stood on the subject of human beings. I knew there were loopholes allowing for indentured servitude that could easily be twisted into what any imperial would view as slavery—that was probably the sort of situation that Sei and I were headed for.

And that brought to mind some ugly possibilities. At one end of the spectrum was respectable indentured servitude. That was by no means a desirable path in life, but it was more or less civilized. At the other end, people bought and sold humans for some nasty things.

It didn't matter which one Willis and Freeber had in mind for us—I had places to be and things to do.

And now it looked like we weren't going to the Bazaar after all.

The station loomed in front of us, but we weren't making for it—we were heading for another establishment built onto an asteroid. This one was obviously a gambling den.

There were quite a few small ships and shuttles in dock around the place.

Freeber skillfully brought in the tug between a Trigan corvette and an Evagardian shuttle. There might have been some very discreet or very heavily guarded imperials inside the Bazaar—but there wouldn't be any here. This Evagardian shuttle was just a symbol of status for a wealthy galactic. And it was brave for them to leave it out here unattended.

Freeber undid his straps and checked his chrono, then leaned over and gently patted Willis' cheek. She stirred, groggily opening her eyes. Seeing we had arrived, she sat up, blinking rapidly. She pushed the blanket aside and staggered to her feet, shuffling off to the lavatory.

Sei and I waited patiently, gazing at the brightly lit gambling den. Lots of flashing lights and advertisements—plenty of brands and products I'd never even heard of. There was always something new to see in Free Trade space.

There was an atmosphere field around the den. You could leave your ship without a pressure suit and just stroll through the door.

Willis returned as Freeber was getting me and Sei out of our seats. Though I wasn't sure how long I'd been unconscious, I knew I had to be coming due for my next injection. I needed regular doses of the antidote to the poison EI had gotten me with until I could find the time for a proper dialysis. But even with my hands free and the ability to speak, my things had been taken—and probably left at Idris' place. I didn't *have* the antidote.

And that was a problem. I already had a headache.

"Just walk them in?" Freeber asked.

Willis shrugged.

"He won't like it."

Willis clearly did not care. She yawned, then stretched.

Freeber tucked a pistol into the back of his waistband and pulled on a jacket.

We left the tug and waited while Willis, grumbling, paid for a lift platform to carry us to the ground. The green and white tiles underfoot stood out sharply from the asteroid rock, and the recycled air smelled distinctly bitter. It was the scent of the rock itself. I felt the tingle of decontamination mist, and the flashing advertisements were making my headache worse.

In time, as the poison reproduced in my bloodstream and the levels rose, it would cause my veins to constrict, gradually reducing blood flow. I'd lose strength, sensation, and motor skills. Eventually it would get bad enough that it would result in less oxygen getting to my brain. I wasn't exactly sure how long it would take to kill me. At full strength, a few minutes.

The antidote pushed it back, but the poison was designed to linger until the job was done, so it wouldn't stop trying.

People emerged from the den and others pushed ahead of us to get inside. We drew a few glances, but apparently two young men wearing control cuffs weren't enough to impress anyone. There were all sorts here—men and women of all ages. There were plenty of pilots, but also people who had the look of being locals. The Bazaar was surrounded by smaller stations, but the cluster itself was fairly isolated. Inside the Bazaar, you could spend years trying to experience everything being offered, but outside it there was only so much to do. Places like this were popular for a reason.

Sei was nearly knocked down by a teenage girl in a Martian singlet, and she was being chased by a boy in a costume that was meant to look like an imperial EV suit. There were a couple of food carts outside the doors, and little tables, lots of people sitting and eating. A band of three with Trigan mariachi synths was playing a set that was getting a great reaction.

It was good music, but Freeber and Willis weren't even slightly interested.

The den's doors opened, and loud music and voices washed over us, along with some very welcome warm air.

The interior was more or less what I expected. Crowded. Gaudy. There was a lot of fake gilding around; the dominant colors were purple, green, and gold.

Chimes and electronic noises filled the air, which was thick with the smell of burning plant and chemical matter, and also ethanol. And sweat.

Waiters and waitresses in uniforms that were equal parts minimalist and theatrical were prancing around the gaming floor, and holoscreens formed corridors that created the illusion of being underwater. Mermaids and exotic fish swam around us. It was the sort of place Prince Dalton would've loved.

A man in fashionable body armor halted Willis.

"Don't just walk past," he said, looking tired.

"Me?" Willis placed a hand on her heart, looking indignant.

"You shouldn't be here," the armored man said, glancing at Freeber.

"Hey." Willis snapped her fingers in front of the man's face. "It's me. You're talking to me. Don't tell him where he should be. He belongs with me."

The man in the armor glowered at her for a moment, then looked at me and Sei. He seemed to be deliberating. He wanted to stand his ground, but he didn't want to make a scene on the gaming floor.

"What is this?"

"None of your business," Willis replied.

The man said something into his holo, then turned and started away.

Willis followed without hesitation. Freeber pushed us along behind her.

Sei was looking around like he wanted to catch someone's eye, but I knew there wasn't likely to be any help for us here. Ideally, Willis and Freeber would sell us. Then we'd get our hands free, or at least the use of our voices. Then maybe we could do something.

Given the state of my health, I was hoping we'd get to that part soon.

We took an abrupt turn, and we were off the main floor. At the end of a narrow corridor was an office. It was roomy, but the dark colors made it seem smaller than it was. A shifting light throbbed in one corner, bathing it all in a soothing light.

The man inside got to his feet, face disbelieving, as the guy in the armor followed us inside. The door closed behind us, shutting out the noise from the floor completely.

There was a big statue in the corner of a nude woman holding a sword and covered in blood, which I recognized instantly. It was a promotional display from a Ganraen drama produced during the war with Evagard, based very loosely on the Grand Duchess. The production had been financed by the Royals, its goal to provoke imperial ire, and it had done it.

As Prince Dalton, I had been at the premiere. It had included numerous historical inaccuracies, a less-than-flattering portrayal of the Heroes of the Unification, and a treatment of the Grand Duchess that included all manner of unflatteringly scandalous antics. None of it with any credible basis in fact, but that was the nature of propaganda.

Not content simply to let a popular Ganraen actress portray the Duchess, the drama's producers had digitally re-created the Grand Duchess' face and voice down to the smallest detail.

I couldn't imagine anything that could possibly offend Evagardians more. As a means of inspiring outrage, the drama had been a smashing success.

That was the only anti-imperial object in the office, but the rest of Heimer's decor was equally tacky.

"Hi," Willis said, doing a good job of sounding very cavalier about it.

The man—Heimer, presumably—gaped at her. He was short and a little paunchy, but normal enough. I placed him at around fifty. He wore an impeccable Frontier suit.

These Free Trade crooks were snappy dressers. I was just assuming he was a crook. There was nothing illegal about running a gambling den, but I doubted Willis would try to sell us to an upstanding citizen. On the other hand, this was Free Trade space. These people were all weird.

Freeber was tense, but Willis kept up her act.

"Got something for you," Willis said, reaching up to put her hand on my head. She rubbed my hair. "What do you think?"

"About what?"

"About them. These two. Evagardian. Come on. Prassa will totally be all over them. I'll give you a discount."

Heimer's mouth moved silently. He pointed a finger at Willis, moved it to Freeber, then back to Willis. A full five seconds went by before he could form words.

"You want to sell me a couple of imperials so I can give them to my wife?"

"What part of that are you not getting?" Willis asked, giving him the most irritating look she could muster. I was starting to have some doubts about her business acumen.

Then they were all pulling guns.

Heimer's had come out of his sleeve, Willis' from her holster, Freeber's from his belt, and the bodyguard's had already been in his hand.

Both Willis and Freeber were aiming at Heimer. Heimer was aiming at Freeber, and the bodyguard had the muzzle of his pistol pressed to the back of Willis' head.

I was impressed; it had happened fast. The chems Willis was using didn't slow her down. Sei's eyes were wide. I knew how he felt.

"You're seriously going to come in here fucked-up on—on whatever you're using, and talk to me about Prassa," Heimer said, glaring at Willis. "And you let her," he said to Freeber.

"Grow up," Willis said, eyes narrowed. "You were there. She'll love these guys. I'm doing you a favor."

"You think this is going to work out for you?" Heimer asked, tone patronizing. "You know, if I kill you both, all I'm doing is saving you some embarrassment. Shut up," he said to Freeber, who had been starting to say something.

"I didn't know," the big man repeated, ignoring him.

"I've heard that before," Heimer shot back.

"Sounds like a personal problem," Willis said, flicking off her safety. "Make me an offer."

Sei and I weren't in the path of any of these bullets, but with so many guns in such a small space, that didn't really matter. Sei had gotten very pale.

"You're insane. You're seriously, actually, totally crazy," Heimer said to her face, "if you think I'm going to do business with you, even if you had something for me that I wanted. Something that *made sense*."

"You think I'm not pissed too?" Willis gave him another maddening look. "She bathes with decon juice. Or I would, if I was her."

"I don't care what she *does*. But now everyone *knows*," Heimer snarled. "*This* brain-damaged piece of meat." He wiggled his pistol at Freeber. "*Him*. Of all people. After the shit they did to him in New Brittia. How's that make me look? Even if it was just in VR."

"Man, you don't want to know how you look," Freeber said.

He was about to do it. Heimer tensed, and I got ready to make my move—but Freeber went on.

"I was being a woman," Freeber said. He didn't say it very loudly.

The words had a profound effect on the room. I was just grateful for the reprieve. For a moment there, it had looked like someone was going to get shot. Maybe a couple people.

Willis looked over at him sharply, and Heimer blinked, taken aback. He lowered his gun slightly.

"Wait. What?"

"You heard me," Freeber said, clearly annoyed.

It wasn't easy to keep looking scared now. Sei was struggling not to laugh. Of course he couldn't really laugh—he was muted, like me. But we had to keep our faces serious.

Heimer stared up at Freeber suspiciously. The big man made an exasperated noise and lowered his gun, spreading his arms. "How am I supposed to know it's your wife when she looks like Prince Dalton?"

Willis' brows rose even higher. This was news to her.

"I didn't know it was her until I added her to my friends list after," Freeber said, putting his pistol away. "Talk to her before you talk to me, jackass."

"That's what you do in VR when I'm not there? Be a woman and hook up with women pretending to be royal dudes?" Willis asked, sounding more impressed than annoyed.

"How am I going to know if it's a man or a woman?" Freeber asked her.

Then he cleared his throat and looked meaningfully at me and Sei.

Heimer had forgotten us completely. Now he looked over at us and seemed to suppress a laugh. Shaking his head, he used a finger to push the barrel of Willis' gun away from his face.

"What do you seriously think I'm going to do with them? Hand them to her and just say, 'Here, have fun'? You're both insane. You need to detox. Take them and get them out of here. I don't want your leftovers. Neither does my wife," he added, scowling. "We don't keep indentureds."

I felt a pang of disappointment. He wasn't going to buy us. We had to get away from Willis and Freeber and out of these control cuffs. Or at the very least unmuted so I could tell them I wasn't well. Otherwise I was just going to die right in front of them.

"What about for gaming?" Willis asked.

"What? What does that even mean? This isn't New Brittia. Is my name Baykara? Go sell them at the Bazaar like everyone else. And get help. You both need help."

Freeber and Willis exchanged a look.

"It was a long shot," the big man said.

Willis scowled at Heimer. "Pussy," she said.

"Even if I wanted some random guys—for some reason—I don't know who these are or where you got them. For all I know, you stole them."

"Of *course* we stole them."

"See? Do you even listen to yourself talk? I don't need this. You two are mental. Get *out*. And don't come back for a while— you really mess with my thing." Heimer waved, annoyed.

The man in the armor firmly shooed us to the door. Willis broke eye contact with Heimer only grudgingly, grabbing my sleeve and hauling me into the corridor, swearing loudly.

We left the den quickly; Willis seemed to have no desire to linger.

As we waited outside, she tapped her foot impatiently. The float platform that would take us back to the ship was taking its time. Mentally, I was tapping my foot as well. Time was passing—time I couldn't afford.

This place seemed like a good time; maybe, instead of such an obvious destination, I should have brought Salmagard somewhere like this. Somewhere a little less structured, some- where fun. Not that Red Yonder wasn't fun.

No, this sort of place was beneath Salmagard. She didn't seem to have much reverence for her station, but at the end of the day she was still the real thing. She was willing to push boundaries, not leap over them.

On the other hand, if I'd brought her here, we probably wouldn't have been kidnapped.

Willis looked up at Freeber, who was stonily fiddling with his holo.

"I didn't know you liked to be a woman in VR," she said.

He pretended to ignore her, tugging at his gloves and check- ing his chrono. There was a lull in the music, and someone laughed loudly as they entered the den. Above, a Trigan skiff passed low over the asteroid.

"Don't think I'm going to just forget," Willis went on.

Freeber didn't reply. It looked like he was sincerely regretting what he'd said in there—but I didn't think he'd had a choice. If he hadn't defused the situation, someone could've gotten hurt. He wasn't stupid.

"What do you look like?" she pressed.

"None of your business."

She reached up and grabbed his ear, twisting fiercely. Wincing, he had to lean over. He reluctantly keyed his holo, calling up an image. His VR avatar was a slim blond with flawless skin and surprisingly realistic proportions. When people could build themselves from scratch, they tended to go overboard. Not Freeber, apparently.

"When I get a new compatibility ring," she said, looking at the image, "I'm going in there with you. I'm going to be like a huge muscle-head guy like you, and I'm going to completely take you to station—I'm going to mess you up, pound you to within an inch of your sanity."

"Sure you will," Freeber said, shaking her off.

"See if I don't," she said, folding her arms and sticking out her tongue at him.

He reached out and tousled her hair. She gave him a look, then noticed that Sei and I were still there. I wondered if we could've just slipped away right there.

"What are you looking at?" she demanded, and slammed her knee into my groin.

6

SALMAGARD squeezed tighter, her arm locked around the man's throat. He was crimson in the face, but she didn't let up. He didn't even try to fight back, not really—certainly not effectively. He just pulled at her arm, as if that were going to help. It took about ten seconds for him to lose consciousness.

She let him fall into the deep carpet. Salmagard was taken aback by how easy that had been. She checked his pulse, then stepped back, dusting off her hands. After a glance at the door, she went into the room's tiny lavatory. In the display, she saw herself wearing the outrageous lingerie that Idris had ordered.

It was a bit daring for her sensibilities, but becoming. She wondered if it was the sort of thing the Admiral would like. Not that this was the time to be thinking about that, but adrenaline always had this effect on her. She had to focus.

She had to find Diana and free her. Then she had to find the Admiral and Sei and free *them*.

Salmagard pulled on her dress and left the room, fastening

her sash. The corridor was narrow and sterile. She could faintly hear loud music thudding somewhere overhead.

Idris had said that Diana would be next door. Left or right?

Salmagard went to the nearer door and hit the reader.

Diana was sitting on the bed, wearing the same silly lingerie Salmagard was—but rather than black, hers was red. The pale woman had her face in her hands, and she was weeping noisily.

Salmagard froze, stricken—had she been too late? She hadn't wasted any time—and no, she wasn't too late.

A man lay on the floor by the wall, which was severely dented. Salmagard didn't understand.

"I'm a monster," Diana moaned.

Salmagard went to the unconscious client and checked his pulse. He was alive. This room was identical to the one she'd been in, to the last detail.

"He's all right," she said.

Diana just groaned into her hands.

"Get dressed. We have to go," Salmagard told her.

"I know."

She noticed the shackles dangling from Diana's wrists and ankles.

She stared at the broken chains, then at the other halves of the four sets of shackles still attached to the bed.

"Did you—" Salmagard began, pointing, then hesitated. "Did you *break* those?"

Diana just covered her head, shoulders shaking.

Salmagard blinked. "How?"

The pale woman didn't answer. Salmagard considered the remains of the shackles and the dented wall. There were explanations, but hadn't Freeber said Diana's body wasn't artificial? She was flesh and blood? That meant she had augmentations.

Organic replacement limbs? Had she been injured when she was in the Service?

Or there were nanomachines that could generate enormous strength; they were used by acolytes and other Evagardian special forces.

At the moment it didn't matter. Salmagard had a mission.

She hesitated for a moment, then moved toward the lavatory door and remembered that Diana's dress had been destroyed. She rolled the unconscious man over and got his jacket off.

"Put this on," she said firmly.

Diana looked up and seemed to rally. She swallowed and got to her feet, taking the jacket. Her red eyes stared down at Salmagard.

"What do we do? Call it in?"

Salmagard nodded. "But we have to go. We have to go after them."

"What? Let the GRs do that," Diana said. She was right—Salmagard had been thinking about Imperial Galactic Rescue too. "That's their job. This is why they exist. For stuff like this. Stuff *exactly* like this."

"No, it has to be us. There's no time. They'll disappear out here," Salmagard told her. "You call for help. I'll go. I'm in the Service. I'm a negotiator."

"No, I'll come," Diana said quickly. "I'm—I'm a vet. Let's just get out of here. I don't like this place."

Salmagard looked up, then at the door. No one was crashing in, pointing guns at them, or trying to get them back under control. "I guess they're not watching."

"Of course not. Nobody would pay to . . . do stuff to us if there were creepers looking."

Salmagard eyed the door. "Can we walk out?"

"Do we even know what this place is?" Diana was waking up quickly. "Doesn't feel like planetside. Can't be."

"I heard music out there. There's something above us."

Diana looked down at the broken shackle hanging from her slender wrist. Her eyes hardened.

"Let's go see," she said.

They went out into the corridor. The door at the far end opened, and Idris emerged, shrugging into his blazer. He froze at the sight of them.

Salmagard sprinted forward at top speed, or as close to top speed as her dress would allow, but he was too fast. Idris retreated back into the room and slammed the door with a bang.

Salmagard reached it and pushed, but it was secure. He'd managed to lock it. Then Diana was there. She touched the plastic, then hauled back and struck it with both palms, knocking it from its fastenings and sending it toppling into the room.

Salmagard didn't question what Diana had just done; she launched herself through the doorway blind. Idris was behind the desk. He was speaking rapidly into his holo, but as the door crashed to the floor, he dropped it and went for a pistol resting on his console. Salmagard vaulted onto the desk, snatching the gun away and kicking him squarely in the chest. The impact sent him staggering back, past his chair and into the wall. As he struggled upright, he found himself looking at the muzzle of the gun.

"Take off your trousers," Diana said, picking up the door.

He stared, Adam's apple bobbing.

Salmagard gave him a meaningful look, and prodded his face with the pistol.

With jerky motions, he undid his belt and obeyed. Diana put the door more or less back in place, then picked the trousers up and pulled them on, cinching the belt tight around her bony hips. She cleared her throat. "What did you do with our friends?"

"I didn't take them," Idris said. His eyes were crossed, fixed on the gun. "Willis and Freebs still have them. They're gone."

"Where did they go?"

"I don't know. I really don't. They're not my people."

Salmagard pressed the pistol into his eye, then pulled it away and grabbed him by the collar, pushing him facedown on the desk. "Hold him," she said to Diana, who wedged her elbow against his neck and leaned in, making him gasp in pain.

Salmagard's eyes fell on a little pile of items on the desk.

The contents of their pockets. Her own holo, and Diana's. The Admiral's. Sei's.

The Admiral's hypos.

The Admiral's hypos containing the antidote to the poison that was still in his system.

Salmagard snatched them up and shoved them into her sash. She tucked away the pistol and grabbed Idris' right hand. Without hesitation, she broke his little finger. He cried out, but Diana gave her elbow a hard shove, choking the breath from him.

One at a time, Salmagard snapped all five of his fingers. Then she went back and broke them all again at the second knuckle. Time was an issue, so this would be an expedited interrogation. Salmagard had never had formal training on this topic, but she could improvise.

Diana had to grip his face tightly and hold him down hard as Idris tried to thrash his way free.

Salmagard circled the table and bent over to get eye level with him.

"Where would they have gone?" she asked, picking up his other hand.

"The Bazaar," Idris croaked, tears running from his eyes. "Heimer's place? The Flashbulb? Rosario's? I don't *know*."

Diana took Idris' holo off his wrist. She grabbed him by the hair.

"This has to be some kind of station. You've got a shuttle, haven't you? Where is it?"

"The first bay," he ground out.

"You said the Bazaar," Salmagard said, getting his attention. "*The* Bazaar?"

"Of course," Diana said. "We're going to borrow your shuttle. You don't mind, do you?"

Idris opened his mouth, and she smashed his face on the desk, knocking him out cold.

"Trick question," she said, letting him slump to the floor.

"How do we fly the shuttle without him?" Salmagard asked, aghast.

"I'm a pilot. Well, I used to be." Diana held up his holo. "Is that our stuff? Let's go. What's in those sketchy hypos?"

Salmagard hesitated. "Medicine."

"Yours? Or your boyfriend's?"

She hesitated, but only for a moment. "His."

"Then we better get a move on. We have to get the GRs on this. This is what they do."

Imperial Galactic Rescue was a small branch of the military exclusively dedicated to extracting Evagardians that got into trouble outside imperial space.

They were one of the most glamorous units in the Service, getting the same kind of recognition as the elite guards and acolytes from Valadilene. There was no shortage of dramas and stories dedicated to their exploits, and it wasn't uncommon for Evagardian children to grow up dreaming of being one of them. Salmagard had no doubt that they were extremely good at their job.

But they couldn't perform miracles.

And the Admiral wouldn't want to be found by the military. She had to try to help him avoid that. She didn't know what they would do with him if they got their hands on him, but he'd been willing to flatline to shake them off, so he obviously felt strongly about it.

And Salmagard knew firsthand that Evagard had tried to kill him before.

"They won't get to them before we do," Salmagard told Diana. "We can notify them, but we're already here."

"I've heard the window for getting people back in this kind of situation is pretty small," Diana said, frowning. "Or maybe I saw that in a drama. But we should go."

They gathered their things and left the office.

It took several minutes to locate the shuttle bays. There were only two of them, but there was quite the little warren of sublevels beneath whatever stood on top of Idris' dungeon.

Idris' personal shuttle was an Isakan model, a civilian flyer for personal use. It was shiny red, and it looked as if someone took meticulously good care of it.

His holo granted them access and launch permissions.

Diana said she was a pilot; Salmagard had to trust her. *She* certainly couldn't fly a shuttle. She could barely manage a personal flyer. Though, with the Admiral's coaching, she had piloted an aircraft once, however briefly.

She shuddered at the memory.

Her heart thudded as she followed Diana up the ramp, expecting an alarm, or something—anything to indicate that their escape was an issue for Idris or the people who worked for him.

But there was nothing. There hadn't been a single person in the halls. Security measures intended to stop them had been conspicuously absent every step of the way. Maybe all Idris' talk of how he had his business down to a science was just that: talk. Bluster. A bluff to keep his frightened victims in line. Salmagard didn't know which was worse: that he would rely on such tactics, or that they had apparently worked for him for this long.

The only thing she was sure of was that Idris hadn't counted on taking women from the Service. That was a mistake he wouldn't make again. He wouldn't have the chance.

After she found the Admiral and got him back, Salmagard was going to report Idris and his establishment to every authority that might even *possibly* have jurisdiction here. Indentured servitude might be legal in Free Trade space, but kidnapping wasn't. Idris was going to go to prison.

Diana closed the ramp, and they hurried into the cockpit. Diana dropped into the pilot's seat and started to power up the shuttle. She pulled off her borrowed jacket, revealing rippling abdominal muscles and protruding ribs. Idris' lingerie was becoming on Salmagard—not on Diana. And the pale woman's chest supporter was soaked with sweat.

"Are you all right?" Salmagard asked.

Diana looked down at herself, then touched her collarbone with a finger, eyeing the beaded moisture on it.

"I have some hormonal issues," she said, pushing the jacket aside and strapping in. "All this excitement isn't helping." Her bare arms glistened, and veins stood out visibly on her taut skin and muscles. Something wasn't quite right about her fingers, but Salmagard wasn't sure what—or maybe it was the nails. Lights from the console reflected in Diana's red eyes, and the red of her eyes was reflected in the readouts. It was unnerving.

Salmagard decided not to press. It was clear to her now that the other woman's singular appearance was not due to deliberate modifications. She was ill, and clearly sensitive about it. Maybe it was genetic; that would explain it. There was nothing worse than a loss of value to one's DNA, and nothing would kill genetic prestige like the impurity of an undesirable mutation.

Or, worse, an unattractive one.

And she'd snapped those shackles with nothing but her muscles. She must have. If she was strong enough to break chains, knock doors out of their frames, and throw men bodily into walls hard enough to crack them, Salmagard was surprised Diana hadn't simply broken free earlier.

But no—even with the strength that was probably coming from an extremely troubled metabolism and adrenal glands, no human could break out of control cuffs, which numbed the hands and wrists.

Salmagard strapped in, looking worriedly at the feeds from the cameras all over the shuttle that showed different angles of the bay. But no one was coming. Certainly not Idris; he was fast asleep, and would be for a while.

Maybe they really could leave without a ripple. That wasn't unreasonable; Salmagard felt she was owed a change of luck. First Nidaros; now this. It didn't seem fair. Of course, Alice Everly had always cautioned Salmagard never to take fairness for granted.

The shuttle was online. Now Diana was feeling out the controls. She noticed Salmagard's worried look.

"I'm a fighter pilot," she snapped. "Give me a second."

Salmagard fixed her holo to her wrist and established an uplink with the Free Trade communications network. She began to compose an alert to send to the nearest consulate, which they could pass on to the GRs—but there weren't many facts to include.

Taken from Red Yonder. Man possibly named Idris. Willis. Freeber.

At the very least, she could draw attention to what Idris was doing, but with so little information, the GRs weren't going to do the Admiral and Sei any good in the immediate future. Only Salmagard and Diana could help them here and now.

Apparently there was an atmosphere field outside, so there was no need to depressurize the little dock. Diana used Idris' holo to open the bay doors.

Salmagard made sure there was no mention of the Admiral, then sent the notification. It wasn't going to help in any meaningful way—not in time to matter—but she had to do it. She looked up as Diana guided the shuttle out.

They saw the fuel stop, the asteroid, and the large restaurant and shop that sat glowing atop it. So this was what was upstairs. The ships in phase lock around the place were all long-range cargo tugs. Under different circumstances, all of this would have struck Salmagard as being very novel and exotic.

"I've got it now," Diana said, tearing her eyes away from the feed and raising the starscape. "I can fly this. Where are they?"

"He said something about the Bazaar. And something called Heimer's place."

"I've got the Bazaar," Diana said, pointing. "Should we check the other place first? Idris has it marked—there's a route in place."

"Is it closer?"

"It's on the way."

"Do it."

Diana punched the location, highlighted the course, and pushed up the throttle.

"It's not a long way," she said. It was difficult to tell if Diana was angry and looking hostile or if it was just her eyes that were scary. She sounded confident. "We'll get them back."

Salmagard leaned back and closed her eyes, hoping the Admiral hadn't tried anything stupid. Those two ruffians, the man and the woman who had kidnapped them, weren't people to trifle with. Salmagard could tell that much by looking at them.

But the Admiral liked to act as if there was nothing that could faze him, as if he couldn't be intimidated. Like he had nothing to lose. He liked to make bold plays and take chances, but Salmagard wasn't completely blind. He wasn't well, and he couldn't be trusted to perform at the level that his ego seemed to demand of him.

She didn't know why he felt the need to put on that show, but Salmagard had a feeling that he would put it on with or without an audience. And it wouldn't end well.

He needed her. There were just too many ways to picture him getting himself killed. Salmagard shook her head.

"Worried?" Diana asked, glancing over.

Salmagard nodded, swallowing her nausea.

"Hey, what's your name?"

Salmagard blinked. Come to think of it, they hadn't really been introduced. Sei had told them Diana's name, but the Admiral had, of course, neglected to give theirs, though surely he had a perfectly safe alias for these situations.

"Tessa," she said.

They shook hands.

7

"HE'S not going to answer," Freeber said, pulling off his headset. "He's going to ignore us."

"The hell he will," Willis muttered, reaching back around her seat to snatch up the reader that Sei had toyed with earlier. "Not unless he wants me to get excited all over his social. I don't think he wants that."

Sei and I were back in our seats in the cockpit of Freeber's tug, securely strapped in.

We were approaching the Bazaar, and I was gazing at the monolithic cubes that made it up, hoping there was someone reasonable in there that would buy us promptly. With my luck, they'd sell us to cannibals that wouldn't even unmute us before they stuffed us in an oven.

If that turned out to be the case, there wouldn't be much we could do about it. That was cheery. It was probably the poison; I couldn't feel my fingertips, but my toes were getting a little cold. It was starting.

Willis, loath to pay the entry fee for four people—two of whom she did not particularly care for—seemed to be trying to lean on someone that owed her a favor.

"Suddenly he wants to talk," Freeber said, looking at a communication notification flashing on the viewport.

"Tell him to let us in. We'll just walk across and go in on foot," Willis said.

"He says his supervisor will see the tug."

"Tell him we're bringing him new technical orders. That's a good one," Willis said. "The supervisor won't know better unless he's good at his job. And what are the odds of that?"

"He doesn't like it."

"I don't care what he likes. Tell him I want a guide path in ten seconds or I'm going to redefine privacy and teach him the definition of pain."

She sounded like she meant it. Sei gave me a look of exaggerated terror. Now that no one was pointing guns at anyone, he wasn't worried at all; he was probably convinced Galactic Rescue would show up at any moment and rescue us. And maybe they would. But *he* wasn't poisoned.

Freeber winced, then relayed the message.

After a moment, a green indicator appeared on the viewport.

"That's what I thought," Willis said, putting the reader aside. "What a little bitch."

"Who are we even going to? Who's buying?" Freeber glanced back at me. "They won't be worth much on the open market, and we don't have codes."

"They're still imperials," Willis said.

"That just makes them hotter without codes."

She let out a hiss of frustration. "There is that. Shit."

"So who?"

"I don't know. We'll have to ask around."

Now Sei wasn't amused. He was starting to think about the sorts of people who would want to buy undocumented humans, and that wasn't a pleasant line of thinking.

It wasn't out of the question that we'd get lucky and be sold to someone who didn't know what they were buying. If someone respectable was tricked into taking us, they'd have no choice but to let us go when they learned of our circumstances—but the odds were against that. Without proof that we had signed ourselves away to servitude, we were nothing more than kidnapped imperials.

There weren't very many respectable people looking to buy those. The people who *would* be buying wouldn't have any interest in hearing our side of things. We weren't people anymore; we were contraband.

"He better open those doors," Willis growled, leaning forward. A moment later a pair of bay doors on the Bazaar's exterior began to vent. Lights flashed and guide paths appeared. Maintenance robots crawled around the outside of the bay doors, and a figure in a tech suit was visible under the big coolant distributors. I could see the glow of his welding torch.

That was a good career. A safe career. Mostly. I could've become a tech. That wasn't where my aptitudes were, but it wasn't like it was beyond me. But it was too late to change now.

The Bazaar was not pretty. It was just a gargantuan cluster of metal boxes, or at least that was the exterior. We weren't seeing its good side.

Someone with an actual right to be here must have allowed the tug to get this close, and now they were guiding us in. I wondered if there was anyone in this sector who Freeber and Willis didn't know. Or anyone who actually liked them.

The tug glided inside and landed. It wasn't a large bay; in fact, it was barely large enough for the tug and its occupants. A small fleet of maintenance robots had been shoved aside to make room for us. They were spindly, ugly little models I'd never seen before. They reminded me of carnivorous plants I'd seen in a drama once.

There were workbenches and big carts filled with tools. Nearly everything was maintained by robots; they were faster and more reliable than humans—but someone had to maintain the robots. In some cases, that would be other robots. But then someone had to maintain *those*. It was thankless work, but without the techs in these bays, no station could function.

The Bazaar was supposed to be all about that key precept of trade: that he who can attract and please the most customers is king—so appearances were important. But here, no one was looking. No one was trying to impress anyone.

Shuttles probably came in to pick the bots up and ferry them where they were needed in the Bazaar. The place was big enough that to get from one end of the station to the other, it would often be faster to take a shuttle than to try to make your way through the markets themselves.

Most reasonably sized stations had trams or multidirectional lifts, something to help people get around.

The Bazaar had neither, but the interior was so large that people actually piloted personal vehicles inside. Not the carts and skiffs that you saw on normal stations, but real flyers and ground cars.

The bay began to pressurize, and Freeber powered down the tug.

Willis released me and Sei, pushing us ahead of her. We watched our captors arm themselves and don jackets to conceal their weapons. Neither of them looked happy.

Freeber muttered something into his holo and nodded to Willis, who hit the release. The doors opened and the ramp lowered.

The service bay was cluttered, and it was an embarrassment. It might as well have had the words *Built by the lowest bidder* stamped on the bulkheads. There was a decidedly flimsy look to all of it, though frankly I got that impression from the rest of the station as well. After all, the Bazaar's cubist design was a cost-cutting measure, not a stylistic choice.

As for the people who worked in this bay—the decals plastered all over the walls told me everything I needed to know about them. No one was safe from advertising, anywhere. All of the holographic ads I could see were for chems and VR compatibility. There were a couple of guys in the far corner clustered around a large holoscreen that was meant for robotic diagnostics, but they were using it to watch a broadcast. They were making a lot of noise, and one of them was holding up a stack of Free Trade currency bonds.

I saw a logo flash on the screen; it was something from the Baykara Network. Maybe they were watching New Brittia, or maybe they were watching something from the Baykara Games. Either way, someone was probably about to die. Gambling was the mechanism of the Baykara business model, and human life was the fuel.

An older man in tech coveralls was making his way toward us looking distinctly ruffled. As he walked, he disengaged a pair of hand protectors that lit up and chirped a warning at him. His eyes flashed, and very suddenly, startling all of us, he flung the protectors to the deck.

"You can push me around until the end of the universe," he snarled at Willis. "But you won't last more than an hour in there without entry codes."

"We will if we take your ride," Willis said, giving me a hard shove. The floor was covered in oil and metal shavings; I managed to keep my balance and stay upright, barely.

"The hell is this?"

"Our merch. Who can unload them for us?"

The guy shrugged. "Just take them to market."

"Can't get as much," Willis said. "And no codes, remember? There has to be somebody."

The older man folded his arms. He looked back at the hatch, then up at a bank of windows high on the wall. He shook his head, nostrils flared, barely controlling his temper. His guys over in the corner weren't paying any attention; they were even louder now, cheering at something on the broadcast.

"What are they?" he asked, looking at me, then at Sei.

"Imperials," Freeber said.

"Undocumented? Of course they are."

Willis gestured impatiently.

"You want someone who wants to buy two Evagardian men who don't want to be bought."

"There has to be a market," Willis said, eyeing the rows of maintenance bots. "Someone who doesn't like imperials. Someone who runs something like Idris does."

"People don't pay much for people they don't plan to keep. And not very many people like to keep people that don't want to be kept."

"Spare me. There has to be someone. There's always someone."

The old man just scowled and opened a holo in the air in front of him. He swiped around a bit. "There might be a guy," he said. "A specialty guy."

"How do we get in touch with him?"

"You don't. He's gray market, cagey. You have to go there physically."

Willis groaned. "Where?"

"His place is in Fenix Cube. He calls himself something weird. The Dane. You know they get all those VIPs from the hotel, and he's that guy, you know."

"I don't know," Freeber said.

"That guy that gets things that people are too shy to ask for."

"Who's shy here?" Willis asked, looking baffled.

The old man wasn't in the mood. "Make it quick."

"Yeah, I want to have a nice romantic weekend at the Bazaar," Willis said, snatching the crystal he was offering.

He didn't even reply. He was already walking away. There was a shout of triumph from the techs in the corner.

"This guy's going to want a commission." Willis groaned. "If he even takes them. God, I'm so *sick* of imperials."

Freeber let her vent. He guided me and Sei along behind her as she stormed off toward the hatch, throwing a venomous glare at the old man, who was ignoring her.

We entered a narrow, dingy corridor with a malfunctioning recycler, then a stairway that rattled and shook underfoot.

For a moment I was struck with vertigo; the stairs extended up and down farther than I could see—there were at least a hundred levels. I thought about bulling into Freeber and knocking him over the railing, but there were nets every few levels to prevent those sorts of accidents. A digital mural at the rear of the stairwell flickered. It was meant to look like an endless strip of blue sky, but the display was pixelized and corrupted. A few floors up, a piece of it several meters across appeared to be missing. It hummed loudly and hurt my eyes.

Maybe the stairs weren't completely steady, or maybe my sense of balance was starting to go. I had to be careful not to trip. It wasn't easy to keep track of time, and I wasn't exactly sure how long it had been since I injected on the shuttle to Imperial Pointe.

One flight down, we were stopped by a locked door. Some crude artwork on the wall depicted the Ganraen flagship crashing into the Royal Capital, and there was a trampled plush toy on the grating beneath it. A fish. No, a shark. A shark wearing a hat. There was a tear, and his stuffing was coming out.

I gazed at it while Willis swore into her com.

The door unlocked; the old man must have keyed it remotely. We went through, into another set of unattractive corridors, but there were faint sounds of life. We were getting closer to the action. A dispenser that had once offered decon cream for hands was covered in some kind of red mold, which had spread onto the bulkhead. Freeber and Willis didn't seem to notice it; Sei and I moved to the other wall and slipped past as far from it as we could get.

The next hatch took us directly into a dark storefront. It was a shop that sold physical components. Robotics, by the look of things. They had to be highly specialized parts, because most businesses would just print their own when something broke down on them. The objects in view were for show; these physical locations were only symbolic. No one had time to actually visit a place like this. The Bazaar was crawling with robotics and services built around delivering physical wares to their buyers.

This guy they were taking us to—the Dane—had a sensitive job. They'd said the words "gray market." I wasn't intimately familiar with the terminology, but I took that to mean he wasn't hung up on the Free Trade Charter. That would necessitate a little more discretion for both him and his patrons.

That seemed normal enough. Free Trade culture wasn't as savage as Evagardians thought it was, and it was nothing if not predictable. Imperials had the Empress, and Free Traders had the bottom line. We all lived to serve.

Willis and Freeber knew where they were going. They had used this route before, and they kept a brisk pace through the store, hustling us to the hatch. The noise on the other side was muted by the air seal, but I knew it would be loud. I braced myself and looked at Sei. He was holding together well. That stood to reason if he was in the Service. And he'd mentioned something about a rough tour. He'd probably seen some things.

Willis checked something on her holo, glanced at me and Sei, then threw back the latch and pushed the door open.

There was a lot going on in the Bazaar, so much that it was difficult to make sense of it. The only thing I could see was the scale. It was probably two hundred meters to the other side of the corridor, and half a kilometer down to the lowest floor. I couldn't even guess how far we were from the top.

A dizzying network of walkways spanned the gap, and personal flyers glided past in glittering lines.

The opposite side of the corridor was a grid of thousands of businesses and enterprises, vendors and merchants. I knew our side was the same. People milled far below, little more than a vague swarm.

The noise was painful, and so were the smells. I'd been in big stations, but never with this kind of open design. It was overwhelming. I couldn't look at any one thing; there was too much, and a lot of it was so far away that I couldn't see it clearly. It was a teeming mess. Even in good health, it would've made me want to pass out. There were limits to what the brain could handle.

Willis made a disgusted sound. "Here we go," she said.

Freeber went to a door a few meters down from the one we'd emerged from. He touched his earpiece and muttered something, and the latch fell out of place. He got the door open, and Willis prodded us through.

It was a tiny bay for a small flyer. The cramped space was made more cramped by tall stacks of boxes with logos from Bazaar delivery services on them. There was an acrid stench in the air, and a single plastic advertisement on the wall for Isakan whiskey.

The flyer was sleek and glossy purple. It had a closed top and a gaudy emblem on the front. It was trying to be the sort of flyer a self-important chem dealer might cruise in on a Trigan world, but it was falling a bit short. Those flyers were much more elaborate and bombastic.

Freeber opened the rear cargo space and unceremoniously shoved Sei inside. That struck me as rude; why couldn't we ride in the back? The flyer had room for four, maybe even five people.

I didn't get to ask. I was muted.

Freeber pushed me in as well and slammed the lid.

8

"DOESN'T look so bad," Diana said, eyeing the bright lights and festive atmosphere of the little casino through the shuttle's front viewport. Young people were dancing spiritedly outside, a small mobile cart was serving drinks, and it looked like a party was getting under way.

"You've got something," Salmagard said, pointing at a notification.

"Registration fee?" Diana looked offended. "Just for docking? Like it's a privilege?"

"I'll pay it."

"No, I've got it." Diana produced her holo and transferred the money. "And will they even guide us? No? I have to do this by hand?"

"You're a good pilot," Salmagard said. It was true. Diana was so deft at the controls that Salmagard had trouble believing this was her first time flying a shuttle. Even if she said she was a fighter pilot, it was clear she could fly anything. Indicators appeared on the display to warn them if they got too close to anything, but no alerts flashed.

"Not good enough for Oen Bjorn," Diana replied bitterly, guiding them deftly into the tight rows of shuttles.

Salmagard didn't know who that was. She hoped Diana wasn't going to turn morose again.

"Remember," Salmagard said. "If we can't get them out, we can't. All we have to do is keep track of them. As long as they're alive and we know where they are, even if things get bad, the GRs can handle it."

"I'm not leaving Sei. Not if they're being mistreated."

Salmagard swallowed. She felt the same way. "Quite," she said, taking Idris' pistol from her sash and checking it.

"How should we do this? You're the negotiator."

Salmagard considered it. "We'll ask to see whoever's in charge."

"And?"

"And we will—" she began, but stopped, considering it. "We will compel them to tell us if they've seen our boys." Salmagard tried to put a little firmness in her voice.

The shuttle locked in place between a Luna yacht and a Free Trade peacekeeping patroller. Local peacekeepers—they wouldn't do them any good. Free Trade authorities only cared about crime relating to money. In Salmagard's mind, that was irrational—the Free Trade economy relied on money from all around the galaxy. If people didn't think Free Trade space was safe, they wouldn't visit it. Free Trade authorities should've felt obliged to be very hard on crime and to cultivate an atmosphere and culture of gentility.

But it didn't work that way at all. At the end of the day, people wanted what they wanted—and for many things, this was the only place to get it. People wouldn't stop patronizing Free Trade space no matter how dangerous it was. It was that simple.

Diana unstrapped from the pilot's seat and pulled on her new jacket, fastening it shut and rolling up the sleeves. It was quite a look: the oversized trousers and a jacket that only fastened in the middle, revealing plenty of pale skin. Diana's hair was a mess and her eyes were blazing. The pale woman opened and closed her hands with a series of soft pops and snaps.

Salmagard got up, politely ignoring those alarming sounds from Diana's joints. She reflected that Diana's peculiarities probably worked in their favor. They would add to their intimidation factor, which Salmagard suspected they were going to need.

They disembarked, boarding a small float platform. Diana swept her holo across the pad, paying for the lift.

"You have to pay for everything here," she complained.

"But it's not very expensive."

"It's barbaric. It's the principle—it's undignified. It's shameless. Desperation isn't pretty, and neither is greed."

Salmagard couldn't argue with that, but Alice Everly had always warned her never to judge galactics. She tightened her sash, and she could feel the cold of the metal underfoot. She'd left her shoes behind at Idris' place. Her hair wasn't ruined, but it was just askew enough to be distracting. She did what she could to adjust her assorted combs and ribbons, but the ride was short and the lift touched down before she could finish.

At first Salmagard had worried that their disheveled appearance would draw attention, but that wasn't the case.

Heimer's Gaming Parlor was packed with such a colorful

array of people that it made the sights and sounds of Imperial Pointe seem mild by comparison. The waiters and waitresses, the dancers, the images on the displays, even the patrons themselves—they were all more interesting to look at than Salmagard and Diana.

A performer in a gravity bubble had some spectacular and distracting anatomical modifications, and there was a woman who wore nothing but a robotic snake covered in blue fur. At least, Salmagard assumed it was robotic. Out here maybe engineered organisms were legal and accepted. She didn't know. The snake hissed at a passing waitress, who twirled by, unperturbed, her holographic skirt spinning and sparkling wildly.

They entered the establishment and paid the cover fee, taking it all in. It was, like so many places Salmagard had found herself in since leaving imperial space, loud. Perhaps Red Yonder was a bit like this, only on a larger scale. And probably a trifle classier.

Salmagard was new to the Service; Diana had already done a combat tour, so she was supposed to be the experienced one. But she was just gaping at the dancer in the bubble, and while Salmagard silently agreed that he was impressive, she was determined to stay on task.

She thought about Willis and Freeber, and felt her fists clench. She turned on the nearest bouncer.

"We need to speak to the proprietor." She had to raise her voice over the music.

He gave her a blank look, then nodded. "You're early," he said, taking her by the shoulder and guiding her past the rows of gaming machines. People seemed to know to get out of his way.

Diana seemed taken aback, but Salmagard wasn't complaining—there was some kind of misunderstanding, but she didn't care about details; she wanted results. She let the man guide her through the rows of screens and gaming machines, wondering if her eyes were going to adjust to all these lights and colors.

She thought about how her family would react to the news that she had set foot in an establishment like this. Forget the circumstances behind it all; this was scandalous. It was alien.

But no worse than everything that had already happened.

There were more dancers, both in bubbles and on a stage. One was actually in a cage. Most of them were female. Salmagard had never given it a lot of thought. She knew her family was privileged, but she'd never thought they were *too* different from everyone else.

But just the gap between her lifestyle and that of the average Evagardian subject was substantial. And the gap between that average Evagardian and *this* was staggering. It was just like Alice Everly had said: it was one thing to know, and another to see.

Salmagard could feel anxiety in her chest. It wasn't just fear for the Admiral—this was too much. Acting alone without orders, seeing the contrast between the Imperium and the rest of the galaxy up close. It was a lot to deal with. It was getting to her.

In a moment they were off the main floor, in a short, dim corridor. There was less noise, and that helped. Salmagard breathed.

The bouncer tapped on a door.

"This is you," he said. "I'll tell him you're here."

He walked off. Salmagard and Diana hesitated. There were no signs, nothing to indicate what these rooms were.

"Does any of this make sense to you?" Diana asked. Salmagard shook her head and hit the release for the door. Inside was a plush circular room. It was ringed by a purple sofa. Above was a zero-g bubble, just like the ones out on the floor.

"Oh," Diana said. "That's flattering."

"What?"

"They must be expecting a new dancer. They think it's you." She snorted and hit the release, sealing them in. "Because they sure as the Empress don't think it's me."

"I see," Salmagard said slowly. "Do I seem like the sort to do that?"

Diana was still gazing up at the bubble. "You're built for it, at least. Must be nice."

"What?"

"Work like this. Lots of attention. And the job skills are more transferable than knowing how to pilot a top secret experimental fighter. No one trying to kill you. Could be worse." Diana looked distant.

Salmagard folded her arms, annoyed. "Is that really what I look like to these people?"

"Different culture." Diana waved a hand. "Don't let galactics offend you; there's no money in it. That guy thinks you're the new dancer, so maybe this is an interview. Maybe he's expecting you to dance for him to get him to hire you. I wonder if he's good-looking. That's the cliché, right? That you sleep with them to get them to hire you? That's what they do in all the dramas."

Salmagard gave her a questioning look.

"What?" Diana asked.

"In any case," Salmagard said, "we can have a word with him. See if he knows anything about that man and woman."

"We'll have him all to ourselves. These people are convenient."

"I'm sure all of this would be a lot more difficult if they were taking us seriously," Salmagard said. "But they aren't expecting trouble. We have to exploit that."

"Why doesn't anyone respect imperials?"

"We are not popular," Salmagard said, surprising herself. It was obvious to her now that she had never properly appreciated how big the universe was, and just how much values and cultures could differ.

She'd known that galactics were different from people raised in the embrace of the Empress, but she'd never thought those differences could be quite so radical.

The door opened, and Diana reacted instantly. She violently yanked the man inside, throwing him onto the sofa. Salmagard leveled her pistol at him, holding a finger to her lips. He was a short, older man in a tremendously expensive suit.

Diana glanced outside, then sealed the door.

"You're not my new holo editor," the man in the suit said, narrowing his eyes.

Salmagard ignored that. "We're looking for a man and a woman who have some friends of ours. A large man, and the woman has red hair. Do you know who I'm talking about? Have you seen them recently?" She couldn't keep the urgency out of her voice, but she worked to keep her tone reasonable. Her expression and the pistol could do the threatening for her.

His eyes grew wide.

"No," he said. "No—no way. Who are you two?"

He *did* know them.

"Imperial Service," Diana said from the door, folding her arms and trying to look tough. It worked.

The man in the suit stared at her and swallowed. "Who were those Evagardian guys?"

Salmagard felt a surge of triumph. This man had seen them.

"Important people." Diana was getting into this. "Are they here?"

"No. No—I didn't touch them. I don't even know why she brought them here. That is *not* my business."

"Where did they go?" Salmagard demanded.

"To the Bazaar," the man said, keeping his hands up. "I'm sure. I mean, where else?"

"Contact them," Diana ordered. "Tell them to let the imperials go. We can all walk away from this."

"I can't," he said.

Salmagard looked at Diana, who strode forward, then seized the man's wrist and put his hand flat on the sofa. Salmagard prepared to start breaking fingers.

"Wait," he said. "Wait—you have to—you have to understand—they're freelancers. You don't just *call* them—you don't know where they are. It's not in their interests to be found—this is who they are—" He gasped. "They come to you—you don't go to them."

"Who are they?"

"Just people. They do jobs."

"What kind of jobs?" Salmagard asked, beginning to bend his middle finger. His body stiffened.

"Anything," he said, starting to sweat. "They're nobody special; they just do their thing. Your guys are probably headed for the meat market. It's the easiest way—that's all I got, I swear."

Salmagard let go of him and got up, thinking hard.

"I can prove it," the man said quickly. "I can show you the feed of them leaving my place with your guys. They're not here, I promise you."

"Let's see it," Diana said.

The man reached into his jacket, and it was painfully obvious to Salmagard what he was doing. Instead of shooting him, she lunged for him before the pistol was even visible, but he was stronger than he looked. He pushed her off and took aim at Diana, pulling the trigger several times. Diana rolled out of the way and dropped her elbow on the control panel for the zero-g bubble, smashing it to pieces.

Salmagard dropped flat as the bubble burst with a deafening roar of feedback, the shock wave throwing the man in the suit against the wall hard enough to stun him.

Salmagard kicked the fallen gun to Diana and raised her own, but the man was out. Diana eyed the pistol but didn't pick it up. She rose to her feet, rubbing her elbow and looking annoyed.

"Do we believe him?" she asked after a moment.

"I think we have to," Salmagard replied, letting out her breath. Her ears were buzzing a little. That had been terribly loud, and they had to assume it would draw attention.

Diana hit the door release and went into the corridor, coming face-to-face with the bouncer who had led them to the back. He had his gun out.

Diana rammed him into the wall and forced his hand up, but he pulled the trigger. The gaming floor was loud, but not loud enough to drown out the sound of gunfire in the open.

Salmagard rushed to Diana's side and sank her fist into the bouncer's solar plexus; then Diana threw him aside. Together, they rushed onto the floor—maybe they could make it out before the other security people figured out what was going on.

They pushed through the packed walkway, where Salmagard's pistol wasn't half as good as Diana's appearance for making people get out of the way.

A screen beside them imploded, and Salmagard spotted another bouncer coming their way, pistol outstretched. She pushed Diana in the opposite direction, and they hurried into the next row. People weren't exactly panicking, but a few were taking notice and looking around, puzzled. Did they even realize someone was shooting? Chems, ethanol, and loud music were all conspiring to kill any semblance of situational awareness in these people. The flashing lights made it difficult to see, and there were bodies everywhere—it was nearly impossible to spot the bouncers among them.

Salmagard had run a thousand simulated scenarios, covering everything from open warfare to shipboard combat. Many of them were designed to be as chaotic as possible, but they'd never given her any trouble.

Somehow, this was different.

They nearly crashed into the woman with the blue snake; the snake hissed loudly at Salmagard, who recoiled and tripped over her dress. Diana caught her and pulled her between two displays, past the bar, where robotic arms were mixing drinks, oblivious to the commotion.

"What do we do now?" Diana demanded.

"Withdraw," Salmagard replied. She saw no other option.

More shots rang out and a machine overhead exploded, causing digital credit chits to shoot out across the floor. Someone had spilled a drink on Salmagard, and she smelled of cherries and ethanol. There was a lot of shouting now, and a woman was announcing something over a broadcast—perhaps an evacuation—and still no one had the good sense to turn off the music.

And the bouncers had actually fired at them, even in such a crowded space.

Salmagard didn't know what she'd expected. She hadn't given this a lot of thought. It had just seemed like the thing to do.

If she didn't save the Admiral, who was going to?

The GRs might eventually catch up with Sei, but what if he was separated from the Admiral? What if he wasn't, and the Admiral was caught and identified? What would the Evagardian authorities do with him?

And who could say what the two of them would have to go through before that happened? It had never even been a question. The situation demanded action.

But what Diana and Salmagard were doing was against all kinds of laws—the victimization they had already suffered, or nearly suffered, didn't legally justify this action.

It was also very impolite to the people caught in the middle.

Salmagard wheeled around to fire repeatedly into the smart carbon showing mermaids and bubbles, sending ionized gas and coolant across the gaming floor and temporarily blinding half of the casino.

She could hardly expect these galactics to take kindly to what she was doing. Maybe this was what galactics were talking about when they complained about Evagardian entitlement. Maybe they had a point.

One of the dancers in a zero-g bubble stared at them as they sheltered behind a smaller bar near the card tables. A bullet sent a large chunk of the bar's faux marble top to the floor as dust, and Diana flinched. A bottle burst, and they were sprayed with cheap wine. Diana wiped it out of her eyes and opened her mouth, indignant.

Salmagard grabbed the back of Diana's jacket and pushed her

down, taking aim at a control panel identical to the one Diana had smashed in the private booth. She fired, and the resulting shock wave was every bit as impactful as she'd hoped for.

The dancer dropped to the ground with a cry. Salmagard dragged Diana up and hurried her forward, firing more shots into the air to warn the people ahead—but there were two guards between her and the door, and one of them had a surprisingly large Trigan submachine gun. A few short minutes before, Salmagard would never have believed he might possibly use it with so many people present—but a lot had happened since then.

She detoured into a row of antique pachinko machines, all chiming, ringing, and flashing brightly. Ahead was a carbon-shield viewport. Someone shouted something very rude and threw a tray at her. Salmagard ducked and stayed focused, still moving.

The area wasn't pressurized; there was an atmosphere field outside that window.

"Can you break that?" she called out over the music.

"Why not?" Diana replied, sounding dazed, still trying to shake off the wine.

Salmagard leveled the pistol at the viewport and emptied what was left of her magazine into it. The rounds didn't get all the way through, but they left impressive cracks.

Diana pulled free and sprinted forward, sinking low, then launching herself shoulder first at the viewport with everything she had, crashing through it like the fragile glass in the windows of historic structures on Old Earth.

Salmagard dropped the empty gun and vaulted out after her, taking off for the rows of shuttles. She paused at the console to call for the float lift, but Diana wasn't having it.

"No time," the pale woman said, grabbing her and effortlessly picking her up. She ignored Salmagard's dismayed squeak, bounding forward without breaking stride.

Diana leapt with truly impossible strength, then landed lightly on the wing of an Isakan shuttle. Salmagard wrapped her arms around Diana's neck and held on for dear life; there was an atmosphere field, and gravity, but they were in the phase rows, so there was nothing beneath them but spacecraft. One misstep here could mean literally falling into open space.

Diana's arms were like steel. She ran the length of the shuttle's wingspan and leapt to the next one, all faster than Salmagard could run on even ground.

"Are you even human?" Salmagard gasped, trying not to look down.

"Not especially," the red-eyed woman replied.

9

IT wasn't the most comfortable ride.

Sei and I were both muted, and control cuffs were not escapable, so there wasn't much to do except lie there together.

We could feel it when we got moving, and there was a slight tremor, a little hum, and a vague sense of motion. I was glad it wasn't enough to make either of us sick; that would've been awkward.

My situation was gradually deteriorating. Lying in a cargo compartment wasn't very demanding, but once I was on my feet, I had a feeling the fatigue would be noticeable. I was getting some light chest pains, and that wasn't a good sign.

It would only get worse, and I was afraid that when the time came to make a move, I'd be too weak, or in too much pain, to be of any use.

This didn't have to be a crisis. The moment someone took this strip away from my throat, I could ask for help, and I stood a good chance of getting it. If I laid on the drama a bit, I could probably convince these guys that things were a little more urgent than they really were. They wouldn't want me to die; I wasn't worth anything dead.

The chems I needed weren't hard to come by. They wouldn't have to go to much trouble to help me.

The flyer came to a stop, and the lid opened a few moments later, letting in the rush of noise. I squinted into the light and felt dizzy, looking up at the Bazaar. High, *high* above, gravity was inverted so that the ceiling a kilometer away was the ground for the people walking on it. It took a lot of fundamental mental adjustment just to be able to look around on the Bazaar without getting a headache, or maybe having a psychotic episode.

It would be easy to erect holographic barriers—barriers that would double as surfaces for even more advertisements—but the Bazaar would never do that. These unobstructed views were part of their brand; they traded on it. They never missed an opportunity to remind people how big it all was, that there was nowhere else you could go to find so *much*.

As Freeber dragged me out, I could see that this corridor was similar to the one we'd seen earlier. Maybe it was a bit smaller, but otherwise there was no difference, except the ground level for this one was built up much more. High-rise structures rose up past us, coated thoroughly in smart carbon displaying advertisements.

This was disorienting. There was no getting used to this. I'd heard that some people used graphics projected directly onto their eyes to limit the stimulus coming in, to make the Bazaar experience easier to handle. I could imagine how that kind of artificial tunnel vision could help.

I'd always wanted to visit the Bazaar, but now I just wanted to leave.

The building directly across from us flashed white, then showed a woman wearing heavy cosmetics and some kind of ceremonial Old Earth garment and eating plant matter. Another structure was displaying cybernetic implants and artificial bodies. A third was showing a colorful wonderland that I could only guess was part of an effort to promote VR or chem use. Or both.

Then Freeber had Sei out of the compartment and standing beside me. A moment later we were being steered toward a door. This part of the station seemed a bit more upscale than what we'd seen earlier; the metal and polymer on display were cleaner, and the design sensibilities in the storefronts and entryways seemed less rigidly utilitarian. There was a little more space. The foot traffic was steady, but not as heavy. Willis and Freeber waited as a small group of young women passed, each of them leading a male android by the hand. Rentals.

Willis shoved us forward when they'd gone, and I took a look at our destination. It was similar to the storefronts that surrounded it, but not quite the same. There were no windows or screens, only a door.

Freeber tried the palm release, but nothing happened. Willis pressed a key on the pad. Several seconds passed, and a light on the door turned green. Freeber tried again, and this time it opened.

It seemed Freeber and Willis were limited to dealing with shadier establishments. All the legitimate businesses would demand the registry that they were clearly so reluctant to pay for.

A powerfully musky scent billowed out of the dim room beyond, enough to make Willis wave a hand and swear.

But not enough to stop her from hurrying in and pulling us after her. She and Freeber seemed keen to stay out of the open. I didn't blame them; the Bazaar had to be good at enforcing its entry restrictions. These two needed to keep their visit short if they wanted to avoid a fine.

We were in a small waiting room, but the style of it was novel. The walls were paneled with polished wood and dyed leather, all held together with brass studs. It was a nostalgic Old Earth aesthetic intended to convey affluence and masculinity. It was popular in the Commonwealth, as well as in certain parts of the Empire.

The illusion was complete. From the light fixtures to the genuine paintings hanging on the walls in real wooden frames, the room was perfect.

Willis wrinkled her nose.

A man in a suit as old-fashioned as the room was in front of us. I immediately recognized him as an android, though he was clearly high-end.

He gestured gracefully at the couches at either end of the room.

"Please wait," he said with a flat galactic accent with maybe a hint of ethnic Trigan in it.

My heart sank. More waiting was not what I needed. I tried to get Willis' attention, giving meaningful looks down, hoping to indicate my mute strip—but she just gave me a warning glare.

Did she think I was making faces at her for my health? Because I *was*.

There was only one more door, and this one presumably led to the real shop, or whatever this place was supposed to be.

Freeber pushed us onto the sofa and joined Willis a few steps away. The android perched on the other sofa, looking on with a mild expression.

Willis and Freeber conferred quietly.

I was never going to take chems for granted again. Or, better yet, maybe I could just never take them again. This was the second time I'd had to go without them at a bad time.

Chemical dependency had been part of being Dalton. The prince had been a notorious chem abuser and party animal—but his habits hadn't done me any favors since I got out of the role.

Come to think of it, Dalton hadn't ever done much for me. I never wanted to be a celebrity. Not that I could blame him.

After all, I'd had to kill him before I could replace him. The one Ganraen Royal that was actually a decent person.

I was getting gloomy. Was it my body chemistry or my circumstances? Being kidnapped and having my plans ruined was more than enough to spoil my mood, so physical illness wasn't likely to help.

This was a very sensitive time. An important time. The *most* important time—no, I decided after a moment. That wasn't true. The most important time of my life had come and gone. I never should have let it go, but how could I have known?

I had only my own conceit to thank for all of this.

In any case, my job was hard enough without people coming along and interfering. Willis and Freeber didn't understand what they were doing.

If I was upset, I was justified.

After about ten minutes, the inner door opened; then a well-dressed woman crossed the waiting room and left without even glancing at us. The android started to get up, but she was gone before he could say anything.

The inner door sealed shut again immediately.

Willis and Freeber watched it expectantly, but more time passed. I could see Willis getting increasingly annoyed. I was right there with her. If whoever ran this place wanted to get around to us *today*, that would be great. This place was trying so hard to be classy, and that android was so polite—so clearly no one had thought to program in the detail that letting me sit here and expire was rude.

Willis glared at the android, who didn't seem to notice. I expected her to go over and harass it, but she continued to wait in silence.

"Please go in," the android said finally, with another of those little gestures.

Freeber jerked his chin at us, and Sei and I got to our feet.

The room beyond was the same size as the waiting room and done up the same way. Rather than sofas, it had several armchairs.

There was no one there.

A painting on the wall depicted a sailboat on the high sea, obviously meant to be Old Earth, but the artist had forgotten that Old Earth had only one sun.

It was still a nice painting.

"Please make yourselves comfortable," said a voice. There were audio projectors all over the room. The speaker was an older man with an extremely refined Evagardian accent. I couldn't say where in the Marragard system he came from, but he had that distinctive lilt. It sounded legit, but it was probably at least partially altered. This guy was a criminal. It didn't matter how hard he worked to make his front look good—he did bad things.

So of course he disguised his voice. People who do bad things have to hide. Or run.

Freeber and Willis exchanged another look. Willis shrugged. They seated themselves in the armchairs.

"How can I help you?" asked the voice.

"Trying to get rid of these two," Willis replied bluntly, looking at me and Sei.

"To clarify, you'd like to trade these two men. As a physical commodity."

"Yeah."

"I assume you were referred to me because these men are undocumented? You'll need to say that part aloud. Also take this opportunity to vocally confirm that you're not law enforcement officers from any of the agencies listed."

"Listed?" Freeber raised an eyebrow.

The door opened and the android entered, opening a scroll-type holo.

"We're not cops," Willis said, waving him away.

"Where do these men come from? Who are they?"

"Imperials." Willis crossed her legs, scowling at us. "We got them at Red Yonder."

"Tourists?"

"I guess."

"What can you tell me about them?"

"They've got spirit," Willis said. "They've been acting scared this whole time. But they're not. At least, that one isn't." She jerked her chin at me.

Maybe I hadn't been giving Willis enough credit. I wondered

who she was, what she'd done before this. My work history proved that I was at least a competent actor, but she'd seen through me.

"Maybe they think the Empire's going to come rescue them," Freeber said.

"Do you think they're military?" the voice asked. "Or gray area?"

"Honestly, I didn't want to know," Willis said, looking tired. "We left their holos behind. No way to know for certain now, unless you want to ask them. I'm ready to swear that one is," she said, looking at Sei. "Not sure about this other one. I'm thinking not, though. He just doesn't look it. He looks like Prince Dalton, if that's worth anything."

"Fair enough. Mysterious Evagardian men, both young, both physically attractive. Are they likely to be missed?"

"Probably."

"That is going to hurt your margin."

"That's my whole goddamn life," Willis said tiredly, slouching down and toying with one of her braids. "I don't care. I just want them gone."

"What sort of figures were you hoping for? In Free Trade credits?"

"I don't know. Idris gave us fifteen each for the girls." Willis rubbed her chin and looked at Freeber. "I don't think we can get that much for these. No tariffs."

"Baseline for dirty meat should be around five thousand," Freeber said.

Willis nodded. "These two should be worth at least double that, though. They're cute; they're imperial."

"An asking price of ten thousand? That's a little low for my clientele. Let's stop looking at the undocumented status as a detractor and paint it as a selling point. These aren't broken-in indentureds; they're pure, wild imperials. And that's something I might be able to sell. You said you got them from Red Yonder?"

"Yeah."

"Let's twist that a little. We'll try valuing them at fifty each."

Willis looked impressed. "You think they're worth that much?"

"To the right individual, I'm sure they are. An individual who's looking for a very exact experience. An individual with refined tastes and habits. An individual with a lot of money but not a lot of time. Someone who likes attractive young men, but not so much that they need those men to return the sentiment. I think there may be someone here at the Bazaar right now who might be interested. Good news for you. Not for these two."

10

"YOU'RE just lucky you're not a first daughter. My family never would have let me become a pilot. Particularly not for an experimental spacecraft. They only encouraged me to join because it was all but guaranteed I'd be a part of a ceremonial detail."

"I know." Diana sat back from the controls, gazing through the viewport. "I'm no different. I wasn't meant to be a fighter pilot; it's because of the aptitude testing. They got people from all different career fields. If you'd shown the stuff they were looking for, they'd have offered it to you. You're lucky."

Idris' shuttle was quite comfortable, and Diana seemed pleased with its performance. It must've cost a fortune.

"And there was action on your first tour?" Salmagard asked. There was a scratch on one of her jade combs, probably from shrapnel during the shooting. She kept fidgeting with it. Though the shuttle was actually traveling very fast, the ride was smooth, and it appeared sedate. It *felt* slow. That bothered her. She was in a hurry.

"Yeah," Diana replied, sighing. "You know, you look so much like the Duchess that you could almost be one of the face kids."

Salmagard turned to her, taken aback. "You know about that?"

"Of course. I'm one of them," Diana said. She cocked her head. "You're saying that you *are* supposed to be the Duchess?"

"Well—well, I resemble her," Salmagard said, taken aback. "I was modified."

Diana shook her head and went back to gazing at the stars. "What are the odds? I'm one of the ones that didn't make it."

"Sorry," Salmagard said on reflex.

"What?"

"I'm just—I'm looking."

Scowling, Diana turned to face Salmagard, putting on a patient expression.

"I know I don't look like much anymore," she said, obviously self-conscious. Salmagard knew this was rude, but she couldn't help herself. As Diana had said, the odds were astronomically against the two of them meeting by chance. She had to know.

Salmagard stared at her intently. Diana's face was thin and her cheeks were almost sunken—but flesh her out a bit, change the eyes from red to green . . . add some color to the lips . . .

Take the black hair and make it blond. Straighten it. Add an inch of height. Round out the hips, swell the bosom.

Her jaw dropped.

"You're the Disciple," she said, eyes wide.

Diana cleared her throat and looked away. "Good eye. A lot of people didn't see it. Even before this. And people don't know her face—not the way they know yours. And the Heir and the Guardian. But before—once in a while someone would spot it."

"Do you have her genes?"

"A little bit somewhere. I don't know if they're legit or not."

"By the Empress."

"Do you know anything about her? The Disciple?"

"Only what I learned in school," Salmagard said. Though the legends of the Heroes of the Unification weren't exactly treated as history lessons, they were ubiquitous. Every Evagardian youth was exposed to them at some point.

New dramas about them were released regularly across the galaxy; buildings, cities, and stations were named after them.

And a handful of people had been given their faces—the well-intentioned but asinine gimmick of an initiative to promote class diversity in the Service.

Diana's eyes were flat. "You and everyone else. Historical perspective is a hell of a thing."

Salmagard blinked. She supposed she couldn't argue that.

"Still, it's an honor for your family to be selected. What line are you?"

"Kladinov. Kladinova for women. You?"

"Salmagard."

"I've heard of you."

"I've heard of *you*."

"I think some of your cousins are supposed to be on my list—you have some extended family on Lyragard, don't you? Or they were on my list before I messed up my genes. Look, you're being polite, and I appreciate that. But I can't tell you why I'm like this. I'm not allowed; Third Fleet would crucify me. Let's just say it's my own fault." Diana rubbed at her eyes. "And he just let me do it."

"I won't ask. The GRs are mobilizing," Salmagard said, checking her holo. She was taken aback; this was an impressively fast response. "They don't want us to move in without them."

"They wouldn't care if we weren't liners. Tell them to go to hell. If they want to get there first, they can be our guests, right?"

"I agree completely," Salmagard murmured. The notification didn't actually call for a reply, and she preferred not to send one. The GRs wouldn't reach the Bazaar for hours. They were making a good effort, but it wasn't enough. Not for Salmagard.

There was no time to spare, and the two of them were only minutes out.

"What is it?" Salmagard asked. This time it was Diana who was looking at her.

"I'm worried too."

"He'll be all right," Salmagard told her, a little irked at being read so easily. "As long as we can get to him soon. Both of them."

For a moment, Diana said nothing. The shuttle was flying itself, and she absently watched the readouts. Finally she glanced over.

"He looks good in black," she said.

Salmagard smiled. "White too."

"It's risky, though."

"What is?"

"I know you don't plan to marry him, but guys like that are bad for your prospects."

"More than you realize," Salmagard replied. Diana hadn't believed her when she'd said the hypos had medicine in them. She thought the Admiral was a chem abuser.

Diana raised an eyebrow, impressed. "Is it serious?"

Salmagard was suddenly uncomfortable. She didn't have a good reply for that.

Diana cocked her head, giving her a maddening look. "First daughter falls for a guy that's no good? We've both seen that holo drama before."

Salmagard cleared her throat. "I don't know him very well."

"Well enough to know he's trouble."

She hesitated. "He did something bad." She hesitated. "But he's not bad."

"Are you an empath?" Diana asked.

"No."

"Then how do you know? Look, it's okay to fall for these guys—you just have to quit while you're ahead."

Salmagard twitched. "I haven't fallen for anyone," she said. "We went through a lot together. I owe him."

"You owe him enough to risk your place in line?"

"I owe him my life."

"So?"

"You should understand. You know what's expected of us. We can't leave debts unpaid."

"We aren't supposed to *have* debts," Diana pointed out. "*They* are supposed to be indebted to us."

Salmagard swallowed. That was quite true, and something she was keenly aware of. Her grip on her armrest tightened. No one had ever promised her that the expectations placed on Evagardian women of noted bloodlines were reasonable, though. Indeed, Alice Everly often bemoaned them.

Diana shook her head suddenly. "What am I saying? I'm just a mess because I got passed over for a woman with no blood, no history. Nothing. You should go for it. Forget your line. If you like him that much, just do it. Who am I to give advice? Look at me."

"I never said I wanted that," Salmagard pointed out.

"What does he want?"

"What?"

"He knows who you are, doesn't he? What does someone like that expect from you?"

Salmagard swallowed. She opened her mouth, but a warning began to flash.

"What's that?"

Diana called it up. "Huh," she said.

"Well?"

"Someone's targeting us." She grabbed the controls and took manual control, throwing them into a dive. She locked in her course on the display, then throttled up. Salmagard felt the sudden jerk and grabbed her straps to make sure they were secure.

"EMP nodes," Diana noted, flipping a switch. The readouts dimmed slightly, and more warnings appeared.

"What?"

"Pretty much the only ship-to-ship weapon that's legal for these people," Diana explained. "What? I'm a fighter pilot. I have to know these things. The launcher's got six barrels because it shoots really fast, and it launches these little nodes that release an EMP in your ship and disable you . . ."

"Not that," Salmagard snapped, seeing the red light now blinking on the scanner. "Who *are* they?"

"Idris' guys? That guy back there? What was his name? Heimer? His guys? Take your pick," Diana said, rolling her eyes. "We're not making friends out here, sweetheart. Oh— now they're shooting. Okay, boys. Have you ever danced with an Everwing in the pale moonlight?" Her red eyes lit up. "Of course," she added, looking annoyed, "this isn't an Everwing."

Salmagard squeezed her eyes shut and held on.

Diana didn't sound even slightly concerned. And she was right: Salmagard had been so fixated on her timetable, on the Admiral, on the mission of rescuing him before his need for his antidote became terminal, before the GRs got to him, before he was forced into something horrible—that she had almost forgotten what she'd done in the gambling den.

"Empress."

"What?" Salmagard asked without opening her eyes, feeling the shuttle shake.

"Well, it's just— This is a shuttle, not a fighter. And it shows, you know? She handles like a . . . I don't know. It's just kind of sad. I feel like I did at my first formal. I had to wear this dress with a malfunctioning temperature control, and it was tight, the collar was choking me, and I almost passed out. Worst night of my life." Diana made a disgusted noise, then went on complaining. "Trying to do a coffee ceremony with all my aunts there watching my every move. I still have nightmares about it. You're lucky. Things are different on Old Earth. The stuff we get up to on Lyragard . . . sometimes I wish I was just some no-blood girl in a sustenance pod trying to get an apprenticeship. I could just play *Five Husbands* all day. But no, I had to join the Service. I had to go kill pirates and get passed over by guys who shouldn't even be allowed to breathe the same air you and I do."

Diana babbled on, all the while diving and banking. Wild streaks shot past the viewers. Salmagard made a strangled noise and tried to control her breathing.

"And it's not like I really blame him," Diana added. "Or her—Well, no. I *do* blame her, because that's fraternization no matter how you look at it, and that's really bad. Yeah, he had his little informal commission or whatever, but he wasn't really an officer. They hooked up so fast after we got back that there's just no way—*no way*—that she wasn't totally into him on the ship. I mean, I don't really know what went on between them. Don't look at me like that," Diana said, glancing over at Salmagard. "It's not what you think. It's not like I was in *love* or anything."

The shuttle shuddered violently, but Diana just kept talking.

"It was just my ego, I guess. You know? Because he was my partner; it was just the two of us—we were the only two-man cell, and I guess I just sort of felt possessive, like I should have first dibs. Who poaches in a situation like that? Who does that? That's why I'm mad, not because of bleeding-heart stuff. I mean, you can't really *fall* for someone on a combat mission like that, especially with your implant on. Or I don't think you can. Or you shouldn't. I don't know. I guess you can. It's not like I didn't like him."

Salmagard didn't know what to say to any of that. She wasn't really listening.

"Will you open your eyes? You're stressing me out. I know how to fly, Tessa. Just relax."

She reluctantly opened her eyes. They were barreling toward the Bazaar at a truly irresponsible speed.

"How is this going to end well?" Salmagard demanded, pressing herself back against her seat, clutching the safety handle.

The Bazaar was gigantic, and growing dizzyingly fast.

"See that?" Diana pointed, banking. "That's a radiation bleed.

There'll be lots of bays in there. We'll find an open one, and that's our way in. All we have to do is stay ahead of this guy."

The shuttle rolled, and Salmagard clearly saw more tracers fly past.

"They're really shooting at us," she said.

"If you don't shoot, you'll never score. Trust me, I know." Diana made another sound of disgust. "I can't even deal with it anymore. Can I just spend the rest of my life in bed and never come out? I'll just go into VR forever. I don't care what my family says—not that they're speaking to me. I mean, *look* at me. Oh, Diana, why would he pass you over for an older woman with nothing to offer? Why do you *think*?"

"Can you focus? Please?" Salmagard was sweating.

"I've got it. Relax."

"You've done this before."

"This? No, not really. But this kind of flying . . . it's so slow that it's more like playing chess. I've got all day to stay ten moves ahead. It's too easy. Kind of stupid, really. I mean, what's the point? And Sei doesn't understand, obviously. He's clueless."

Ships, waypoints, signs, advertisements, guide paths—they were all flashing past the shuttle in a blur.

"This is slow?" The shuttle's buffers were doing a good job counteracting the force from their extreme speed, but Salmagard still felt a tug at her core.

Diana shrugged. "Compared to a fighter. We're barely moving." Diana wasn't kidding. She had only one hand on the stick; she was rubbing at her eyes with the other.

The red-eyed woman looked bored.

More warnings flashed on the screen, but Diana ignored them. Salmagard saw indications that there was incoming fire, that they were moving at illegal speeds, that they were performing illegal maneuvers, and that they were in violation of Free Trade law and Bazaar regulations.

More lights joined the chaser on their tail on the scanner. It was at least a dozen vessels, all of them moving faster than the shuttle, closing in visibly.

"Are those Bazaar enforcers? They'd better be. But are they after us or him? It's got to be against the rules for him to shoot at us this close to the station, right?" Diana wondered aloud, throwing them into a spin that made Salmagard feel physically ill. She covered her mouth and shut her eyes again, praying to God and the Empress. "No time to do it the right way; these guys probably have the law on their side since you shot up that casino," Diana said.

Salmagard chose not to comment on Diana's decision to exclude herself from responsibility on that one. She was afraid that if she opened her mouth, she'd be sick.

"If they EMP us and board, the cops can't do anything about it—they've got first claim. Free Trade law is the worst. Hey—once we do get in there, you better be ready to run. Because we're not going to want to be anywhere near this shuttle when Bazaar security gets to it," Diana said, taking a hand off the stick to shake it. Her knuckles popped alarmingly.

They shot underneath the station, and Diana flipped the shuttle so that they were abruptly above it, skimming a mere ten meters from the surface of the cube. More warnings strobed madly on the display. The shuttle was traveling faster than it was supposed to; Salmagard could hear the chassis groaning under the strain from the overheating engines.

A deep trough lay ahead. Diana pulled right, then spun out and in, turning the shuttle sideways to fit. Now the impression of speed was even more pronounced. The walls streaked past like gray liquid.

"You know, he's not bad to stay with me for this long," Diana said, watching the rear feed. Salmagard didn't think she was talking to anyone in particular at this point. "But he's not good either." She pulled up sharply, taking the shuttle in a dizzying loop that terminated with them racing toward a glowing bay.

Diana killed thrust and did an emergency burn on the starboard side, sending the shuttle into a wild spin. She hit thrust again, now with the shuttle facing the opposite direction, using the engines to kill the momentum as they entered the bay.

The impact was jarring, but Diana had lessened their speed to the point that it was little more than a series of hard bumps, then a terrible grind as the shuttle slid across the bay floor, leaving wide molten gouges behind it.

They screeched to a stop. Coolant was venting all over the bay.

The chaser had vanished from the scanner. The Bazaar security ships hadn't, but Diana had left them all behind, and they had some catching up to do.

Salmagard stared straight ahead, frozen. She was shaking all over, feeling a terrible chill. Salmagard wondered if she could walk.

"We're here," Diana said.

11

SEI and I were in the cargo space of the borrowed flyer again.

The words of the bodiless Evagardian voice in that stuffy, old-fashioned room hadn't set us up for a relaxing journey. He hadn't pointed out anything we couldn't have guessed for ourselves about the sort of people who would want to buy us, but it hadn't felt good to hear it all laid out that way. We didn't need to be reminded that it was probable someone would only want us so they could mistreat us, in all likelihood simply because we happened to be imperials.

I didn't like Frontiersmen. I never had. Their planets were all right, and it wasn't even their culture that bothered me, but I couldn't stand the people. Even as Dalton, I'd made a point of avoiding them when I could. In my years as a Ganraen Royal, I'd traveled to the Frontier system only twice, and both times I'd visited only New Earth.

Every visit had made my opinion of those people lower. The sentiment wasn't rational, and I knew it. The people I encountered, my experiences and impressions—they weren't properly representative of Frontiersmen as a whole. My judgments were unfair. But that didn't change anything.

I couldn't stand those people.

But I still wasn't going to buy them on the black market and treat them poorly just to get it out of my system.

I was starting to develop some pretty negative feelings about Free Traders too, but that was a common enough prejudice wherever you went.

Free Traders weren't all criminals, but criminals were all I'd seen lately. It was skewing my perception, and the poison was killing my mood even faster than it was killing the rest of me.

I decided to think about Salmagard instead. She wasn't in any real danger; Idris hadn't given any indication that he knew that he had Service members on his hands, so her ability to handle herself would take him by surprise. I had no doubt that Salmagard could deal with people of Idris' caliber with ease, and she had Diana with her. I didn't know the pale girl's story, but I remembered the way she'd opened that bottle of Evagardian Ale and drained it. On that alone, I suspected she was someone that was better to have on your side.

Salmagard would escape from Idris and make for the nearest Evagardian consulate, and that was all well and good. She knew better than to send GRs after me, but there were also Diana and Sei to consider. Diana would want help for Sei, and she wouldn't have much sympathy for my unique circumstances. Salmagard would agree that rescuing Sei trumped being considerate of me—and rightfully so. So rescue was on the way. Well, rescue for Sei. Trouble for me.

But the GRs probably wouldn't know they were looking for me. If they did manage to rescue us, I might have a chance to slip away before they identified me. I just had to hope I had enough strength for it when that time came. I couldn't let the GRs treat me—doing so would expose them to my DNA, which was flagged on every watch list in the Imperium. It would reveal that I was still alive, and I wouldn't be in any position to get away. The GRs were good at chasing people.

The latent poison in my system was starting to approach the severity of the detox I'd dealt with on Nidaros.

I thought about how I would handle Freeber, if that was what it came to. He was massive and strong. Willis wasn't helpless either. Even if I was healthy, a physical confrontation wouldn't be practical.

If things got ugly, maybe Sei would help.

The flyer came to another halt, and in moments we were being pulled out and dragged to our feet. We were in a covered vehicle repository. Very clean, very quiet. The other flyers around looked expensive. This was a hotel. I'd seen plenty of places like this as Dalton. I rarely got to go in anywhere through the front while the war was on.

Doors at the far end led to a lobby, but Freeber and Willis had other ideas. We entered a service stairwell. They were avoiding the surveillance in the elevators, which would prob-ably scan their faces and check for codes.

It was a long climb. I lost count of the flights, but it had to be close to twenty.

We were still far from the top when we stopped, and not one of us was breathing normally. I considered just dropping on the spot and forcing them to address the state of my health—but Willis could probably think I was faking, and if she beat me up I'd just be that much worse off when the time came to do something.

Willis wiped her brow with her sleeve and swore under her breath.

She and Freeber both checked their weapons, then opened the door and moved into the corridor, pushing us ahead of them.

This was a nice hotel. The floor was smart suede, and the walls were infused carbon, refracting light to creating calming, shifting hues. Somehow, the color scheme created the illusion of openness and space, as though there were skies and oceans beyond these walls instead of metal and vacuum. Quiet music played, and that was the only sound. These rooms were absolutely soundproof.

I wasn't sure that was a good thing, considering.

We halted at the door at the very end of the hall: a suite. A night in there probably cost as much as a night at Red Yonder. I'd heard housing costs were outrageous in the Bazaar, so lodging was probably inflated too.

Willis hit the door chime, and several moments passed.

The door opened, revealing a woman around Willis' age who clearly took much better care of herself. She was wearing slacks and a blouse. Her hair was damp, as if we'd pulled her away from the heater she'd been using to dry it. She was tying her hair back with a silk ribbon and holding a jeweled clasp in her mouth.

"Come in," she said around the clasp, stepping aside without pausing her tying. Freeber pushed us over the threshold; then she nudged the door shut with a hip and put on the hair clip. It looked nice.

She had a few glossy highlights in her hair, which was otherwise an unremarkable brown. Her skin tone suggested a life without too much exposure to UV light, but she was obviously in good health.

The woman dried her hands on a kerchief, then stepped up

to me and took my face in her hands, probing in a businesslike fashion. She was searching for implants. She ran her fingers through my hair, poked around in mouth, and gazed into my eyes.

Then she patted me down, very thoroughly. I didn't know if she was searching for concealed weapons or more implants, checking my physique, seeing if I had all the required parts, or just feeling me up because she felt like it. If she was hoping for a reaction, I didn't give her one.

"Okay," she said, and moved to Sei. She repeated the process with him, and he bore it stoically. He was a pilot, so he'd been trained to deal with capture by enemy forces. This wasn't *exactly* an enemy force, but many of the same principles applied.

It was hard to view this woman as the torture-happy slave-owning type; she looked ordinary enough to me. And there was nothing to say that she was that type; the disembodied voice in the room of the procurement agent had simply implied that someone who would want two nonconsenting undocumented imperials was *likely* to be the type to treat his or her things roughly.

"No one mentioned that this one prefers men," she said, stepping back from Sei. So she was an empath. And an extremely good one; she was making calls on us after a few minutes of inspection. That was fast.

"We didn't know. Does it matter?" Willis asked, annoyed.

"It does. We won't take that one." She turned her attention back to me. "But this one has potential." She looked into my eyes again. "Though he's a mess in here," she said, prodding my forehead with a finger. "Give me one second."

She disappeared into the bedroom. Willis put her head back and mouthed some swearing.

The woman returned donning an earpiece, the sort that was for secure business use. She touched it, and I realized she was streaming a feed to someone else.

"Yes," she said. "Good all around. Lot of scarring." Was she talking about me? I didn't have any scars. "Complicated." That struck me as an interesting thing for her to say. I wondered if I ought to be flattered.

I was out of my league.

"Could be a keeper," the woman went on. "In fact, I think he was made for you. He's not well, but it seems to be chemical. Can we have the clothes off?" This was directed at Willis.

"Sure. But if you want a test drive, it'll cost you."

"No need—that's not what we want him for."

Willis cocked her head. "Then what's wrong with this one?" She pointed at Sei.

The woman gave her a look, then touched her ear. "And never mind on the clothes," she said, then went back to walking her slow circle around me. She came to a stop, locking eyes with me yet again. Whoever was watching this stream was looking at my face.

I couldn't help but be curious. I wanted to know who was out there thinking about buying me. And what they had in mind for me. The GRs weren't a sure thing, but they were good at their job, and I didn't know how good Willis and Freeber were at covering their tracks. If the GRs were going to show, assuming Salmagard had escaped from Idris promptly, then it was probably only a matter of hours.

A lot could happen in that amount of time if I was sold to someone unwholesome, and if there was such a thing as prime escape condition, I wasn't in it. And that annoyed me, because getting out of bad situations was something I was actually pretty good at. It didn't seem fair that I was being held back by a mute strip. My voice was my best weapon.

The woman's expression, which had been one of mild disinterest, turned to surprise. Her eyes fixed on me, and now they were much more thoughtful. I was dying to know what she was hearing.

"Is he really?" she asked, glancing away. She took a step back from me, and something passed across her face. Fear? It was gone too quickly to be sure.

I smiled at her.

"Okay," the woman said, tearing her eyes away from me. She smoothed her blouse and addressed Willis. "This one's no good either," she said. "Sorry. I can't take either of these. And they *are* illegal—I have to ask you to go." She walked briskly past us and opened the door, holding it open.

For a moment I thought Willis might explode and make a scene, but she recovered quickly and simply stalked out. Freeber grabbed me and Sei, nodded politely to the woman, who bowed. He guided us into the corridor.

Willis made straight for the lift; she didn't want to deal with all those stairs back to the vehicles—she didn't care if it was risky. For once, Sei, Freeber, and I were all thinking the same thing: that right at this moment, we did not want to be in a lift with her.

Willis obviously wasn't worried about Bazaar authorities right now.

We rode down in silence. Me and Sei, because we were muted. Willis, because she was fuming. Freeber, because he didn't want to make her any angrier. Sei and I hadn't been professionally or romantically involved with Willis for a long period of time—as Freeber clearly had—but it was equally obvious to us that anything that anyone said would set her off. None of us wanted that. I was dying. I didn't need this drama.

We followed her as she stomped off toward the flyer. When she reached it, she just bent over, laying her cheek against the metal of the cargo lid and letting out a long, frustrated groan.

It echoed through the repository. We could vaguely hear the noise of the station, but it was still pretty quiet. The place had interesting acoustics—or maybe that was my ears. What would Willis and Freeber do if I really did pass out? Probably just dump me down the nearest exhaust vent.

A woman paused in the act of getting into her flyer, glanced in our direction, then ignored us.

Freeber looked tired. Willis abruptly stood up and whirled on Sei.

"So you don't like women," she said.

He shook his head, looking apologetic.

She punched him in the face, knocking him flat. Then she whirled on me, grabbing for my groin. I tried to pull away, but she found what she was looking for and squeezed savagely, dropping me to my knees. Her elbow crashed into my temple, laying me out beside Sei, seeing stars, and feeling profoundly grateful that I was muted.

I didn't want anyone to ever hear the noises that I would've been making just then.

"Imperials!" She groaned again, raising a boot, clearly intending to start stomping Sei—but Freeber put his arms around her and pulled her back.

"That's not nice," he said.

She struggled a little, but her heart wasn't in it. Then she gave up and sagged into him.

"But I don't even know what this one's defect is." She moaned into his chest, pointing a finger at me.

No. She didn't.

But I did. There was only one explanation for the sudden reversal up there.

Whoever had been on the other end of that feed had recognized me.

But recognized me as who?

12

DIANA and Salmagard burst into the open.

The noise, the motion, the smell—it was like hitting the water after a long fall. The Bazaar's interior was a sickening kaleidoscope.

Gasping for breath, Salmagard seized the railing and looked down, immediately feeling ill. They had to be near the top of the station; it couldn't be less than a kilometer drop in front of her. She staggered back, covering her mouth, and Diana caught her.

The red-eyed woman wasn't even winded, despite the mad dash they'd made from the bay. This place didn't bother her at all.

"You all right? Still with me?"

Salmagard pulled free, nodding vigorously.

Civilian flyers hummed past by the hundred. Lifts shot up and down, and walkways were everywhere, extending, retracting, rising, and falling.

"Do you need a minute?"

Salmagard shook her head, trying to suppress her gag reflex.

"Come on," Diana said, hustling her onto the public walkway.

"Damn this dress," Salmagard swore. She was sweating, and she suddenly gagged. "What's that smell?"

"It's galactics. Come on, we can get some clothes."

"No time. We've already taken too long." Struggling to loosen her sash, Salmagard stared at the colorful people around them. She considered her deeply crimson Isakan dress bold—even approaching gaudy.

She hadn't chosen it. Fatima, her bunkmate aboard the *Julian*, had. Salmagard hadn't known what to wear, and Fatima, appalled by her wardrobe, had assured Salmagard that her own fashion sense would unquestionably ruin any attempt at a romantic rendezvous.

Fatima had been right. The Admiral had liked the dress—and it was clear now that it was not at all gaudy. Apparently, before today, Salmagard hadn't properly understood the meaning of "gaudy."

The people of the Bazaar were gaudy, just like the people at that gaming parlor.

Salmagard looked down at herself. Fatima had said the Isakan cut would make Salmagard seem open-minded instead of stodgy. The dress didn't show any skin to speak of, so it was dignified, and it fit her status, but the bright colors and figure-hugging design made sure there wasn't even a trace of masculinity.

Furthermore, the sash removed the need for a clutch or bag.

The extent of Salmagard's fashion sense was to copy the conservative masculine clothes favored by her mentor, Alice Everly.

Fatima's views on the matter had struck Salmagard as

impressively cosmopolitan and sophisticated. Clearly, this was an area where her privileged upbringing had failed her.

Salmagard had felt uncommonly daring to go forth in this ensemble. Now she saw that if she ever wanted to characterize her mode of dress as bold or daring, she had a lot to learn.

Their arrival had set off plenty of alarms, but so far there hadn't been any sign of pursuit. In imperial space, the authorities would've been all over them by now—but just as cultures and values seemed to differ in Free Trade sectors, so did standards.

Salmagard didn't believe for a second that there would be no consequences for crashing in on the Bazaar this way, but perhaps Bazaar station security wasn't as omnipresent as its Evagardian equivalent. Perhaps they really could walk away from this.

"How do people find their way in here?" Diana asked wonderingly, gazing around at the crowds of people and uncountable enterprises. Flying transports passed overhead, alarmingly low. A holographic woman dashed through Salmagard, making her jump in surprise. Was someone exploring the Bazaar remotely, and was that their avatar? Or was that an AI? A guide? Whoever or whatever it was, it needed to learn some manners. So did a lot of these people.

Diana was getting some looks. Her jacket's fastener had broken at some point, so both her strikingly thin, contoured torso and the chest supporter she'd been forced to wear at Idris' place were on display. But people weren't looking at that; they were looking at her eyes. There were plenty of body mods on display here, but nobody had glowing red eyes.

Salmagard keyed her holo. The Bazaar had its own public network, and she connected to it.

Diana guided her out of the path of a big man wearing armor, then pulled her into an alcove between two shop fronts. It was close quarters, but it cut down the noise a little, and it was dangerous to walk around such a crowded place buried in one's holo. That wasn't stopping anyone.

"I need a buyer's account," Salmagard reported.

"So get one."

"I'm trying to make it. But I need an entry code. I think you get that when you come in here the right way."

"Can you pay and get it remotely?"

"I don't think so." Salmagard was trying, but the system wasn't very intuitive. Or maybe it didn't make sense to her because she was an imperial.

Suddenly she was alone. Alarmed, she looked around, but spotted Diana entering a shop a few meters away. Salmagard hurried after her.

It was a café.

"That, that, and five of those," Diana said at the counter. "I can pay by transfer, right? I don't need a buyer's account?"

The café smelled heavenly, but, more important, it was enclosed. It was a relief not to have the Bazaar swirling around her with all its noise and distractions. Salmagard was still dizzy, but she could feel her equilibrium coming back. She joined Diana.

"And coffee," Diana added. "The strongest you got."

"What are you doing?"

"I'm hungry."

"You ate all those calorie bars, though," Salmagard said, concerned. "Back in the shuttle." There had been a thousand calories in each of them; Diana had wolfed down at least four.

"I'm hungry again," the red-eyed woman replied, shrugging.

Her stomach rumbled. The android behind the counter was asking for details about her coffee. "I don't care, just make it happen," Diana snapped, snatching her bag of pastries from the second robot.

"We don't have time for this."

"I thought you were trying to figure out where we were going next," Diana said through a mouthful of pastry. She grabbed her cup and took a large gulp.

That stopped Salmagard. "I was."

"You have one too," Diana said, using a napkin to take a pastry from the bag and offering it to her.

Salmagard took it and dropped into a seat at a table for two by the window, feeling gloriously depraved. She was a mess. She was here illegally, doing illegal things, eating without utensils while walking about like a common galactic—it was a good thing the Admiral wasn't seeing her this way.

Diana offered her coffee, and she took a drink, eyes still on her holo.

"I don't think we can get into the big catalogs without going back out, then coming back in the right way and getting these entry codes," she said.

"We're not here to buy," Diana said, shoving another pastry into her mouth whole and immediately beginning to choke. Salmagard distractedly pounded her back. The red-eyed woman drained the rest of her coffee and got up, then went to the counter for more.

"But we—we should, though. It's the easiest way to get them back," Salmagard called after her.

"Buy them?"

"It's peaceful."

"It's stupid," Diana said, bringing back her cup. "How much do they cost? I'm not in the good graces of my family right now; all I have is my salary."

"I can afford them," Salmagard said confidently.

"Must be nice."

"Must be nice to have that metabolism," Salmagard shot back, watching Diana devour another pastry.

Diana opened her mouth, looking hurt—then she gazed down at the pastry in her other hand, swallowed, and bit into it.

"But I can't get into the buyer's directories without a real account. You've got to have this number they assign you that legitimizes you to do business here, and we haven't got it. So I can't search for them. All we can do is"—Salmagard waved a hand—"buy lunch."

"What about a physical directory? Can't we just find out where they're being sold and go track them down?"

"We'll have to, but look at the size of all this. There could be a hundred places selling people," Salmagard said, feeling the beginnings of panic.

"We have net access here. All we have to do is search on an independent database. *They* won't care if we haven't got these codes. Here we are. It's a little outdated, but what are we looking for? People? Humans?"

"We can try. No. No, this is no good. I'm getting nothing but organ growers and propaganda and marketing firms. Slaves?" Salmagard swiped down the list.

"Try that."

"This looks promising—no, these are all comfort android vendors and training schools."

"Training schools?"

"For your human property, I presume . . . eurgh."

"What?"

"Nothing." Salmagard swallowed.

"Don't be a prude."

Salmagard bristled a little at that, but said nothing, continuing to search. "'Indentured servitude,' that's what these people call it. Oh, yes." Her eyes widened. "I've found it."

"Found what?"

"The Open Market. That's actually what they call it. The Open Market."

"For?"

"For people. This has to be it." She straightened up, excited.

"Oh." Diana stopped chewing for a moment, then began again, slowly. "And?"

"It's in the innermost cube. Apparently it's quite substantial."

Diana cocked her head. "Is the industry really that big?"

"And that's just here physically. This can only be a part of it."

The café was warm. It was cozy. It smelled mouthwatering. There was quiet music and a comforting murmur of relatively well-mannered customers.

But outside was the Bazaar. Bigger than a city, and infinitely more dangerous.

Somewhere, out in that sea of people, was the Admiral.

"How do we get there?"

"Take a flyer, I suppose." Salmagard looked out the window at the passing vehicles. "There must be a system."

"A system we can't access," Diana reminded her. "We can't get a ride that way. Is there something else? A tram?"

"Not that I can see. We may have to go on foot."

"How far is it?"

"In a straight line, from here to there, two kilometers. With the route we'd have to take"—Salmagard chewed her lip—"closer to five."

Diana sighed and pushed away the bag of pastries, getting to her feet. "But you love running in that dress," she said.

13

FREEBER pulled us out of the cargo compartment, more roughly this time. He had more patience than Willis, but at some point he had to get tired of dragging us around. That was fine with me; I was anxious to part ways too.

I'd braced myself for bright, painful light, but I didn't get it. We weren't in the open. My eyes adjusted, and I realized this was a residential district, a closed corridor with only a limited amount of space for vehicular travel. I could hear the vague roar of business from somewhere above, reverberating through the station's superstructure.

Even by Free Trade station standards, this was a slum. Narrow little apartments lined long, tall, featureless blocks that flanked the passage. The ceiling wasn't even smart carbon; someone had actually painted it blue. It couldn't even simulate the look of sky. And that paint had been applied a long time ago; now it was coated with grime and buildup.

The walls near the ground were covered in crude adhesives

and amateur artwork. Loud, grinding music was audible from one of the apartments, and I could smell controlled chemicals in the air.

Recyclers coughed and rattled, and half the light fixtures were dead, leaving the corridor's lighting gray and grainy.

Sei looked around with obvious distaste. I'd seen places like this before, though not for a while. Still, the corridor itself was spacious, and the apartments were more or less intact—so no matter how shabby it all looked, this probably wasn't, by Bazaar standards, a bad place to live. Compared to the Bazaar proper, it was wonderfully peaceful. That alone was almost enough to make me forget that the control cuffs now seemed to weigh about twice what they had half an hour before. The same for my shoes.

Freeber guided us toward a stairwell. There were lifts, but it didn't look like any of them worked. The carbon shield over emergency levers and biohazard sensors had all been broken long ago. There were safety violations everywhere.

At least down here these two probably didn't have to worry about station security catching up to them. If the lights weren't being maintained, surveillance probably wasn't either.

It probably cost a thousand Free Trade credits a month to rent one of these apartments. Maybe more, since lodging within the Bazaar was so scarce.

In the Empire, you could live in a vastly nicer—though perhaps slightly smaller—sustenance apartment for absolutely nothing. You'd have your own combiner and a small living stipend, all courtesy of the Empress. For nothing. Just for being Evagardian. What about health care? Education? These people had to struggle for everything that the poorest imperial took for granted.

They worked hard to live here. Even Cohengard, the most reviled city in the Empress' embrace, was like a fantasy ideal compared with this block.

True, it was humiliating to live on sustenance and depend on the Empress, but was it worse than this? In the Imperium, that was a contentious topic.

We climbed up two flights, making our way down the row. Below, some kids were playing a game with cling boots and a holographic ball, swatting it back and forth across the corridor as they ran up the walls to get at it when it bounced. None of them was wearing any protective gear—that reminded me a bit of Cohengard.

It looked fun. I wished I had that kind of energy.

Willis jabbed the chime for a door. Nothing happened. No light, no audio cue. She prodded it again. Then again.

She rolled her eyes and started to pound on the metal door. Minutes passed. She looked at her chrono.

"You do it," she said to Freeber, who gave it a try. He was much louder; his blows actually shook the door in its frame.

More time passed. Finally, the door opened.

The bleary woman inside was a little older than I was. She was reasonably fit, completely bald, and wearing only plain underwear and an undershirt with a bird on it. There were some blocky, angular tattoos on her shoulders, and she had a big scar on her left thigh.

She was rubbing her eyes and yawning. Her eyes focused on Willis, and she immediately tried to slam the door shut.

Freeber pushed it open and let himself in. Willis dragged Sei and me inside.

The apartment was humble, but spotlessly clean. The bald woman didn't seem to have much, but everything she had was in its place. The temperature control wasn't working—it was far too warm.

She stared at Willis and Freeber for a moment, then scratched tiredly at her stomach and padded into the kitchen without another word.

We all followed.

"Who are they?" she asked, taking a cup and filling it with coffee from a beverage combiner.

"Just meat," Willis said. "Imperials."

The bald woman said nothing. She stirred something white into the coffee and drank half of it in a single gulp. She put the cup aside, her back still to us, placing her hands on the tile surface and leaning forward, bowing her head. Praying for patience? Trying to wake up? Collecting herself?

Finally she straightened and faced us, folding her arms and leaning back against the counter.

"You're going to have to tell me what you want," she said, looking resigned. "I'm not guessing. I'm not an empath."

"Put these two on the market for us."

"Why can't you do it?" Her eyes narrowed. "Did you sneak in again?"

"What's the problem? You have codes."

"How much do I get?"

"Nothing. Take care of it today and we're even."

The bald woman scowled. "Give me their contracts."

"They don't have any."

"Of course. Leave me out of it. If people want to sign their lives away, that's on them. But you can't go around just grabbing people to make a credit. Take them to Idris."

Willis produced her holo and called something up. She showed it to the other woman, whose eyes widened.

She gathered herself quickly. "How did you get that?"

"How do you think, Nora?"

"I was drunk."

"I can tell."

Freeber was angling to see the feed, but Willis quickly covered it. "Not for you," she said sternly. Nora pushed him back. "Nope," Willis said.

Bemused, Freeber went back to watching Sei and me.

"Do people have to record *everything*?" Nora put her face in her hand, groaning. She rubbed at her smooth scalp and eyed the two of us. "Who *are* they?"

"I told you. Imperials."

"They'll be missed. Someone will find them. Those people don't just let folks disappear."

"Must be nice."

"I have to sell them unlisted, miscellaneous. You won't get much, even if they are Evagardian. Who wants imperials with no contracts? Nobody needs that stress."

"Someone'll take them off the listing. They always do. Even if it's just for parts."

I saw Sei swallow. It looked like we were moving toward the worst-case scenario.

"I'm telling you," Nora said firmly, "the price is going to be low."

"I know that. Just take care of it. We need to get out of here before our number comes up and we get fined. And I'm done with them. Okay? I'm done."

"Just pay and stay as long as you want. Get a membership. You're here often enough. Jesus. Or don't. God knows, I don't want you here."

Willis took a controller out of her pocket and tossed it to Nora, who caught it, looking disgusted.

Willis blew a kiss at her and walked out.

Freeber nodded to Nora, then to us, and he followed Willis. A moment passed, and the front door opened and closed.

Nora looked glumly at the controller in her hand for a long time. "Sorry, guys." She looked up at us. "I'm going to check this to make sure it works. If it doesn't, good news: you're free to go."

I braced myself; Nora shocked us with the power low and kept it as brief as she could.

She winced as Sei and I did. It really wasn't that bad.

"Sorry, sorry. It does work. Um. Okay, sit down." She pulled chairs out from the table, and Sei and I seated ourselves. "And don't get up," she added, thinking fast. This was all coming at her suddenly, and she was trying to keep up. However reluctant she might be, she hadn't put her foot down. So she owed Willis something, and dealing with us was a small price to pay to balance the scales.

Nora refilled her coffee and sat down across from us, placing her holo on the table and calling up a browser.

"There goes my morning," she muttered, taking another drink. "I'd unmute you guys, but men who don't talk are actually kind of nice . . . Let's see what you're going for. Yeah. It's just like I thought. You don't go unlisted unless you're desperate. This is stupid." She leaned on her elbow, eyes tracking the scrolling menus. "This guy just went for fifteen hundred. I don't even want to know where they found him. That girl got twenty-five. You guys are imperials, though."

She looked up at us. "You're young, and you look good.

You look like Prince Dalton. What are the cute ones going for?" She continued to search. "This kid pulled three thousand, but he's only sixteen, so he's gray—why doesn't he get more? Must be something wrong with him—the only people who buy kids are the ones with enough money to smuggle them out without getting caught . . . Can't sell you to them. Too bad there isn't a gray option for you, but I guess if there was, they'd have already found it." She sighed and stared at us.

"Who wants to buy you? Who would want to buy two guys like you? You don't want to be sold, do you?"

We both shook our heads.

"See? Exactly. So it's not like you'd make good indentureds. Whoever buys you has to try and hold you. Hmm." She went back to the reader. "I'm going to say you're virgins. You probably aren't, but everyone else is lying on here, and the perverts that buy people like you probably like that."

She captured images of our faces, then listed us for sale.

"And we'll offer a little discount if someone wants to buy you both," she added. "So three apiece, or five and a half for both. Don't look at me like that," she said, giving us a pained look. "I'm not a merchant. I don't know what I'm doing. There."

She put the reader down and got up, arching her back and stretching. "You guys better sell fast—I have to get to work." Yawning, she turned to leave the room, then turned back. "I guess taking my eyes off you probably isn't a good idea." She sighed. "Are you hungry?"

Sei and I exchanged a look, then nodded.

Was it really morning? Of course not; there was no morning here. Everyone on this station was running on a different schedule. But our arrival had clearly gotten Nora out of bed.

She went to the counter and pulled out a flat heating element, then switched it on. She took a bottle of protein solution from the cooler and plugged it into the nutrient combiner, then dialed in a code I couldn't see. Yellow streams of liquid began to mix with the clear protein, quickly changing the bottle's color to a pale gold.

She sprinkled something green on the cooking surface, and it began to sizzle. Sei and I watched as she took thin, flat starch discs and put them on the surface, where they began to fry.

Sei was pleased with this delay; in his mind, it brought him closer to being rescued before something bad could happen to him.

This wasn't good. We could be in the hands of someone very shady in a matter of minutes if we sold quickly. In that case, the poison in my body was the least of my worries.

Nora was appropriately wary. She'd see anything we did—anything at all—as an attempt to escape. There were two of us, and only one of her. Anything I did to try to get her to unmute me, she'd see as a ruse—and she wouldn't hesitate to dial up the electricity and teach me a lesson.

Though she seemed decent enough, she wasn't in a position to help us. Freeber and Willis were dangerous. She didn't want to defy them. And dealing with us was illegal. Her best move was to sell us quickly and hope her involvement wouldn't come back to bite her in some way. Because taking us to the authorities or setting us free certainly would.

Freeber and Willis had put her in an awkward position, but I didn't have much sympathy for her.

Nora skillfully flipped the discs a few times, then pushed them aside and took the bottle from the combiner. She poured the yellow fluid onto the heating element, where it began to solidify. She used a pair of metal slicers to chop it, push it around, and do a lot of things we couldn't see clearly, all the while seasoning the mixture with things from the cabinet.

She was quietly humming an Evagardian pop song that was horribly overplayed across the entire galaxy at the moment.

She removed the circles of starch from the heat, then distributed the yellow mixture among them. Next, she rolled them into tight, cylindrical bundles, then put them back on the heat, placing them so they stayed shut.

It took her perhaps a minute to clean up her utensils; then she switched off the heat and took a bowl of something red from the cooler and put it on the table. She tipped the three cylinders onto a plate and rejoined us at the table.

"Don't make this weird," she warned, holding up the controller and giving us a threatening look.

We both tried to look cooperative.

"Okay," she said, her eyes flicking between us. "You're cuter," she said to Sei. "So you're first. Did someone hit you?" she asked, looking at his blackening eye. "Whatever. I don't want to know." She picked up a cylinder, removed the cover from the bowl, and dipped it in the sauce, which appeared to contain some finely chopped vegetable matter.

It was an awkward arrangement, but the cylindrical design of Nora's breakfast made it easy for her to feed it to us. It was good; the starch covering was crispy and, I suspected, genuine—not made in a combiner. The filling was soft, hot, and savory. The red dip was a little spicy.

But being fed by a woman who was going to sell us made it difficult to enjoy her cooking. Still, I was feeling weaker by the minute, so eating couldn't hurt. I probably didn't look so good at this point, but Nora was ignoring that. She just wanted to be rid of us. Worrying about my health would only complicate her situation.

Nora was a maintenance technician. The professional way she did everything was a giveaway, and so was her lack of hair. Fully clothed and wearing a wig, she would look like any other woman, and that was probably how she presented herself outside. But with her spending ten hours a day inside a low-end tech suit, hair would only get in the way.

Sei and I both started when the headless android emerged from the bedroom. Nora scowled at it.

"You take longer to charge every day," she complained. It was an extremely old-fashioned model, one that was only in the shape of a human. Even with a head, it was obviously a robot. It wasn't a serving or comfort model—it had probably begun its life as some kind of industrial labor unit.

"My apologies, ma'am. We have guests."

"Don't worry about them."

"Very good, ma'am." The android circled the table to stand behind her. It began to rub her shoulders with metal fingers covered in slip-resistant rubber. Nora barely noticed, and kept feeding us.

After Sei and I had eaten, Nora munched her own breakfast as she scanned headlines on her holo. She continued for several minutes.

"Ma'am, would you like me to bring you a robe?" the robot asked as it wiped down the heating element and folded it up. Nora didn't even hear him; she was too absorbed in what she was doing. After a moment her eyes lifted to us, and she sighed.

"Okay. Okay, look, you two. I'm trying to keep you out of the worst of it, you know? The people getting sold for five hundred credits so people can eat them, or whatever they do with bottom-shelf meat. So if you sell at this price, even though it's not much, whoever pays it probably wants their money's worth out of you. It'll probably be pirates who want to ransom you back to the Empire. If it is, just let them. If it's someone else, you know the drill. You're imperials. Your government has people to help you, right?"

We nodded.

"Yeah," she said. "So even if they don't find you themselves, you just have to do what indentureds do when they get into a tight spot. Build some trust, then take advantage of it to call for help or report mistreatment or whatever. Okay? It sucks, but that's how it works. The next couple weeks probably aren't going to be a lot of fun for you, but you'll probably be okay. At least, that's what I'm telling myself. And you should too."

She stared at us for a moment, then groaned and went back to her holo, chewing gloomily. Her analysis of our situation and chances wasn't completely off, but she'd left out a few scenarios, and she knew it.

The holo chimed, and she looked surprised.

"Look at that," she said. "Someone's interested."

14

"OH, Empress."

Salmagard stood in front of the gates, looking down at the market. The size of the Bazaar itself was staggering because of how open it was, but she'd never expected something like this. It was called the Open Market, but she hadn't expected it to be *this* open. Surely this was the sort of business one would want to conduct behind closed doors, the sort of thing people would not want to be publicly associated with—at least, that was what she'd thought.

A man shoving a woman in control cuffs pushed past them. Salmagard was covered in sweat now, and badly winded. She stared at the crowds below. There was a stage with a big screen behind it, smaller auctions, booths, offices, all of it laid out for everyone to see.

There were eight gates at this entrance, and lines at all of them. It was packed.

The public walkway was high over the trading ground; you

had to pay to get in, then ride a lift down to where things were actually happening.

Diana, not even breathing hard, was still thinking straight. She guided Salmagard into a line. There was no shortcut for them. They had to wait with everyone else.

Salmagard stared at the people around her. A family a short distance off was extremely distraught. A woman was weeping openly. A couple of station security men were hurrying toward her. Diana and Salmagard turned away.

"You all right?" Diana asked, concerned.

"Tired," Salmagard replied.

Salmagard was a negotiator; she could run all day if she had to, but keeping up with Diana had been a struggle. Salmagard was in a daze, but not from the run. It was from what was around her. There were people controlling other hooded and masked people, and no one was batting an eye. That wasn't the worst part.

There were the tourists too. Some of them were Evagardian. Of course it was illegal in the Empire to own another human being. There were some strict debt-collection laws that were a little similar in some respects, but even those were light-years away from this.

But these imperials weren't here to buy or sell; they just wanted to look. And commemorate this exotic adventure, where they got to see things they appeared to find fascinating.

Salmagard remembered what Alice Everly had told her about cultures and people. There were people in the Imperium with different views as well. Nothing Salmagard hadn't already known, but to actually see it only made her feel more ill.

"If they check our IDs, we're in trouble," Diana murmured,

craning her neck to get a look at the front of the line. "But I think we're okay; they're just skimming to get more money. It's just ticket entry. Got your holo?"

But Salmagard wasn't listening. She was looking over the railing at the sheer drop and the scene below. The teeming crowds, the number of people who were a part of this trade. She couldn't comprehend it.

They were already at the front of the line. Diana paid both their entries and pulled her through.

"Wake up," she said, snapping her white fingers in front of Salmagard's face. "It's showtime. Let's do this."

Salmagard focused, but it wasn't much. Her universe was tilting around her. "How? How do we find him?" she asked.

"Them, you mean?"

"Please step into the lift," an android said, and they did so. The enclosure sealed, and they began to descend.

Salmagard opened her mouth to reply, but sweat stung her eyes, and she wiped her brow with her sleeve. Her eyes fell on the stage in the center of it all. A young boy in control cuffs stood blindfolded with several bright lights shining on him. The interior of the lift muted the noise from outside, but they could still hear the roar of the bidding.

That was illegal. It had to be. Free Trade space had their indentured servitude, but it applied only to people of legal age to govern their decisions. One had to consent. Obviously the boy was too young.

But it wasn't illegal *inside* the Bazaar.

Diana was consulting her holo. "That's the big stage. It's the best spot in the market. The most expensive people go up there— you have to pay a fortune to get that exposure. Apparently it's like its own brand, like there's a lot of prestige associated with buying someone off the big stage. I don't think they're going to be up there."

Salmagard nodded. The boy on the stage was trembling. She could see the light catching on the mute strip on his throat. Not that he had to be muted—there were thousands of people there, and the noise was deafening.

The lift reached the bottom and they gratefully got out. At least from down here Salmagard couldn't see as much of the market. That was a good thing.

There was a service desk nearby. Diana headed for it, and Salmagard followed, praying for strength and focus, but with a bitter taste in her mouth.

For some reason, her faith in both God and the Empress just wasn't as comforting as it had been this time the day before.

Diana pushed her way to the counter and leaned over; there were several smartly dressed people ready to take questions.

"Welcome," the man in front of them said, smiling. "You two look like you're having quite a day. How can I help you?"

"We need to find someone," Salmagard said without thinking.

"She means we need something specific," Diana cut in. "How do we shop for that?"

"Well, most folks use the index," the man replied cheerily. "But if you're willing to spend a little extra, consider an agent. They're experts who can help you locate and barter for exactly what you want."

"That sounds good," Diana said. "We can afford it. Where?"

"See those sound pods?" The man got up and pointed. There was a line of transparent cubes along a far wall, past the main stage. Inside each cube were a desk and a person. Some cubes were frosted over; perhaps those agents had clients. "You can walk right in, and they'll be glad to help you."

"Thanks," Diana said, gazing at the cubes.

"Enjoy your shopping." The man smiled, bowed, and sat back down, politely pretending not to notice Salmagard's visible distress.

"Hold it together," Diana hissed. Salmagard followed her back into the crowd, afraid she was going to pass out. "For the Empress' sake, *please*. I can't do this by myself," she added. They made straight for the nearest cube and hurried up the steps.

The door opened as they approached, and the woman behind the desk shot to her feet, breaking into a sparkling grin. She'd had plenty of physical augmentation, and she was wearing so many cosmetics that her age was impossible to guess.

"Ladies," she said, rubbing her hands together. "Come in, sit."

The door closed behind them, shutting out the noise of the market completely.

They hesitated, then took the two chairs in front of the desk. Salmagard fanned herself with a hand, and it was all she could do not to wheeze.

"Are you all right?" the woman asked.

"Fine," Salmagard lied, shaking her head. "Fine."

"Welcome," the woman said. The plaque on her desk read: *Steph*. "I work for Dynamic Galaxy Limited. We're the foremost staffing professionals in Free Trade space, and one of the largest and most respected placement services in the business." As she spoke, the smart carbon behind her lit up, showing company logos, testimonials, and promotional presentations in a dizzying collage. "Full accreditations. No gray area services offered, I'm afraid. Everything we do here is aboveboard and in accordance with the Free Trade Charter, and most common galactic law. If you have any questions about specific locality statutes for any post-Bazaar plans you might have, I can answer those. I'm a registered Free Trade attorney, and I can authenticate and document any purchases you might make. Everything that happens here is easy and airtight."

The clear walls around them frosted over.

"So, now that we've gotten that out of the way, do you have business needs that conventional Free Trade Employment Charter rules fall short for? Do you have professional needs that require an extraordinary degree of discretion from your people? Because if it's for work, we've got personnel for every conceivable need. If you need help at home, we've got you covered there too. Androids have come a long way, but they have their shortcomings, and to be perfectly honest, a lot of us just don't trust them." She gestured, and the walls were immediately covered with headlines and video clips related to dangerous and malfunctioning robotics.

Her smile widened. "At the end of the day, you really are better off with the real thing. Looking for men? We've got men. We've got men for every day of the week. Women? Look at our most recent spotlight: Grandma Hawkins from New Earth. They say she's the best cook on the entire planet; you get her for two years, only a hundred thousand. She's trying to put her grandson through school. We've got Mogwi Tandela, winner of the Forty-Ninth Commonwealth Gladiatorial Tournament. He's a veteran of the Ganraen Royal Navy *and* a New Brittia survivor. He's got a special tier-three addition to his servitude that extends to *combat*. First time I've ever seen that." She glanced up at the hulking man on the screen.

"Destroy your bedroom, then your enemies. Only two million for two months. But of course, we're not restricted to our featured premium offers; I've got the whole Bazaar index. And remember, the more you pay, the less I get. I'm on your side, ladies. So. What are you looking for?"

Diana and Salmagard exchanged a look.

"Men," Diana said.

Steph twitched her eyebrows. "Right? Hey, you're doing the right thing. I tried to go vanilla for a long time, but it wasn't happening. Look at this." She turned around a hologram on her desk so they could see. It showed a young man, dark skinned, superbly muscled, and shirtless.

"Best decision I ever made," Steph said fondly. "Ten thousand for four years, tier two." She shook her head. "Only six months left. I don't want him to leave. So what do you two have in mind?"

"Two. Two men," Salmagard said, distinctly uncomfortable.

"The perfect double date," Steph said, nodding gravely. "The one where you call the shots. You've got the right idea. I wish I had when I was your age. What kind of guys we talking? You want showpieces, or something you can use?"

"We're actually looking for very specific men," Diana said.

"Picky eaters, huh? That's the right way to be if you ask me," Steph said with an approving smile. "It's good to know what you want. If you don't want to buy off the rack, you've still got options. You can buy cheap, then negotiate to get whatever mods you need. Say you pick up this guy," Steph said, pointing to a hologram of a skinny, nondescript man. "Then you cut his service time, but in exchange he has to get bone growth, muscle mass implants, penile augmentation, facial restructuring, whatever you guys want. You can get great leverage on those bargains because you're footing the bill. Not only does this guy get his time shortened, but he gets all this work done for free. You both win. Get me? The more you offer, the faster it happens, and you can go wild with this. I've seen people go full hermaphrodite with as little cost to the client as twenty percent off total service time and a payout of something like twenty thousand. It was dirt cheap. It was ridiculous. They still had to pay for the changes, but that's a steal. So, what sounds good?"

"We're actually looking for something that we can get here and now," Diana said.

"Fantastic. When you need it, you need it. I know how that is. Why wait?" Steph pulled up her search index. "What's your fancy?"

"Evagardian," Diana said.

. Steph winced. "Ouch. You *are* picky. Look, I'll be real with you. Imperial stock on hand is always going to be low. They just don't sign for this very often, and when they do, you pay for it. They also get snapped up pretty quickly. You're usually going to be much better off to try to reserve something in advance."

"Let's see what's out there," Diana said.

"And just so we're on the same page, which tier of servitude are you looking for?"

"What's that mean?"

Steph raised an eyebrow. "First timers? Um, well, I've never had to explain this before. There are guidelines. Okay. Tier-one servitude is just that. Servitude. Your servant works for you in a professional context, protected by numerous professional guidelines, as seen here." She lit up a hologram. "You can only work them so hard, and they have . . . you know, rights and dignity. Tier two gives them a little less freedom, in exchange for more of an investment on your part, and more of a payoff for them when they complete their contract."

Diana and Salmagard looked at her blankly.

"If I take home a tier-one servant," Steph said, tenting her hands, "I can tell him to do the laundry and rub my feet. If he's signed to tier two, I can treat him like I would a comfort android, or a construct in VR, but of course I'm still held to whatever safety guarantees and personal sustenance terms are in our agreement, as notarized by his representation, as assigned by the charter or third party."

"Oh," Diana said.

Salmagard's head spun. This indentured servitude—sexual activity seemed to play a central role in it. In the whole industry. But that made no sense; if all people wanted was sex, that was what VR was for. All one had to do was put on a VR collar and hook up with strangers over the network, or just choose from millions of idealized AIs. There was something virtual for everyone's tastes.

Buying and selling real people was a *terribly* inefficient way to go about getting a sexual experience, even a particularly specific one.

Salmagard could see it now. This industry wasn't really about sex; it was about ego. Ownership was just the ultimate way for people to assert themselves over others. And nothing showcased domination like absolute control.

None of this was actually about sex; sex just seemed to be the form it took. Salmagard had believed she understood what Alice Everly had tried to tell her. She'd been wrong. Comprehension was only now beginning to dawn on her.

"We'd like to see both," Salmagard said.

"Good decision," Steph said. "You can always negotiate. If you find someone you want who's tier one, you can talk to him before you buy and work something out. Then you just submit a proposal to his broker with the new terms. You know, same drill. Cut his time down, and he'll agree to go to tier two. Then you've got him. Most of them are willing to negotiate. Very rare that you have a tier one who won't go to tier two for the right price, especially for buyers like you two. You have preferences for your Evagardian men? Age?"

"Twenties," Diana said.

"All right. See? Only a few dozen of them in the system right now—half of them are gone already. These are locked for VIP bidders with line priority. Okay." Steph spun the hologram. "See anything you like?"

Together, Diana and Salmagard looked up at the grid of faces in front of them.

They leapt to their feet at the same instant. Relief flooded through Salmagard as Diana threw her arms around her, squeezing her much more tightly than was comfortable.

"Oh, Empress!" Diana said.

"Those two." Salmagard gasped, pointing. "We need those two. How much?"

Steph, obviously taken aback by their exuberance, leaned across the desk to look.

"Aw," she said. "Too bad. Those two have already sold."

Diana and Salmagard froze.

"What?"

"See that symbol? They're already bought and paid for. Maybe you can place a bid with their new owner," she said quickly, seeing their faces fall.

"Yes," Salmagard said, mouth suddenly dry. "Yes, we'd like to do that."

"Let me see." Steph dissolved the hologram and sat down, pulling her chair to the desk and turning to her console. "No. Sorry. They're already off the station, and the buyer's anonymous. It usually is. But don't worry," she added. "There's plenty more where they came from."

A sudden pounding on the door startled all three of them. It was pretty fierce to get through the sound buffering.

There wasn't time to do or say anything. Steph just hit a release on the desk, and the door opened. Men and women in armor flooded into the small room so quickly that even if Salmagard had wanted to fight back, there wouldn't have been much she could do. They all had weapons drawn. Gloved hands roughly seized Diana and Salmagard, hauling them to their feet. Salmagard's arms were pulled back, and she felt control cuffs lock into place to restrain her.

"Station security. You're under arrest," the lead officer said, jamming a stunner into Salmagard's neck.

15

I felt my body jolt, and I instinctively put my hands out as the hiss of the breaking seal filled my ears. The canopy was opening, but too slowly. I pushed against it, tasting blood in my mouth and choking.

I toppled out of the sleeper, and the deck beneath me wasn't what I expected. It wasn't deck at all. It was ground. It wasn't metal or polymer; it was something else, and it was freezing. I rolled onto my back, my head pounding.

My wrist blurred and doubled in front of my eyes. I didn't feel up to this, but if I didn't go through with it, I had about thirty seconds to live.

I brought my wrist to my mouth, tested, then bit. The capsule embedded beneath the skin came free, and I used the last of my strength to throw my head back and swallow it.

Then I sagged to the ground. That was the best I could do. My wrist was bleeding, but that was the least of my problems. I kept my eyes shut, content just to lie there. I didn't know where I was, and though I was completely helpless to anyone who might come along, that just wasn't the issue.

When I'd seen that our new owners intended to put us in sleepers, I'd used my implanted suicide capsule. Its effects were slowed by forced sleep, but not halted. Just as planned, the sleeper noticed the medical emergency and spit me out, leaving me free to take the reversal pill in my wrist. This was my chance.

But the sleeper would also notify my captors that I needed medical attention, so I couldn't just lie around. The last thing my body needed was *more* poison, but I hadn't seen another option.

The strategy of playing along and building trust as an escape plan was potentially workable, but it was also the one any illegal buyer would be looking for. It wasn't a sure thing, and I didn't have the luxury of time. I preferred to strike first, and ideally I wanted to hit hard enough that I wouldn't have to hit a second time.

I was no longer wearing control cuffs. I couldn't feel my fingertips, but I had the use of my hands. It was a start.

I sat up and looked around. I didn't understand what I was seeing. Stone walls? No. Not stone, stones. Stones held together with mortar. The floor was wood. Real wood, by the feel of it.

There was Sei's sleeper, standing beside mine.

There was nothing else to see. The chamber was small and bare, lit only by a fixture on the wall that was trying to simulate an actual flame.

I picked myself up. There was no sign of my clothes. Obviously being weak, sick, and captive in a strange place wasn't enough. I had to be naked too. I shouldn't have been surprised.

I considered the sleeper models. It was perfectly safe to let people wear undergarments in these. I wondered what our new owners were thinking.

I went to Sei's sleeper and initiated his wake-up, then staggered to the door and pressed my ear to it, listening. I couldn't hear anything, but the door looked like serious, very heavy wood. It had a big metal handle and several locks, all accessible from this side.

Sei's seal broke, and I hurried back to catch him before he fell out. Sleepers were designed to be kept upright so people wouldn't suffocate if something was out of balance and there was gravity in play. They were also designed to *keep* you from falling out, but people were always too keen as they awoke, and they'd fall out despite the unit's best efforts. That was just a fact of life, and the main reason that proper, respectable sleeper bays had padded floors and safety straps.

Sei pulled in a long, shuddering breath, clinging to me. He wasn't sick, but he was having a bad wake-up. I held him up until he was strong enough to stand.

"What's going on?" he asked, looking around blearily.

"We're making our move," I told him, watching the door.

"We are?"

"Yeah."

"Where are we?"

"That's what I want to know," I said, reaching out to touch the door. Sei pulled free of me to stand on his own.

I tested the first lock curiously, twisting the knob. I'd never actually touched anything like this before. I'd seen dramas. I'd studied history. I understood the concept.

Something slid out of place. I tried the next lock, then undid the chain.

"Are we planetside?" Sei asked, reaching out toward the artificial flame. He drew his hand back quickly. "That's real," he said.

"What?"

"I said it's real. Empress, that's hot."

"Feels like planet gravity," I told him, closing my eyes and thinking about it. "Can't say which, though."

Sei rubbed the stones of the wall. "I've never seen anything like this, except in dramas."

"Me neither." I opened the door, revealing a short corridor leading to a staircase. It wasn't lost on me that no one had come running when we awoke unscheduled, and I wasn't sure what to make of that. Considering the location of our storage, the most likely explanation was that the sleepers weren't set up to report to anyone in the case of a malfunction.

Our new owners were counting on us sleeping peacefully.

There was also the detail that this didn't feel like normal ship or station gravity. I was running down the list of planets we could be on. Old Earth sprang to mind, not because of the gravity, but because of the materials on display around us.

But how could we be there? That would mean we'd been bought by imperials. Imperials who, rather than set us free, put us to sleep. I wondered how much time had passed and recalled the moment in that hotel room when I realized I'd been recognized.

Who would recognize me? I resembled Dalton, but right now I was wearing my own face—or my face as it would look at my current age. The last time I'd seen my *own* face I'd still been a teenager. Records of my old face were mostly gone by now, purged by people trying to control the narrative of what had happened to the Ganraen capital station.

Who knew me? There were people from my life before the war, but they didn't know what I'd been up to. They all thought I was dead.

Who knew the whole truth? Not very many people. But there were a few people left in Evagardian Intelligence who *thought* they did. Perhaps a few in the government as well.

People who liked to shop for humans through proxies at the Bazaar? Well, corruption had been around for a long time. No reason to think it was going anywhere.

I thought it over. It wasn't implausible. Evagardians loved their deniability. Turning their own people into tools was common practice. Imperials liked to keep things clean when they could.

I knew all about that.

But Old Earth wasn't the only option, and that meant that we hadn't necessarily been bought by imperials. There were lots of small colonies, and some not so small, that had settled on Earth-like planets but forsaken modern technology. There were dozens of them, all living in the past to different degrees for their own reasons.

Looking at the stone walls and floor, and the actual fire being used to light the space, I couldn't help but think about those sorts of places. I'd heard that Evagardians regularly joined such colonies and communes. A few of them had even been founded by imperials out of a desire to get back to a simpler time.

I'd always thought that sort of thing sounded interesting, even appealing. But only for a holiday. I would always want to be able to get back to civilization. A romantic weekend in a rustic little novelty colony? I could think of worse things.

Sei and I reached the top of the stairs, where another door was closed and locked.

I listened again, but there was nothing to hear. I looked at Sei.

"Can you think of a reason we shouldn't just go for it?" I asked.

"Might be better to wait and get the jump on someone," he said. "We're going out there blind."

He was right. I rubbed at my temples, but I knew this headache wasn't going away until I could get my antidote. "But who knows how long they were going to keep us down there? Could be a long time before anyone shows up. If they show up."

"How'd you wake us?"

"I'm detoxing. Don't ask. The sleeper picked it up and spat me out."

Sei nodded. "That's a stroke of luck."

"But I'm not healthy. If we do run into trouble and get physical, I'm looking at you. I'm not big on fighting."

"No problem." Sei cracked his knuckles. "I've got you covered. So we're doing it?"

"I think so. Maybe we can find some clothes."

"That wouldn't hurt."

I undid the locks and eased the door open, pulling back and wincing from the bright light. It took me a moment to realize it was sunlight.

Incredulous, I pushed the door wide open, staring. It wasn't that I didn't know what I was seeing; it was that I was having some trouble accepting it.

We were in the countryside. There was no other way to look at it. Green grass. Blue sky.

Gravestones.

Here was something else I'd seen only in dramas: burying the dead in the ground and marking the site. It had been centuries since that had been a common practice in the Empire. There were probably some people out there who still did it— well, there obviously were. They were right in front of us.

There was no one in sight. I took in the rolling hills, dotted with trees. There was a nice breeze, and it was warm, though not so warm that I didn't want clothes.

"Empress," Sei murmured beside me.

I looked around for a moment, then emerged from the doorway, turning to look up at the structure we'd be placed in.

It was a mausoleum. How appropriate.

"That's supposed to be a place for the dead, right?" Sei asked, squinting at it. It wasn't elaborate, but there were some artistic touches, including a stone carving of a winged child decorating the crest of the roof.

"I think so," I replied.

Sort of an odd place to leave a pair of sleepers containing living men unattended, wasn't it? I turned in a circle, looking around suspiciously. Fluffy white clouds drifted overhead, and a breeze blew just hard enough to make me break out in goose-flesh.

Sei padded over to the nearest headstone and took a look.

"Edward Softly," he read aloud. "AD 1890 to 1937. Before the calendar changed. Before the Unification?"

"Quite a bit before." I took a look at the grave marker closest to me. "Humphrey Littlewit. AD 1890 to 1937. Same as yours."

"You heard of these guys?"

I shook my head. "No. I only know the Old Earth people that everyone else does. Shakespeare. Jesus. The Duchess. That's about it. And who's to say these guys are important? They could just be locals."

"Yeah." Sei ran his hand through his hair, gazing around him. "But the dates are the same. Why are they the same? Where is everybody?"

"Good question." I didn't mind that we were alone. We were two naked men standing around, looking confused in an archaic graveyard. This wasn't something people needed to see.

"So where are we?" Sei asked.

I didn't even have a guess.

16

THE room was rectangular and cramped. Four meters by three. There were a table and three chairs. The walls and floor were smooth carbon. There was a mirrored strip at eye level that ringed the chamber. Surveillance. A biohazard sensor and a decon cream dispenser.

"I'm hungry," Diana complained, pacing restlessly. It was about the fourth time she'd said that.

Salmagard sat at the table with her face in her hands. Every minute was crucial, and they'd been there for hours already.

The Admiral was off the station, in transit; maybe he'd already reached wherever his buyer was taking him. Now the GRs really were his best hope.

Salmagard had her breath back, but that was all. She had nothing to fall back on. All her good sense, everything she was supposed to know, had been pushed aside—all to get him back. If she just could have done that, she wouldn't have cared what the consequences were.

The door opened, and a lean man around forty entered, wearing business clothes with an armored vest. The holster at his hip was empty, and he had a big reader under his arm.

"Ladies," he said, sealing the door behind him. "You look like you've had a long one. I'm here to tell you where you stand." He loosened his collar, gesturing for Diana to sit.

She took the seat beside Salmagard, looking nervous. The man in the vest sat down across from them.

"We've positively identified you as imperial citizens, so don't worry. We're going to keep you comfortable. As things are right now, you're guilty of being here without codes, and also of crashing a shuttle into a maintenance bay. I'm not actually sure what regulations that breaks . . . I guess it depends how we spin it." He shrugged. "We could call it criminal trespass, maybe even an attempted terrorist attack, but we do know that you were being pursued and fired on, so I don't think that's likely. We could just call it an accident. Either way, you're looking at some fines and maybe even some confinement. They aren't the most serious charges, but it's not a joke. I know you imperials think everyone outside your systems are lawless savages, but that's not the case. We do have laws. And there are consequences for breaking them."

He leaned back and folded his arms. "And what I mean to say is that's what you would be looking at if the patrollers weren't so interested in you. Apparently, you're wanted in connection to an incident at a gaming establishment just outside Bazaar space, and that, if I'm reading this correctly, involved some small-arms fire and serious property damage. To the effect of . . . ten million credits."

Diana balked, and Salmagard nudged her in the ribs before she could say anything.

The man watched them.

"That probably includes anticipated legal fees. I foresee some litigation. Anything to say?" he prodded.

"We've been the victims of a crime," Salmagard stated flatly. "We were abducted and separated from our friends. Everything we've done has been to find them and get them back."

She didn't know how else to say it. It sounded ridiculous. There was nothing to do but try to be succinct. Salmagard felt her temper start to rise, and she stared at the officer, silently challenging him not to believe her.

His brows rose. He looked at his reader, then pinched the bridge of his nose. "I can't reply to that," he said. "I'm just here to tell you what's going on. We don't want you thinking we're just leaving you in here to sweat, because we're not. The Bazaar isn't going to charge you or fine you, because FT Patrol wants you in relation to this other ruckus you caused. So we're just going to detain you until their guys get here. I'm not interested in a jurisdictional dispute over you. They're going to take you into custody officially. Right now you're in an investigatory detention period; we've got another six hours before we're required to charge you. Once Free Trade has custody of you, you'll be able to properly report anything you believe has happened to you. You'll also be able to contact the imperial consulate, but by then you're no longer my problem. If you really were kidnapped, I imagine that'll help you, but you're still going to be facing a lot of fines no matter how this shakes out. Damages have to be paid for, and nobody wants to hear excuses." He didn't look terribly sympathetic. "That's where we're at. I think we're all just glad no one's been killed, though apparently you did put some people into care. Do you both understand?"

They nodded.

"We can't contact the consulate now?" Salmagard asked.

"No. And the enforcers know you're not going to like that, but they're ordering it anyway. I don't know what they have in mind, but you can file a complaint if you feel the wait was unreasonable or harmful. You'll get your pound of flesh eventually. So you're in this room for another hour or two; then you're with them, and you'll probably go to the hub. Things should open up for you there. You can tell your side of things, and if you're telling the truth, it won't be the end of your world. Okay?" He tapped his fingers on the desk. "You tracking?"

There was nothing to argue. No play to make. Station security had them dead to rights, and they were being held in the security headquarters.

They weren't going anywhere.

The officer got up and left.

Salmagard rested her head on her arms as the hatch closed. This was it. The Admiral really was gone. Even if they could somehow clear all this up—and that didn't seem likely with the mess they'd made—it would take too long.

Abducted people disappeared all the time. Even in Evagardian space, the law could never have *all* the answers. It couldn't find everyone.

Out here, the odds weren't in the Empire's favor. The universe was just too big, and people buying undocumented humans would be careful to cover their tracks. Once the trail was cold, it was as good as gone.

Salmagard wasn't going to get the Admiral back. She shut her eyes and blotted them miserably on the sleeves of her ruined dress.

A woman of her station was expected to protect her husbands.

No, she hadn't been married to the Admiral, and no, she wasn't sure that was possible—even if she wanted to—and that was a question that was by no means settled. Or even raised, really.

But the principle was the same. Salmagard wasn't just any imperial girl; she was the first daughter of a bloodline that predated the Unification. For her to allow a gentleman in her company to be taken and sold into slavery—it was shame on a scale that she'd never even entertained thoughts of.

And apart from the shame, there was the matter of the Admiral himself. She didn't even have the faintest idea what would become of him. Would he be sold to people who would mistreat him? Kill him? Would he be killed by the poison in his body?

Or would the GRs catch up to him and free him, along with Sei? If so, would he vanish? Or would they discover his identity and arrest him? What would Evagard do with him?

On top of that, there were criminal charges. There was the stigma of going unsupervised—or attempting to, at any rate—to Red Yonder with a man who could only be seen as . . . disreputable.

And this was Free Trade space. If she were convicted here, would she be sent to New Brittia? No. That was impossible; New Brittia was a prison for men. There was probably a female equivalent, though. It didn't matter.

She would be extradited, but that was small comfort. It would almost be better to die alone and forgotten in a galactic prison.

Her military career was over. Any chance she might've had of taking control of the bloodline was gone as well.

Even if people could get past her association with the Admiral—and they would not be able to—she was finished. Her intentions were noble in creating this mess. Getting him back was what would be expected of her, whoever he might be—but she had failed. It was that simple.

Good intentions were lovely, but they didn't win wars. Evagardian women with value got results. There was no credit given for effort.

Everyone knew that. It didn't matter how hard you tried, or why. In the end, it was all down to what you had to show when the dust settled. That was how you could tell the winners from the losers, and Evagard's gentry had no place for women who did not win.

Salmagard had spoiled herself. She was largely rational. She'd always been good at the things she tried to do, but she'd been ready for the alternative. She could handle setbacks; she could bear them with grace and dignity, the way she was supposed to.

But she'd never expected to fail this profoundly, on this level. She wanted to disappear.

Diana got up and started to pace again.

"This sucks," she said.

Salmagard didn't argue. She just pressed her face harder into her sleeve.

Diana paused at the far wall, looking up at a tiny black nub on the wall. "Is that an environment scanner?"

Salmagard looked up, puzzled. "Of course."

"Right. So it can see chemicals and biohazards," Diana said slowly, and her eyes lit up alarmingly. "I'm a genius."

Salmagard tilted her head, feeling pain start to throb in her temples. "I don't quite follow." It was taking all of her self-control to be civil. She didn't believe any of this was Diana's fault, but . . .

Salmagard really needed to be alone. Since that wasn't going to happen, she needed quiet.

"I'm a *genius*," Diana repeated, grinning as she stepped back. "I know how we can get out of here. I know how we can get out of here and find out where the boys are. I know how we can catch up to them." Her knuckles and joints had started to pop, and the look in her eyes had grown even more disturbing.

She had Salmagard's attention.

"Did they take your hairpins? And your combs? They did, didn't they—? Damn it, I don't care." Diana put her thumb in her mouth and bit, drawing blood. Salmagard's eyes widened.

The red-eyed girl grabbed a chair, climbed on, and rubbed the blood on the scanner.

"There," she said, climbing down and smirking. "Too easy."

Salmagard just stared at her.

A moment later, Klaxons began to wail.

17

"THIS way," I said, pointing. "There's something over there." We could see something pointy standing out over the hills in that direction, and that was the way the road seemed to be going.

"Not going to lie," Sei said, catching up. "I'm not completely comfortable going for this kind of stroll without trousers."

"I know how you feel," I replied, looking back at the graveyard we'd left behind.

"I like this, though," he said, looking down at the soft grass.

The grass did feel nice, but it only reminded me how heavy my limbs felt, and how quickly I was losing sensation.

"It's just like Old Earth," Sei said.

"You've been there?"

"Only in simulation. Wherever this place is, it's been seriously terraformed to mimic it exactly."

He was right. I knelt and touched the grass, feeling at the

soil beneath. I didn't really know how to gauge it. New Earth was, in terms of environment, supposed to be quite similar to Old Earth. I'd never set foot on Old Earth, so I didn't know how true that was, but I had been to New Earth—and this was definitely similar.

"We could be in the Frontier system," I said, getting back up. "They hang on to a lot of Old Earth traditions there. Holidays, religion. Maybe even putting bodies in the ground. You saw those markers, didn't you? With the perpendicular lines in the symbol?"

"The crosses? Sure."

"That's a spiritual thing."

"I know what it is—I'm catholic."

"Oh. Well, yeah. That stuff's really prevalent on Frontier worlds."

"It would make sense," Sei said, putting his hands on his hips and looking up at the sky. "Pretty direct route from the Bazaar into Commonwealth space. Lots of ways to make that trip fast."

"That's the thing," I said. "Whoever bought us must have a serious ship and a lot of jump priority, because we went from the Bazaar to planetside awfully fast. I know we weren't in those sleepers for more than a few hours." Any more than that, and I'd probably be dead.

"If you've got the money to buy people, you can buy speed."

Yes, but that raised another question. For a journey so short, why put us in sleepers at all?

"I know. But it doesn't make sense," I said, scratching my head. "They bought us cheap, remember?"

"Look around you. Someone owns all this land. It's got to be worth a fortune, and it's got to be private. I mean, we're contraband. This can't be a public space. Say what you want about the Commonwealth, but all three of those systems are civilized enough to have laws against kidnapping and slavery."

"I know," I said, shaking my head. "This is obviously someone with a lot of money to throw around. So why'd he buy us instead of someone better?"

Sei frowned. "We're both here, so they must've gone for the package deal, huh?"

"Exactly. The rich, landowning bargain hunter? I don't think so."

"I see your point. I don't like it much, though."

"Right?" I nodded toward the shape beyond the hill. "Let's go."

"We're at a big disadvantage out here," Sei pointed out, hurrying after me. "These people aren't going to let us just walk home to the Empress. Are you okay?"

"I'm not feeling well. And don't get ahead of yourself," I cautioned. "I think we're better off trying to talk our way out of this. These people may not know exactly what they have on their hands. In case you haven't picked up on it yet, I'm wanted by Imperial Security and Evagardian Intelligence."

"I picked up that you're shady as hell," Sei said, though there wasn't any judgment in his voice. He was just glad to have another imperial around. "What are you? New Unity? Actually, I don't want to know. Do they know you're here? Are they coming for you?"

"Probably not, but these people don't need to know that. Didn't your friend say you were a war hero?"

He shrugged. "She is too."

"Well, these folks might not want that kind of trouble. We might be able to get them to cut us loose just by telling them who we are. Might not be so bad; they didn't spend much on us. The Free Trade credit's pretty weak against the Imperial Julian right now, isn't it?"

"It usually is. I guess it's worth a shot. And if that doesn't work, then we take the direct approach."

"If you're up to it," I said, looking down at my hands. They weren't shaking, but I didn't know how much good they would do me. "Because I'm not."

"I am more than up to it. We're supposed to be at Red Yonder right now. I had *plans*, man."

"So did I," I said, sighing.

We crested the hill. A house lay below. I was still adjusting. I'd prepared myself for this. It wasn't an alien sight; it just wasn't something I was prepared to see with my own eyes. It was the sort of thing you'd see in a projection or a hologram.

We both knelt to make ourselves less visible; we were horribly exposed on the top of the hill. It was broad daylight, and there was very little cover. "What do you think?" Sei asked, looking down at the place. There was a fence and a small garden.

"Twentieth century," I said. "Give or take. No animals, no vehicle." I raised an eyebrow at him. "Nobody home?"

"If a guy lives there, he'll have clothes."

"I'd wear a dress at this point."

We took one last look around, then hurried down the hillside, quickly crossing the ground to the structure. For a place like this on land like this—on Old Earth—you would need incredible wealth. On a Frontier world, it might not be quite as flamboyant, but there was nothing more valuable than land, and by the look of things, there was plenty of it around with nothing on it. On a terraformed body, no matter how you looked at it, that signaled wealth.

We made our way around the side of the house.

The door in the back was locked.

"It's mechanical," I said, rattling the handle. "It's just metal."

Sei took a flat gardening tool from the wooden box on the porch and slipped it into the narrow gap between the door and the frame, levering it sharply upward. There was a cracking noise, and he pulled the door open.

It was immediately clear that the illusion here was deep. The house's occupants had gone to great lengths to get the details correct. There were still a few modern amenities mixed in with the old props. The ancient cooler in the kitchen was just a shell, but inside was a proper one.

In addition to some strange foodstuffs that I didn't recognize, there were protein gel and some modern beverages. I was sure that if I looked around a bit, I'd probably find a combiner, or at least an injection system camouflaged in one of these strange old contraptions.

We didn't linger in the kitchen. I tried to think about dramas, about what I knew about these architectural sensibilities.

Sei pointed at the ceiling, and I nodded in agreement. We'd find clothes on the next floor up, where bedrooms would be.

It was nearly impossible to be stealthy in this place; the wooden floors creaked ruthlessly. It seemed unlikely that the house was as old as it looked, which meant it had been built with a deliberate look of age. There was a lot of real wood. That was just more evidence of wealth.

We climbed the stairs and found a bedroom belonging to a man.

Sei and I raided his closet as quietly as possible. The clothes seemed to be authentic to the era, though I was having trouble determining exactly when this was supposed to be. I'd never been good with history.

All through the twentieth and twenty-first centuries, men had worn dark slacks, light shirts, jackets to match the slacks, and a neck ornament to complete the look. None of it was *that* different from what we wore today, just more primitive. The core aesthetic principles from this period were still alive and well in the Empire, and across the galaxy.

The man who lived here was a little smaller than me and a little bigger than Sei. His clothes actually fit us rather well. They weren't so small on me that it was an issue, and Sei just had to roll up the cuffs of his trousers a bit. Shoes would've been too convenient, though.

I didn't want to wear antique shoes anyway. The last time I'd dressed up like this, I'd been back on Cohengard, waltzing around with a tray balanced on my hand, serving drinks.

It felt like centuries had passed since then. And fond memories wouldn't get me out of this.

With minimal fumbling, we belted on old-fashioned trousers, fastened our shirts, and, feeling much more prepared to face our captors, went back downstairs.

"Did you look outside?" I asked Sei.

He nodded. "I didn't see anything, but there're all these trees. There can't be any major cities nearby, or we'd see them. There might be something that way, but I'm not sure." He pointed through the kitchen window.

"That's where the road goes," I said, securing my cuffs and straightening my collar.

"We should stay off the road, but we can't do much until we know where we are."

"We could try to get a vehicle and take off." I pulled the curtains aside and peered out at the yard. "But without knowing where we're going, we might not be making things better."

We left the house and jogged toward the trees. The sky was clouding over, but that wasn't right. There wasn't any wind. Or not much of it.

"Hey," I said, pausing. It wasn't just the sudden change in the weather, but I didn't have the strength to do a lot of hurrying. "Didn't that come on a little fast?" I gazed up. The sky, previously bright, gorgeous blue, was turning gray.

"You see a sun?"

"It was over there," I said, pointing. "Just the one, looked a bit like Solari."

"So it could be New Earth. And judging from the house, whatever it rains here isn't toxic," Sei said. "We should be all right."

"We haven't had any vaccines for this biome," I pointed out.

"They probably gave them to us while we were asleep. Come on, we can't stay in the open."

We pushed on. I was worried about our bare feet, but the grass and soil were both soft and welcoming. There was nothing objectionable to step on. Not a single sharp rock.

More low hills waited past the trees, and I could see something ahead.

What was more, I knew what it was. A steeple. As we climbed toward it, I recalled the towering spires on Nidaros and how they had called to mind this very thing, just on a much grander scale.

"It's a temple."

"Church," Sei corrected.

We'd found some people. There were about twenty vehicles arranged outside the structure.

"There," I said, pointing. There were more houses less than a kilometer away, all of them just as old-fashioned as the one

Sei and I had invaded a few minutes earlier. There was an entire village of them. I tried to count. There might be four or more individuals to a house, and thirty to forty houses at least. It wasn't a large colony, if that was what this was.

But what was a colony without a colony ship? What was more, where was the spaceport? The landing site? Was this a seeded colony where the inhabitants were simply dropped off with the materials they would use to start their new lives? What if it *wasn't* a colony? Was this really just a settlement on New Earth?

It didn't fit. None of it fit.

The sky was dark; the cloud cover was getting heavier, but no rain was falling.

Sei gazed down at the church.

"Look at those huge birds," he said. I saw them. They were perched along the pointy black metal fence that ringed the place. Their feathers were black, like the fence, and they were making some loud, truly grating noises.

The church was visibly overgrown with weeds and vines, like the mausoleum we'd emerged from. Did these people not have the time to maintain their grounds? That was odd— everything else was nicely done. The grass was all neat. The house we'd seen had been taken care of. Why was the church different?

Perhaps they chose not to maintain it. That was a thought. This arrangement fairly reeked of a sort of theatrical mentality. Maybe someone had set it up to look this way deliberately.

Before I could get too far into thinking about that, the church doors opened and people began to spill out.

Sei and I stiffened, but they were being boisterous in a so-ciable sort of way, not because they were alarmed. We both got down and watched as they returned to their vehicles. There were more in there than I'd estimated, and they were all dressed like we were, in authentic period clothes.

Several set off along the road on foot, talking animatedly.

These people were excited about something. I couldn't hear enough individual voices to identify accents or dialects.

We watched them disperse. They looked genuinely happy.

"Look at the vehicles," Sei said. "Would you trust something like that?"

"Do you smell it?"

"No."

"They're fakes. Real ones used fossil fuels. The air here's clean. Come on."

The people on foot were already well on their way back to their village. If they looked back and saw us, we'd just look like locals. We were dressed for the part, though we were barefoot, and from the concerned looks Sei was giving me, my condition was growing increasingly obvious.

I started down the hill, toward the church.

"What are we going to find in there?" Sei asked, drawing even with me. He put his hands in his pockets and looked back toward the trees.

"I don't know. Maybe some answers." I was lost. None of this made any sense to me. I wouldn't have thought there was a situation that I couldn't create some kind of picture out of—but here I was without a clue. Even on Nidaros, I'd been able to draw conclusions from what was around me. That situation had been bizarre, but it had nothing on this.

The clean air and quiet was good, though. The smells and crowds of the Bazaar had been awful, particularly coupled with my physical discomfort.

As usual, the only way was forward. My growing weakness was not helping my temper.

I didn't have *time* for this.

I went up to the big doors and listened briefly, then pushed them inward and peered inside. The sanctuary was dark. In the gloom I could see rows of wooden benches and hints of what appeared to be some impressive architecture.

Spirituality was a complex subject in the Empire. Obviously, there could be no higher power than the Empress herself, but she permitted the free practice of religion as long as it fell within the confines of Imperial Law.

Many people saw this as an inexplicable contradiction. There had been occasional moves to bar religion from imperial life, even from within the government itself, but they were always shut down before they could gain traction.

That wasn't my area of expertise, though I knew more about it than some imperials. As a child of Cohengard, I was well-read on the subject of imperial philosophy and the common objections to it. Growing up, I'd even associated with people involved in the New Unity movement—not the radical terrorists, just the ones who didn't fully believe in the Evagardian ideal.

I knew the Grand Duchess had written a great deal on the subject of religion, its role in humanity's development, and its value as a cultural keepsake, but most of that had tied in to her views on the crucial importance of freedom of thought. She considered the question of religion's rationality secondary; she said it didn't matter if it was rational. The Duchess always argued that as long as people obeyed the law, they could believe whatever they liked and always be protected from persecution.

Or something like that. I didn't really remember.

Maybe it was all the chems I'd used as Prince Dalton that

had softened my memory. There were procedures I could have in the Empire that would help me recover some of that, but the Empire and I were in the final phase of our relationship, and it was an awkward one.

That operation would never happen, and I was just making excuses. That reading had been a long time ago, before the war, before Dalton.

Back then I hadn't been sure what I wanted to do with my life. New Unity had courted me—thanks to the company I kept—but I'd never gotten too close. Well, not too close to the movement.

Growing up in Cohengard, I'd seen the aftermath of the revolt close up. And I knew how much of a disadvantage it could be to be born there, though I'd never had strong feelings about it the way some of my friends had. Griffith. And Larsen.

In fact, it was at a New Unity rally that I was—that *we* were—scouted and offered the opportunity to serve.

Griffith had attended the rally because of Larsen. And I had attended because of Griffith.

And now here I was.

"Who's there?"

Sei and I whirled. A man in black emerged from a doorway at the rear. His sleeves were rolled up, and he was drying his hands with a white towel.

At first he'd sounded mildly curious, but now that he saw us, he stopped in his tracks. A long, agonizing moment passed. He had instinctively reached for the light controls, but now his hand froze just short of the panel. He dropped it to his side, cocking his head at us.

"My word. What are you boys doing awake?"

18

"**WHAT'S** this?" Salmagard asked, looking up in panic.

"Biohazard detected," a female voice said over the intercom.

A second set of emergency locks clanked into place inside the door, and the air seal was audible.

"Remain calm," the voice added. "Quarantine in effect. Remain calm. Biohazard containment personnel are mobilizing to address the situation. Remain calm. Do not attempt to leave your immediate area. Remain calm. All personnel, this is not a drill."

Diana smirked.

Salmagard sat up. "Did you do this?"

"No. Absolutely not," Diana replied. "Let's just wait it out. Stay cool."

It took her a moment, but Salmagard understood. She nodded.

"I hope it's nothing serious."

"Me too," Diana said, leaning against the wall and folding her arms.

After about five minutes, the Klaxons stopped.

"Thank you for your patience," the female voice announced. "Normal operations may resume. If any anomalies occur with quarantine measures failing to disengage, please report them to your department maintenance representative. Thank you for your cooperation. Remember, adherence to Free Trade Commission biohazard response protocols is of vital importance to us all. Have a pleasant day."

Salmagard waited, but the door locks did not disengage. She was getting nervous. She watched Diana suck on her bleeding thumb. The red-eyed woman was trying to look nonchalant, but she hadn't taken her eyes off the door.

It was a full ten minutes before the locks thudded out of place and the door opened, admitting a tall man with an impeccable goatee. He wore formal Isakan robes, though he was obviously not of Earth Asian descent. He waved off a security officer and yanked the door shut behind him.

For a moment he gazed at the two of them; then he took a hypo from his pocket and pressed it to his wrist.

"My name's Price," he said. "I'm on the board. I represent the Bazaar's interests. I understand there's been some unpleasantness with the two of you, a crime you were hoping to report." His eyes flicked around the room, lingering for a moment on the smear of Diana's blood over the environment scanner. "But I'm here to help you clear that up. You know we don't like trouble with imperials around here."

"Are we okay to talk?" Diana asked.

Price looked puzzled. "Why wouldn't we be?"

She let out her breath. "Thank the Empress."

"Diana, what's going on?" Salmagard asked.

"This guy's a spy," Diana said, pointing a finger at Price. "There's something in my blood that shouldn't be there. It's not supposed to exist outside of some very tightly controlled laboratories in Evagardian space. So when it shows up on a bio scanner here at the Bazaar, obviously EI has to check it out. And here he is. Right on time. Are you really a board rep?"

Price looked nonplussed. "What a novel idea," he said. "But since we're getting to the point, what I really need from you, ma'am, is to tell me your name is Diana Kladinova. Because if you're not Diana Kladinova, that would be bad for everyone."

"I am." Diana lit up her holo, and Price checked her ID.

"All right," he said, looking relieved. "There's no visual in here, so I couldn't confirm. And audio's disabled, obviously."

"Obviously. Let me guess—my tracker went dark when we were taken, and everybody's panicking."

"So you were abducted? You didn't run? How'd you end up here? You've got a lot of explaining to do, Lieutenant."

"I'm not in the Service anymore. It's a long story, but we've got more pressing business right now."

"Maybe you think you do. Who are you?" he asked Salmagard.

She showed her own ID, intensely conscious of her appearance. Her throat tightened, but Salmagard made herself speak. "PFC Tessa Salmagard, sir. First Fleet, assigned to the *Julian*. Security Forces, Negotiations, Ceremonial Guard."

Price didn't reply, but his eyes shifted back to Diana. "Tell me how you got here from Imperial Pointe."

"We were taken by some kind of freelancer hustlers," she

said. "They sold us to a guy running a fuel depot outside the Bazaar. We were traveling with friends. Those friends got separated from us. We've been trying to locate them before they were sold, but we were too late. They're already gone. That's why I called for you."

"Is that how you view me, Miss Kladinova? Someone to be summoned? If what you're saying is true, and you really were taken, then that would be good. But regardless, we need to get you back where you belong."

"Not going to happen," Diana said. "We might still have a time advantage over the GRs. We're going after our friends. I'll do whatever the Garden wants. I've played by the rules. I've been good—but I'm not leaving until I know Sei is safe. Lieutenant Ibuki Sei. He was with me on the Tenbrook tour."

"Your little stunt here worked," Price said frankly, giving her a stern look. "It worked brilliantly. Because I'm going to scumbag you two out of here, and all your problems are going to go away. If you do have friends out there in trouble, I sympathize. But I have a job, and for the love of the Empress, so do you. The GRs have *their* job, and they're good at it. Now, I can't *wait* to hear all about what you two have been up to, because while you're on the way to the consulate, I'm going to be submitting a long and detailed report about you, Miss Kladinova. Because this is a mess."

"I don't think you're hearing me."

"No, *you're* not hearing me," Price said firmly. "You're an asset, Kladinova. More than that, you're a biohazard. You're a walking security risk. The Garden has given you too much freedom, particularly in light of your extremely disturbing record of nonexistent judgment. Now, you ending up here may or may not be your fault. I don't care. You need to grow up, appreciate what you are, and accept the consequences. Do you realize we're at maximum alert status right now? There is an imminent terror threat from New Unity. Do you have any idea what it looks like when this kind of alert hits on a station like this? Do you know how scary that is? Do you know how many people's days you just completely ruined? Biohazards that a station is not prepared to counter can kill *millions*, Miss Kladinova. Look at Oasis."

"Like I said," Diana replied, unimpressed, "you're not hearing me. Ibuki Sei is an imperial hero. He serves, just like you do. One way or another, we are getting him back safe. That hasn't changed, has it?" She looked to Salmagard, who nodded agreement.

Diana got up and went to the door, putting her hand on the handle. "I'm giving you a choice," she said to Price.

"What choice is that?"

"Are you going to help with the rescue, or are you going to have to get rescued?"

"I know about your family. Don't try to threaten me. And don't bother. The door's sealed. You aren't going anywhere without me."

Diana wrenched the hatch open. Metal squealed and groaned; the mangled lock tore free of the wall, and sparks scattered across the deck.

A woman who had been walking past stood frozen, staring. Diana gave a look with her red eyes, and she quickly went on her way.

"Sir," Diana said calmly, "what's it going to be?"

She held up her fist suggestively.

Price was more than twice their age. He'd probably been in intelligence for as long as they'd been alive, maybe longer. He knew how to be unflappable. But he was posing as a commercial operator. He wasn't carrying a weapon, and even if he was, what was he going to do against a pilot with extraordinary strength and a negotiator?

He was under no illusions. He didn't have the upper hand.

Diana rammed the door back into place and rejoined them at the table.

"This is not going to go well for you," Price said.

"Just help us," Diana snapped.

He tapped his temple. Of course; he was a spy. He didn't wear a physical holo; he just used implants.

"We need to find out who bought Lieutenant Ibuki," Diana said, taking her seat. "The sale would've been a few hours ago now, so you'll have to go back. I know the sales are public record."

"But the buyers aren't," Price pointed out.

"Like you don't have access to that," Diana said derisively. "Use his official Service portrait. Search it against the index. You'll find his record of sale."

"I'm already doing it," Price said, sighing. "You two do realize this is crazy, don't you? I don't care if you're as strong as an EVX—you're in over your heads."

"Let us worry about that," Salmagard said, following Diana's aggressive lead. There was an opportunity here. Salmagard was already ruined. Her career was over and her good name was gone. That was settled. What wasn't settled was whether she would live out her life knowing that she had saved the Admiral or knowing that she had failed. If she got him back, that would be a costly victory.

But it would still be a victory. Win or die trying—there could hardly be anything more Evagardian. Absurd as it was, only by defying Price's authority could Salmagard hope to snatch back at least a scrap of honor from this appalling disaster of a day.

Diana was doing the right thing. Salmagard would back her, and she would see this through.

"Looks like he was sold along with another guy. Let's see who this is. Huh." Price frowned.

"What is it?" Salmagard asked, feeling her stomach drop.

"This face is flagged on my list. Looks like there was a tip a couple hours ago. Doesn't say for what, but he's a priority threat. And he's marked as deceased . . . except, the time stamp—so he's *not* dead. And there's no personnel file." Price's eyes had gone glassy; he was completely withdrawn. He was deep in his implant.

Salmagard's mouth was dry.

After a moment he abruptly focused and looked up, staring at them with new eyes.

"Well," he said. "Well—all right. All right, now I'm working with you guys. You want to find your guy, you have to find this guy too. Now we're getting something done." He touched his temple and flicked his eyelids, probably scanning records.

Salmagard felt sick. She knew exactly what had just happened. In the act of caving to Diana's demands, Price had looked up Sei's purchase—and stumbled onto the Admiral, who he'd probably had checked out on principle, just because of his connection to the sale.

And Evagard had caught it. They'd recognized him. Now the Empire knew the Admiral was involved. The Admiral had faked his death for nothing; it was all coming into the open.

"Okay. His buyer masked the transaction—that's normal. These two *were* illegal. Maybe you did get kidnapped. By the Empress—what's going on?" It was obvious that Price was seeing things he wasn't prepared for, and it was all coming at him fast. "Marcus DeSantos? No way that's not an alias; you aren't from Triga." He got up from the table and started to pace, folding his arms and smiling. His eyes widened, and he turned on Diana and Salmagard, watching them closely.

Then he keyed something and spoke quietly into his com. "Yeah, go ahead and give us some privacy. These two are being difficult, but we might be onto something here. Let's play it out. Push them back."

"Thank you," Diana said.

"Don't thank me yet. If you think you're going to get away with threatening me, then you're farther gone than I thought. But we can deal with that later. Who *is* this guy that bought your friend? And what are *you* doing with a priority guy on my list with ties to New Unity? You both have problems, but *you* aren't New Unity. And this is a dead man. A dead man with no name. Does this have to do with our alert level? Is *this* the guy everyone's so afraid of? Why doesn't he have a name? Hmm."

He paused for a moment, then started moving again. "Oh, of course. Private Salmagard, you didn't tell me you'd had contact with this man."

"I can't see what you're looking at," she said weakly. "So I could hardly comment."

"Hmm. All right, I've got our buyer's real name. Let's see who he is."

Diana and Salmagard watched Price as he read things they couldn't see and spoke to people they couldn't hear.

"Okay, so he's nobody. So who's he *work* for?" Price demanded, nearly shouting. He touched his ear. "Got anything? He's from the Montoya system. Check those cartels. Clean? How can he be clean? He just bought two unregistered slaves. That's not any kind of clean I ever heard of, Tom. Get me something on this guy—every minute we lose, that fish is swimming. This guy with no name is a big one." He clapped his hands, then rubbed them together restlessly, returning to the present. He turned on them. "All right, you two. We're going to make a deal."

"What kind of deal?" Diana asked, suspicious.

"We're on high alert. I have no one to spare. I shouldn't even be here now. You said you wanted to go after these guys, right? Get them back? That is what you said, isn't it?"

"Damn right," Diana said.

"You're former Service. And you—you're active. What if I said you could go? What would you say?"

"Yes," Salmagard said, worrying she was about to throw up.

"You could get in there and intervene, buy time for the GRs to catch up. You two have made a hell of a mess, but if you help bring this guy in, you can come out of this on top instead of ruined. Get me? Yes, I read. What have you got? Okay, so he's not on our radar. Check every association, every flag, every system, every agency, every database. We need to know where he's going—he's got some precious cargo." Price was shouting again.

Salmagard had to get up. She went to the far wall and leaned on it, taking deep breaths. Diana appeared beside her, concerned.

"What's wrong?" she asked, rubbing Salmagard's back. "He's going to come through for us."

"He's *what*?" Price yelled.

They both jumped at Price's outburst, turning around.

"By the Empress," he said, the blood draining from his face.

"What? What is it?" Salmagard asked, swallowing. "Who's got them?"

19

"CYRIL," the man in black said, stepping forward. "My name's Cyril. Now, don't look like that."

Sei and I had both tensed. We didn't move, but he was coming toward us, making a show of not looking threatening.

He paused, frowning. "Are those my clothes?"

Sei and I glanced down at ourselves.

"Could be," I said. "Do you live in a big house behind those trees?"

"As a matter of fact, I do." Cyril's eyes narrowed—but only for a moment. He seemed to deflate a little. "But I can understand why you wanted to get dressed. I imagine the two of you must be feeling a bit disoriented, but I'm glad to see you seem to have found your feet. May I ask who woke you up?"

"No one," I replied. "The sleeper malfunctioned."

Cyril winced. "That's embarrassing. We'll have to make the best of it. Welcome to my parish, gentlemen. It's your new home."

"I don't think so," I stated bluntly. Balance was needed here. Aggression—but not abrasion, if we could help it. This was a delicate situation.

"Sir, we were abducted and sold against our will," I told Cyril. "Though you must've paid for us, you haven't actually got any legal claim. That's why you don't have any official documentation. Anything you do have is fake, fabricated by the people that took us. I'm sorry, but you're going to have to let us go and put in a claim with the Bazaar for your money. We're imperial subjects, and holding us is in violation of basically everybody's laws. If you're reasonable here and now, you can avoid the worst of it."

"Whoa, whoa," Cyril said, looking taken aback. "Slow down. That's—that's quite a story. I should tell you that though you were acquired on my instructions, I wasn't the one to buy you, and I certainly had no idea you were undocumented. My understanding was that you're on open contract, tier-one service. This is disturbing. Let's sit." He perched on one of the wooden benches and gestured for us to do the same.

Sei and I moved to stand over him. We needed to keep the upper hand here. I'd have to try to let my behavior make up for my appearance. In the dark, I probably looked more scary than sickly. We could use that.

Cyril swallowed.

"Where are we?" I asked.

He blinked. A moment passed. "Well, that's difficult to state precisely without the exact numbers in front of me," Cyril said slowly. "But we're in unregulated space."

Sei and I exchanged a look. That wasn't good. Conventional laws wouldn't apply if Cyril was telling the truth about that. That didn't mean he had *no* obligation to treat us fairly, but it didn't work in our favor. It stacked things against us. He went on.

"Past the Free Trade curvature on the Kakugo side." Not New Earth, then.

"I didn't know there was a Terra type out here," I said, frowning. "Not that I would, I suppose."

Cyril's expression flickered. "Look, I can see you're both very single-minded right now, and I promise you that I—well, at the very least I *think* that I can understand your distress," he said, searching our faces. "But I'm afraid if what you say is true, you're in for some inconvenience." He pointed toward the doors, his eyes still on our faces. "As I'm sure you saw out there, there's no spaceport here. We can't just send you on your way. We're quite isolated. We don't even have long-range communications. Now, once I review the documents associated with your purchase and speak with the man I asked to do the buying—if we can confirm your story, of course—I will see to it that you have berths on the next supply ship. But if you're asking me to snap my fingers and spirit you away, I'm afraid that's just not possible. I'm just the pastor, boys—I don't actually do the miracles."

He looked genuinely sympathetic. "In the meantime, if you're not in servitude, you'll be guests. And I don't think you'll mind so much; this is not a difficult community to live in."

"If you're so friendly," Sei said, "why are you buying people?"

Cyril got to his feet, appearing to choose his words carefully. "As I said before, this is a very *isolated* community. There are things we need that demand assistance from outside. Something our people are incapable of providing." Cyril sighed. He was careful not to make any sudden movements. "This is difficult to explain, especially because I don't know if I have lawful authority over you or not, but honesty's always the best policy. Look, our community is—as I'm sure you can see—a bit eccentric about certain things. Not everyone sees us in a positive light. In fact, I'd guess most people out there look at us in a negative one."

"What are you?" I asked bluntly.

"Just people looking for answers," Cyril said, spreading his arms. "Spiritual answers."

"What do you need us for?"

"DNA," he replied immediately. "Use your eyes. It's a small community. Fewer than two hundred of us in all. When it comes to making deposits to the gene bank, who better than imperials?"

"Are you talking about the old-fashioned way, or do you have a clinic hidden here somewhere?"

Cyril fidgeted a little. "The old-fashioned way."

Sei and I exchanged a look. Sei snorted.

"Our public image doesn't make this easy," Cyril went on. "People are not very trusting of groups like ours. But once they get to know us, see it from the inside, they actually tend to be rather impressed. It's not the most elegant route, but we need what we need. This life isn't for everyone, but it does have a strong allure to those who feel downtrodden by galactic society at large."

His gaze flicked between us, settling on me.

"Whether you'll be staying here for the duration of your contract or returned if you're here wrongfully, you will be here for a short period of time. Ten days at least. Let me show you around. Tell you about what we believe. It'll help to see us up close. I'm sure that'll put you at ease. With a story like yours, I can believe you'd be suspicious."

"Give us a second," I told him, stepping away with Sei.

"What do you think of him?" Sei asked quietly, glancing at Cyril.

"I think he has an answer for everything. But he's a spiritual leader, so that's his job. Doesn't make him a bad guy." I rubbed my chin. "He's right, though. We aren't going anywhere by ourselves. We could knock him out and make a run for it, but where are we going? It'll be dark soon, and it won't get any warmer. We don't have any supplies, and these people know the land and have transportation. We'd just be wasting our time. I'm in no condition to commit to running. At least, not a very long run."

"This is the part where we build trust, right?"

"Hardly. I tipped our hand. They know we don't want to be here. They won't let their guard down."

We returned to Cyril.

"Sure," I said. "Show us around. But let's make it a priority to get this cleared up. You don't want us to think you're stalling." I could've put on the facade of a meeker, more cooperative individual, but Cyril was already suspicious of us because of our unscheduled wake-up. It was better to go with a more believable persona. "We can't be at ease until we know where we stand. We've been kidnapped, and it has been a long day. I need you to appreciate how serious this is. We were *kidnapped*. Look at him." I glanced toward Sei, whose eye was still black from Willis' punch.

"Of course," Cyril replied, nodding. "You'd have every right to be upset, but I hope you'll make the best of it."

"We've spent the last day being dragged around and mistreated by criminals. If spending a few nights with you guys is the worst we've got waiting for us, we'll manage," Sei said.

Cyril looked grateful. "Thank you." He put out his hand. "Welcome to our community. Whether your stay is long or short, we're all friends here."

We both shook his hand.

Cyril led us out of the dark sanctuary and into the gathering evening. The sky had cleared up a little, and we could hear the big black birds cawing. He ambled off toward the road, looking completely at peace. Under different circumstances, this would've been nice.

We followed.

"What's the theme here? Some kind of Judeo-Christian thing?" I asked.

Cyril shook his head. "No, but I can see why you'd think so," he said, glancing back at the church. "Our community isn't really about a particular belief, so to speak. It's about exploring our beliefs. We investigate the notion that reality is more layered than our senses allow us to perceive. That there are things out there that we can't see or touch, but that are seeing us and touching us all the time, to put it simply."

"Of course there are. They're called microorganisms," I said.

Cyril smiled. "A similar concept." He stopped and pointed up, making it a grand gesture. "Space. The great infinity. Are the two of you reasonably well-traveled?"

"Reasonably," Sei replied.

"Then you know there are a lot of strange things out there."

"Of course."

"A lot of it we can explain," Cyril said, beginning to walk again. "Some of it we can't. There are signals, impulses, particles, and even organisms, microorganisms, that we do not understand. Signals with no origin that can only be picked up under specific circumstances. I'm not suggesting anything fantastical, mind you," he said, giving us a look. "Everything seems fantastical before it is explained. Then it becomes commonplace. Let's just say that some of us infer greater meaning in some of these phenomena than others."

"That's a little vague."

"It's a complex subject," Cyril admitted. "Not easy to talk about to strangers. You've no doubt noticed our quaint little stylings?"

"Of course."

"Why do you think we do this?"

"Because your spiritual doctrine frowns on modern technology?"

"No," Cyril replied. "We have no doctrine. Well, no hard-and-fast doctrine. Admittedly, this aesthetic has a certain symbolic value with relation to the founder of our beliefs, but it's really just a mental exercise. A form of therapy. You see, gentlemen, topics like existence, reality, and cosmic truth require a certain frame of mind to effectively explore. The purpose of this isolated environment is to cultivate that state of mind. We've adopted a lifestyle that massages the mind to its most flexible and receptive state. You're imperials. May I ask what you do, if you aren't really indentured servants?"

"I'm a pilot," Sei said.

"Stressful work," Cyril said. "When you go home at night, do you have the mental energy to think about the nature of the universe?"

Sei seemed taken aback by the question. "Not usually," he admitted.

"Just so. Our views are considered controversial, all the

more so because among us are some noted men and women of science who are dedicated to proving the truth through purely quantifiable means. We can talk about mysterious things until the sun sets, but someone's got to get in there and try to figure out what's really going on."

"Is it your approach or your findings that get you into trouble?" I asked plainly.

"Both," Cyril replied. "People have a very narrow view of existence. That we are real, and that everything that can't be mapped isn't. That we exist in certain dimensions, which are large, possibly infinite, filled with planets filled with organisms that might differ from us biologically, but still fit more or less the same definition of life."

"Sounds about right."

"They don't like to hear that life, as such, isn't as rigid a label as they believe."

"You're starting to lose me."

"Forgive me," Cyril said, rolling down his sleeves and buttoning his cuffs.

We were nearly in the village now. A vehicle rolled past with barely a whisper. It definitely didn't have a real combustion engine.

There were people on little walkways that flanked the road, and lights in the windows. There was no proper white light; it was all yellowish and very warm-looking. Bricks. Masonry. Wood. Metal.

Very little polymer and plastic.

"And here we are. It's time for you boys to meet our fair village. You're going to like it." Cyril grinned over his shoulder at us. "Trust me."

20

THE noise was incredible.

Price was walking so fast that Diana and Salmagard had to jog to keep up. He had a dampening field active so he could talk to his colleagues and handlers as he moved, but it was only protecting him, no one else.

They were on a walkway a hundred meters over a large dry dock. Below, repairs and maintenance were being performed on a huge pleasure yacht that was all blue and gray, with sweeping wings and lines, and openings—openings normally covered by force screens. It was the sort of spectacular ship that you saw in dramas, belonging to wealthy celebrities and powerful villains.

"Here. Here," Price said suddenly, grimacing at the noise. He pointed to a hatch leading to a break room. "Get in there."

Once Price had learned the apparent value of the Admiral, things had begun to move very quickly. Diana and Salmagard had been in a persistent state of confusion ever since. Diana might have gained some initiative in the interrogation room, but Price had since taken it back.

The two of them entered the small room, and the door slid shut behind them, leaving Price on the other side.

"What the hell?" Diana demanded. She went to the window and looked through, but Price spotted her and waved her away. The room kept out some of the noise, but not all.

Diana scowled and started to pace. "Your boyfriend is in trouble," she said to Salmagard, who just nodded miserably. "But there's no choice. You get that, right?"

She nodded again.

"Did you know?"

"Know what?"

"How serious it was? Look at him—look at them. They're panicking. Is he a terrorist? Is he *New Unity*?"

Salmagard opened her mouth, but the hatch hissed open and Price came through, sealing it behind him and putting a cube on the table. It was a secure communication device.

"Look smart," he said sharply, and Diana and Salmagard instinctively went to attention, despite the fact that they were not in uniform. Diana was no longer in the Service, but no one could just turn it off.

A hologram appeared with a waiting symbol. Price bit his thumbnail and leaned against the bulkhead. He noticed the window, scowled, and switched it to opaque.

A man's face appeared, projected over the table. This was a secure communication, and both Diana and Salmagard recognized him.

This was Dashiell Sirpras, deputy head of Evagardian Intelligence.

"Do you know who I am?" he asked bluntly.

"Yes, sir," they replied in unison. Salmagard started to sweat. There were few people in the Empire with more power than this man. He was bigger than a general or an admiral. Bigger than a Tetrarch.

"This situation's developing fast. I don't have all the details—but it seems like we have a confirmed lead on this individual, and the two of you are in the best position to get him for us. Is that right, Price?"

"I've got field agents, but pulling them while we're at this alert level could be costly. It could expose us, sir. We still don't know what the target is."

Sirpras rubbed his chin. "We'll go with it. Listen to me very closely. You, Kladinova, I know about you. There's a big smear on your record, and if what I'm reading is correct, today's only going to make it worse. And you, Private Salmagard, not only are you under some scrutiny right now, but in light of these events, you're finished. You might even be looking at criminal prosecution. I'm ordering you to assist in the rescue of Lieutenant Ibuki, and in securing the man who is with him. If you do this, you might have a chance at having a life someday. You can't put a price tag on trust, Private. If you don't believe that, ask your acquaintance Lieutenant Deilani how life's been treating her since she lost the Empress' trust. Am I making myself heard?"

"Yes, sir," they replied.

"Good. Secure that man. Deliver him to the agents that are following, and not only will I make it my personal mission to fix your lives and careers, but to push you out of this with something to show for it. This is an opportunity. We're not asking you for much, but apparently this man is notoriously slippery. Price, how much time do we gain by using these two?"

"Thirty minutes at most."

"Might be enough to make a difference. Ladies, the stakes aren't just high for you personally. I don't know how I can articulate the danger this man poses to the Imperium. We need control of him. Make it happen."

The hologram vanished.

"About time he got some good news," Price said, stepping away from the wall. "You heard him. This isn't your show anymore, but you're still onstage. Follow me—there's no time."

He went back out onto the walkway, and Diana and Salmagard hurried after him.

"He's not telling you the whole story," Price shouted over his shoulder. "We're not doing this because you *might* buy us some time—we need you. You've got to get there before they go dark, and they will. And then you need to broadcast so the GRs can find you."

"What do you mean, 'go dark'?" Diana asked as they hurried down a set of metal stairs to another catwalk. The wall of the bay was ahead, and there was a short corridor to another bay. This one was smaller and deserted.

"Shangri La," Price said, setting off across the metal floor. "It's the gravitational lensing. Once you get too close, you can't trust your scanners. You have to get there first and broadcast, or we'll lose our signal before the GRs catch up. And there's only one way for you to make it in time."

"What's that?"

Salmagard was glad that Diana seemed willing to do all the talking; it was all she could do to stay conscious. Her heart was pounding and her brain felt fuzzy.

"Speed," Price replied. "It's a good thing you're a pilot, because I haven't got one to spare for you, and this isn't something we can outsource."

A large set of blast doors opened in front of them, revealing a small antechamber. There were four guards, all wearing mismatched galactic-looking armor. They were imperials, even if they weren't dressed like it. Intelligence security forces, made up to look like common mercenaries.

They let Price pass without a word. A woman keyed something on a console, and the inner doors opened, revealing another dry dock. There were techs swarming about, prepping the section for launch clearance—but there was no ship.

A woman wearing expensive formal wear and a fearsome scowl stormed up out of nowhere.

"You got it from here?" Price asked.

"Yes, go," she snapped at him, grabbing Salmagard's arm, then Diana's, and pulling them both through a hatch into an office. The man behind the desk got up and left without a word.

"Put these on," the woman said brusquely, throwing a pair of matte gray ground ops EV suits at them. As they began to change, she disconnected a crystal from her holo. "See this? This is your override. There shouldn't be anything out there it can't get you through. This is your SOS codec that we'll be looking for. You'll have to find some kind of com array to broadcast it, but it doesn't matter if it's secure or not. That's all it'll take. It's idiotproof. Stabilize the situation, get positive control of the target, then keep your heads down. Once the GRs are locked in, they'll make assisted jumps to reach you faster, and they'll take care of the rest."

"How are we getting there?" Diana asked, beginning to slip into her EV. "How do we catch up?"

"There's only one way," the woman said, pacing. "Only one ship that's fast enough."

"Yeah," Diana said, snorting. "An Everwing."

"That's right."

The pale woman froze, EV suit half on, red eyes wide. She turned to look at the woman, cocking her head.

"You're joking."

"No, Miss Kladinova," the woman replied, clearly making an enormous effort to keep her temper under control. "I am not."

"Where are we going to get an Everwing?"

"There's already one here."

Diana balked. "Bullshit," she said. "Why would you have one here?" Then her face fell. "No," she said. "No, it's not yours. Someone's got one. And they're trying to sell it here. Oh, Empress. How? They're still experimental. How did we lose one already?"

"We didn't," the woman snarled. A vein throbbed at her temple. She folded her arms and squared herself. "It's not one of ours. Not really. It's a copy. Reverse engineered."

"How?" Diana demanded.

Salmagard, not following the conversation at all, had finished putting on her EV. Diana was still only half dressed, and the woman—whose bearing suggested to Salmagard that she worked for IS—was about to have an aneurysm.

"One of our units was captured in combat. It was analyzed, and that data was sold," she snapped.

"Captured? Oh." Diana groaned and put her face in her hands. Then she looked up, mouth open. "I remember. But you want to trust a copy? A fake?"

"Apparently it's quite a good fake," the woman replied, though it seemed to pain her to say it. "We were watching it to see where it ended up before seizing it."

"Everwings are short-range fighters. They aren't made for this."

"It's a one-way trip," the woman stated flatly. "The only way anyone lives through it is if you stick to the script. Get there and secure the situation. Then let the GRs hold it down until *my* men get there."

"Are all ops this far from home like this?"

"I don't need that right now," the woman snarled. "You want to have lives? This is the only way."

"Price made that quite clear," Salmagard murmured, and the woman whirled on her, her hand shooting out. Salmagard was so startled that she didn't do anything to protect herself; the woman grabbed her by the face, her fingers pinching her cheeks, keeping her mouth shut.

"I know about you," she hissed. "I know about Nidaros. I know about *him*. What do *you* know?"

Salmagard couldn't reply; she was too startled, and she couldn't speak in this state anyway. The woman went on.

"You know nothing except what he's *told* you. You don't know anything at all," she said venomously, letting go and shoving her away. "I know you're both liners. You're used to bending the rules, getting what you want, and having everyone look the other way on everything you do. I doubt you appreciate the stakes here."

Too distraught to be offended, Salmagard barely heard what the woman was saying.

"If there was anyone else, this would not be you," she went on. "That doesn't mean you can get some ideas," she said, her eyes lingering on Salmagard. "If something goes wrong, you better hope you end up in Shangri La. Because you're going to wish you had."

She held out the crystal.

Salmagard took it and tucked it into her pouch.

Without another word, they went out into the bay, where Price appeared, holding out two hypos.

"Just do it," he said. "In front of me. Don't argue."

Salmagard took the stimulant and pressed it to her neck, squeezing the trigger. She didn't object. She needed the boost. Diana probably didn't.

"Do you have any questions for me?" Price asked, putting his hands on their shoulders and leaning in. "Because this is the time. Last chance." He had to shout over the noise in the bay.

"What the hell is this threat that's so bad you're making us do this?" Diana demanded. "This is a circus. It's ridiculous. What was she even talking about?" She jerked a thumb at the woman, who was red in the face, shouting into her holo a short distance away.

"New Unity. They're planning something big. Apparently this guy you were with might have something to do with it." Price shook his head. "But I don't know the real details, and if I did, I wouldn't be able to tell you. But we've never been on alert on this scale before. The threat is real, and it's immediate. Every office, every asset, every sleeper activated, every field agent operational. *Something* is going to happen, and somebody obviously thinks we need to take it seriously. So that's what we're doing. But that's got nothing to do with you two. You have a job to do. It's a good thing that you did what you did to bring it to our attention. Don't let Collins give you the wrong idea. You're going to come out of this heroes—just do what the Empress needs you to do. Are you ready?"

They nodded.

"Good. The Everwing is flight-ready, but we still have to get it. And I can't use my people. My operation here is an open secret, but I can't have it compromised. That would disrupt my defensive line, and we can't give New Unity that opportunity, not now of all times. A bunch of them just got busted for buying Mactex."

Diana and Salmagard both flinched. That was a savage, filthy weapon. Nothing less from New Unity. "Attack" was a vague term. Bringing something like Mactex in made things a bit less ambiguous and a lot more frightening. Salmagard felt a chill.

"Yes. Exactly," Price said, seeing their faces. "That's why my people are needed here. The Everwing is in a dock on this strut. We have to do this fast; we're losing time. You have to do two things. Neutralize the vendors and secure the hangar. Then you move the fighter onto the skiff maintenance pad."

Salmagard's eyes widened. They weren't even securing the craft with an official arrest—of course they weren't. Evagardians had no authority here. Any action they took would be illegal. Price was speaking quickly, but he was proposing something rather outrageous—in the Service, this could only be called a special operation.

And Salmagard didn't understand. Hangars were large, so skiffs were used to navigate them. In big docks, there were elevators and built-in transport systems for maintenance. When your skiff needed maintenance, you put it on a cargo pad, and the lift would carry it off to wherever the technicians were, then bring it back ready to use.

"You can't move a ship with that," she said. "It's too small."

"No," Diana said, realization dawning on her face. "You might be able to fit an Everwing. It's not like the fighters you're thinking of, Tessa. It's small. That's clever—then you can move it here and launch it without anyone seeing. The Bazaar people will never know. But you said we had to secure it? Just the two of us? You mean we have to take it away from the people who have it? How many are there?"

"Could be just a few. Could be as many as a dozen," Price said, waving to a tech driving a small transport cart.

Diana's red eyes grew large, and she glanced at Salmagard. "Against us? Just us two?"

"No. Just her," Price said, looking meaningfully at Salmagard. The tech drove up in the cart and got out. Price climbed into the driver's seat and beckoned impatiently.

Diana climbed in immediately, but Salmagard didn't move. What Price was proposing wasn't just shocking and contrary to the Service's way of doing things; it was a major crime—particularly in the Bazaar, where such importance was placed on merchandise.

And just a few moments earlier these people had been reminding her that she was criminally culpable for her actions at Heimer's gambling den.

Diana yanked her into the seat beside her.

"Why?" the pale woman was demanding. "Why just her? It's ridiculous."

"Hardly," Price said over his shoulder, beginning to drive. "You're literally the only person on this station that can pilot that Everwing. We can't let anything happen to you, or we'll never catch up to our guy."

"Guys," Diana corrected. "I'll help you get this other one, but I only care about Sei. He's one of us; don't you understand that?"

"You're the one who doesn't understand," Price snapped. The cart jolted as he drove it off the hangar's landing pad onto the maintenance walkway. The techs ahead were doing something with the pressure door for the outer corridor—it wasn't meant to accommodate vehicles, but Price didn't care about the rules. The doors opened, and one of the techs used some kind of tool to keep a sensor depressed so they wouldn't close automatically.

Price accelerated, and they shot through. The little cart's wheels hummed noisily in the close quarters of the maintenance tunnel. Ahead, blinking lights and chirping noises signaled robots getting out of the way.

"She's a negotiator," he went on. "And I won't send her in blind; we have access to all the surveillance in this sector. They aren't expecting her, and I'll handle her personally. Private. Private!"

"Yes?" Salmagard said, trying to straighten up. There were viewports on their left, and she could see space beyond. The stars didn't move, but the struts did. Much too quickly. The cart hit a bump, and she felt light-headed.

"Are you ready to work?"

"Yes, sir."

Salmagard knew she had to pull herself together. This man *was* her superior. Senior officers in EI and IS had the authority to command her when she was separate from the Fleet, as long as there was no compromise to her operational orders.

By themselves, the things Price wanted her to do—neutralize a few hostiles and help move a ship before attempting a rescue—were all functions she was trained to perform. It was the circumstances *framing* these functions that were holding her back.

The Service had just spent several years teaching her that

there was a certain way things had to be done. And here she was, no briefings, no published orders, no real chain of command, no intelligence. Just authority and necessity. It was Nidaros all over again.

"You know, that's the thing," Diana said, reaching forward to tap Price's shoulder as he pushed the cart even harder, clipping a tiny robot that didn't scuttle out of the way fast enough. "Everwings *are* small."

"Yes," he said impatiently, hitting another bump and struggling to maintain control of the cart. They were moving fast, but hangars and dry docks were massive—even on just one strut, the physical distance that needed to be covered was enormous.

"They're not meant for two," Diana said bluntly.

"I know," Price replied. "But apparently it's been done."

"What? Oh." Diana made an angry noise and did something with her hands that made it look like she was throttling someone invisible. "Bjorn! Why? *Why?*"

Price abruptly cut the throttle and halted the cart. He touched his ear, then looked at the side of the passage. "This is it." He climbed out and knelt in front of a release. Salmagard and Diana got out as he tapped in a code and pulled down the lever. The crawl space opened and he stepped aside.

"Kladinova stays with me." He touched his ear and spoke through Salmagard's holo. "We're synced. Go."

Salmagard didn't hesitate. She crawled through the opening, and Price sealed the hatch behind her. It wasn't pretty, but there were functioning lights, and everything was in good repair. This was no Evagardian station, but it was a good deal better than Captain Tremma's freighter.

"Twenty meters ahead," Price said in her ear. "I'm checking the hangar."

Salmagard got moving. Every second she wasted was time that needed to be spent in pursuit of the Admiral.

"There're seven of them in there," Price reported. "But three of them are in the break room. If you can keep it quiet, we can remotely seal that room so you won't have to deal with them. I'll talk you through the other four. But if we seal it now, they'll know we're coming—and if you tip them off, they'll come out, and you'll have to deal with all of them. No mistakes, Private."

Salmagard paused. Above her was a grate, and through it she could see lights and the ceiling of a hangar—but the ceiling wasn't far off. It wasn't a large hangar.

"Not that one," Price said. "Keep moving. Take this right. This can work; you just have to follow my orders."

Salmagard crawled through a slightly tighter opening, into a space with a ladder.

"Up one level. You've got to neutralize the eyes up there."

Salmagard had to take Price's word for it. She was more than qualified to devise her own plan of attack, but she couldn't see what Price could. She mounted the ladder and climbed quietly, climbing into the next opening and wiggling through.

"Take the first panel. Get a visual."

Salmagard got down flat and squinted through the dirty carbon. The panel opened onto a catwalk that ringed the hangar and led to an enclosed room that overlooked the space. There was a man just a few meters away sitting with his back against the railing, his legs stretched carelessly across the catwalk. He was busy with his holo.

"I'm going to find a way," Price began—and Salmagard knew what he was going to say. Trip an alarm somewhere, do something to get this guy to get up and move, to turn his back on Salmagard to give her a chance to get into the hangar.

"No," Salmagard whispered, cutting him off. "There's no time." She hit the release, and the panel opened. The man didn't even notice. Salmagard rose to a crouch and coughed. When that didn't get his attention, she coughed louder.

The man looked up, blinking several times. His eyes immediately fell on the opening. Leaving his holo glowing on his wrist, he got up and walked over, leaning down to look.

Salmagard pulled him into the crawl space, covering his mouth and lodging her knee on his throat. She held him down with her body, keeping the pressure on his windpipe. He kicked and grabbed at her with his free hand, but that just wasted energy. He was unconscious in seconds. Salmagard got off him, checked his pulse, then wormed her way out onto the catwalk.

It was too dangerous to go to the edge; she could be seen by people below. She didn't know where anyone was, so she had to rely on Price.

"You've got one more up there, in the control room. He has to be next."

Salmagard took a peek. She could see the viewports, but not the man inside that room. The door was open. The room itself would muffle any noise—she just had to get there without being spotted.

She dropped flat to the deck and crawled, trying not to think about the seconds ticking by.

"You're good like that," Price said. "They can't see you."

The hangar was choked with cargo—that was why they couldn't launch from here. There were big crates and a strange lumpy shape covered with some kind of plastic sheeting. Was that the Everwing?

Salmagard couldn't spare any attention for the hangar, though—the metal under her liked to rattle, and she had to keep that to a minimum. She got as close as she could, then got up and slipped to the wall, pressing herself to the metal beside the door and listening.

"He's got his headset on. He can't hear you—just get him," Price said impatiently.

That was all Salmagard needed. She flitted into the control room and dragged the man out of the chair, locking his arm behind his back to immobilize him and covering his mouth. She put her knee on his carotid, and in moments he was asleep.

"Go back out, keep low, go three meters and stop," Price said. "Go."

Salmagard went out the door in a crouch, then dropped flat. One meter, two, three. She stayed prone, waiting for Price.

"Wait for it," he said. "Wait."

She held her breath, listening to the sounds of the hangar. A footstep echoed. Quiet music. A laugh from the far end— that was where the break room was. It wasn't nearly enough noise to cover for her if she made a mistake.

"Now, Private. He's right under you."

Salmagard leapt up and vaulted over the railing. The man didn't even notice her falling toward him. He was crushed to the deck, her full weight on top of him. The impact took his breath away, and before he could even think about getting it back or making a sound, Salmagard put him in a choke hold. The landing had broken some of his ribs at the very least; when he woke up, he'd be in a lot of pain.

He went limp, and she let go of him to get behind the nearest cover, a carbon backdrop for washing mechanical components.

"The last one's by the fighter," Price said. "You can't sneak up on him. Make your move and I'll seal the room."

Salmagard leaned out to take a look. There was a man by that covered shape, and he was looking up at the control room and frowning. He hadn't seen her drop from the walkway, but he knew something was wrong—people who had been visible a moment ago were no longer in sight.

There was no time.

She snatched a heavy wrench from the belt of the man she'd jumped on and slid into the open. The man spotted her, and she flung it at him. It wasn't a terribly practical thing to throw, but it was heavy and it would hurt, so it had the desired effect. The man dodged aside, giving her the time she needed.

He went for a gun, but Salmagard was already on top of him. He was pretty big, so it wasn't a fight to win with finesse. She rammed her elbow beneath his rib cage, all of her speed and weight behind it. The blow staggered the man, and he hit the plastic wrapping.

"Not the fighter!" Price yelled.

Salmagard grabbed him and went for his groin with her knee, but he grabbed her back, and he was much stronger than she was. She dropped, kicking his legs out and taking him to the deck. They landed with a crash, and gravity hurt him, as the heavier one, a great deal more than it hurt her. Salmagard locked her leg around his neck, twisting her torso and letting her lower body do the work. The man's face turned red, and he tried to reach for his fallen pistol—but Salmagard just turned her hips and increased the pressure.

In a moment he was out. He'd be sore when he woke up too. Salmagard was grateful for the EV; she wouldn't have been able to do that in a dress.

She climbed off him and snatched up the pistol, getting to her feet and looking around—but the break room was sealed. She could see three men at the viewport staring at her. None of her other victims was up yet.

"Clear," she said to Price.

A hatch opened, and she whirled, raising the pistol—but it was Diana running toward her.

"Let's go," the pale woman called out. "Price is going to get us launch clearance. Quick, before station security gets here." She spotted the three trapped men in the break room and waved to them. "Come on, help me."

"Right." Salmagard began disconnecting the straps keeping the cover on the Everwing. Diana tore them off, revealing the fighter. Her mouth grew into a wide smile.

"Hello, beautiful."

Salmagard stared at the craft. It was little more than a carbon bubble with some machinery on it. It didn't look very sturdy. It certainly wasn't beautiful.

"Is this it? There's no mistake?" she asked uncertainly.

"It's definitely fake," Diana said, patting it lovingly. "But if it works, I don't care. Price! Break in and pop the canopy," she ordered, dragging the covers out of the way. She pointed. "There's our pad. You couldn't even launch a kite out of this bay," she added, wrinkling her nose and looking around at the clutter. Her eyes fell on the man who'd been guarding the fighter. "That's why you don't steal imperial designs, jackass," she said.

The bubble unsealed, and the fighter's canopy rose open.

Diana didn't hesitate. She climbed up and leapt in, and while many things she did appeared awkward and unnatural, perhaps due to her appearance, she looked as though this was something she'd been doing since birth.

"So I'm not going, then?" Salmagard said, going up on her toes to look into the cockpit.

"What? Of course you are. I can't do this by myself."

"But there's only one seat."

Diana paused what she was doing. "Right. I know. Come on." She got up and put her hand out.

"Empress, save me." Salmagard took Diana's hand, and the pale woman lifted her into the cockpit.

"It's fine. This'll be a short flight." Diana dropped back into the seat and went back to checking the systems. The interior lit up, and there was a hum of power.

A moment before, while subduing that man, Salmagard had felt very small. Now, sharing this space with Diana, she felt very large. Before she could decide how to best arrange herself, Diana pulled her into her lap and fastened the straps in a businesslike fashion. The bubble closed, sealing them in.

"You can't be serious," Salmagard said.

"Isn't this cozy? Just pretend I'm someone you like," Diana replied, but she wasn't really paying attention to Salmagard; she was busy with the fighter. And Salmagard had never seen her happier.

"How desperate do they have to be," Diana went on, "to let me fly this like this? My flying clearance is dead and buried. I'm not supposed to be allowed within ten meters of a control stick. I should be in big trouble just for flying that shuttle before. I wonder if I am, and they just aren't telling me yet. This is pretty well made. I wonder who built it."

She reached for a switch and flipped the cover up. There was a cracking sound, and the cover fell onto Salmagard's lap. Salmagard looked down at it, feeling a new sort of queasiness begin to squirm in her belly.

"Oh," Diana said. "Well, maybe they did a better job on the engines. Have we got O$_2$? Okay." She activated something, and twin glowing orbs appeared in the air. She reached under Salmagard's arms to grip them and nudged something with her toe. "Mind your feet," she murmured, and Salmagard hastily tried to comply. The last thing she wanted to do was touch this peculiar vessel's controls. Diana's thumbs moved, and the fighter rose slightly.

Salmagard saw the machinery, previously tight to the sides of the bubble, begin to expand and deploy. Diana's chin was on Salmagard's shoulder, and the red eyes flicked over toward her for a moment.

"Look, I know you like this guy, but I didn't realize he was some kind of terrorist—and obviously you didn't either. You have to get your head on straight. Who *is* he? They have this massive New Unity threat that literally all of Evagardian Intelligence and Imperial Security are getting bent out of shape over, and they're still taking time to do something this crazy over one guy? *One guy?*"

"It doesn't make sense," Salmagard said as the Everwing began to move, drifting slowly toward the maintenance pad.

"Yeah. I've been there. You think you know someone. Special ops." The red-eyed woman sighed theatrically.

"No. No, why are they sending us? Why not just let him go? Using us to help GR . . ." She felt hot. She tugged at the neck of her EV, trying to get some oxygen. "Using us to help GR—it's like they want him alive." She pulled at the straps, but there was nothing for it; they were going to be suffocatingly tight. They were meant for only one person.

"Obviously they do. And even if they didn't, they want Sei alive," Diana said, bringing the Everwing to a halt over the pad. She checked her feeds and lowered it. The craft shuddered as clamps locked it down, readying it for transport.

"They've tried to kill him before, though," Salmagard said softly. "And they haven't cared about killing other people to get to him. What's changed? Why do they want him alive now?"

21

THE community's remarkable attention to period detail was in full effect on the town's main street. There weren't just houses; there were businesses as well. I looked at the signs, and the oddly hypnotic red-and-blue pole across the street. I could see the vehicles up close now. Ground cars and crawlers had come a long way.

There were people out and about, and Cyril introduced us to a few of them. The town's residents seemed remarkably happy to see us, but also surprised. I was starting to believe what Cyril had said about cultivating a peaceful and relaxed mind-set. These were some of the most high-spirited people I'd ever encountered. And why shouldn't they have been?

It was a nice evening, and they lived in a beautiful town, apparently without much in the way of worries. I wondered if they even knew the war had stopped. Maybe they hadn't even known it had started. Cyril said there were no communications with the outside here; most of these people probably didn't have a clue what was going on in the rest of the galaxy.

Maybe they were happier that way.

It was clear they took this simulation of twentieth-century life seriously, but they weren't slaves to it. I wasn't an expert, but no one looked uncomfortable, despite the outrageous clothing. Everyone was properly groomed and perfectly healthy. It was all for show. These were modern people living in an old-fashioned setting with all of its strengths and none of its weaknesses.

I looked in through the windows of the businesses. Some had people running them; others appeared to have androids. Apparently Cyril didn't want his flock working too hard. Maybe he was afraid it might distract them from the more important issues. For my part, I'd never spent much time thinking about spiritualism. I'd always had other things on my mind. Other priorities.

I wondered what that said about me.

I watched the people on the street as we passed. For the most part, they seemed to be enjoying their evening, but there was something else. That sense of excitement I'd picked up on earlier. No one was like this all the time—these might be cheerful, fun-loving people, but there was something extra. A spark. Something special was going on.

"Here," Cyril said, stopping in front of one of the shops. "Let me buy you a malt."

Inside, there were only two other patrons: two women around my age. We seemed to have their undivided attention, but Sei and I were more interested in the novelty of the establishment itself. We sat down at the counter, and Cyril joined us, ordering malts.

I didn't know what a malt was.

The android behind the bar looked like a pretty girl with an outrageous hairstyle, wearing a neat pink uniform. She deftly operated combiners made to look like old-fashioned machinery, pouring mixtures into large metal cups, which were then put in another machine that shook them savagely. Sei and I stared, taken aback by the brutality of it.

The android removed the cups, put in spoons and straws, and handed the concoctions over. We didn't try to conceal our suspicion, but we'd watched the android make them, and Cyril was already working on his. We were afraid of the substance itself, not the danger of being poisoned or drugged. We both knew how abysmal nutrition had been in this era.

Going from the sickly-sweet taste, there were more carbo-hydrates in a single spoonful of this stuff than a human was supposed to eat in a week. It was tasty, though.

"I don't want to be rude," Cyril said, wiping his mouth with a napkin. "But are you all right, sir? You don't look so good. We don't have a real clinic, or at least not one that would impress imperials. But we do have a medical android if you need attention."

"I've got an imbalance," I replied, naming the particular cocktail that was best suited to neutralizing the poison still in my body. Initially I'd decided not to disclose my condition in the interest of not showing weakness, but I didn't know how much longer I had on my feet.

Cyril looked troubled. "I'll see what I can do to get that for you. In the meantime, we've got stimulants and painkillers."

"Better not to mix my intake," I said. "I have a feeling my chemistry's a bit fragile right now."

"You look like you're in pain."

"I am. I still have to be careful. I'm not out of danger yet, and I don't want to take unnecessary risks. Pain I can live with, but putting myself in a coma—this isn't the best time for it." That was the truth. I stirred my malt and watched the android clerk wipe down the counter.

"As you think best. I'm a little concerned that we purchased a man with an outstanding medical condition. I think some mistakes may have been made after all. I'm terribly sorry."

"Let's just call it a misunderstanding," I said. "As long as we stay on task."

"How does your economy work?" Sei asked, curious.

"It doesn't. It's all controlled," Cyril replied immediately.

"I thought so. Who's footing the bill?"

"A number of people, some of whom prefer not to be thanked for their generosity, I'm afraid. Building all of this involved some expense, but in truth it's all surprisingly cheap to run."

"With so few people, I guess it would be." I looked out the window. A young couple passed, chatting animatedly.

Cyril did his best to hide it. He had to have practiced.

But I saw it. I saw it because I was looking for it.

He had had a neural uplink, and he'd just gotten some kind of update from it. His eyes flicked ever so slightly to the side. He camouflaged the disruption by picking up his cup and using his straw to take a drink. That was him assimilating whatever he'd just learned.

There was nothing overtly sinister about having an uplink—but that kind of implanted technology wasn't terribly rustic.

When Cyril put the cup down, there was a tension in him that hadn't been there before. Something was stressing him now. How was he supposed to contemplate the nature of the universe like this?

I kept quiet.

"Well, gentlemen—we've got to start somewhere," he said, pushing the cup away. "And it's about time I have that talk, so I can figure out where we really stand with you two. I'm sure you're telling the truth—you seem like honest guys. Since we don't really have guests here, we don't have a . . . bed-and-breakfast. But I'm going to find someone to put you up, and they're going to treat you like royalty. Okay?"

Royalty. I knew what it was like to be treated like royalty. I didn't miss it.

"I could say we appreciate your hospitality," I said, "but it might sound disingenuous. Thanks for being reasonable."

"It goes both ways." Cyril got up, but motioned for us to stay. "You're not prisoners. I'm not going to keep an eye on you or lock you up. There's no tactful way to say it; there's nowhere for you to go. If you go far enough east, there's a really nice lake. But the only other habitation on this body is . . . Let's just say it's prohibitively far away."

"We're not going to run on you," Sei said, stirring his malt. "We just want to get this straightened out and get home. We're going to press charges against the people that mistreated us. Not the people who acted with decency."

"Point taken. Wait here. Someone'll be along to take you home for the night. Tomorrow I'll know exactly what's going on, and I'll be able to give you the answers you want. Please understand that I can't make you any promises until there's due diligence on my end."

"Do what you have to," I said.

"If you change your mind about medical attention, just ask anyone. They'll take you to our physician."

"Thanks."

"Don't mention it. Have a good evening."

He smiled at us and left the shop. The android clerk had come out from behind the counter and was sweeping the floor. She paused by the big device that I recognized as a music cabinet, or something like that.

"Would you like to hear a song?" she asked, beaming at us.

"No, thanks."

She went back to cleaning. The two women at the table by the window watched Cyril go, then swooped down on us. I'd expected that.

"So who are you guys?" the taller one asked, taking the stool behind me. The other one moved in on Sei. "Are you okay?"

"I'm fine," I replied. "I'm just not good with sleepers. I'm having a bad wake-up. We're just visitors. We're taking a look."

"Oh—oh, you're thinking of joining us," the shorter one said, breaking into a wide smile. "What's your background?"

"Well," I replied, looking at Sei, "we're both former military."

The two women exchanged a look. "Oh," the tall one said, looking impressed. "You must've seen some things."

"You could say that," Sei replied. He was as puzzled as I was, but he knew better than to let on. Neither one of us knew what to expect from these people, but this exchange didn't feel quite right.

"Can you tell us anything about Cyril?" I asked, eating a spoonful of my malt. "We like it here, but he's the one we're not sure about."

"Cyril's amazing," the shorter woman said immediately, and I could tell she meant it. There was so much positive energy radiating from her that it was a little stifling. Was this what happened when you lived the simple life?

"What do you mean?" Sei asked.

"He knows things," the taller one said.

"What kinds of things?" I raised an eyebrow.

"Things that . . . you wouldn't expect him to know. He's special."

"Is he an empath?"

"No, not like that."

Interesting.

"So," the shorter one said, eyes lighting up, "you want to come with us? We can show you around."

I put my arm around Sei and pulled him close. "It's been a long one," I said. They could see how bad I looked—let them think it was exhaustion. "We're probably about to turn in."

Surprised, they drew back a little.

"But we'll see you around," I added.

They excused themselves and left the shop.

Now Sei and I were alone with the android. I let him go and rubbed my chin, thinking hard.

"I didn't expect that," Sei said.

"We don't have time for them right now."

He saw me gazing at the android.

"You said she was a negotiator, right? Your girl?" He looked concerned.

"Yeah, she is." Why was he asking this?

"Then she'll be fine. It's actually kind of rude to worry about her."

I looked down at my malt. There was a misunderstanding here. I felt a stab of guilt; I hadn't been thinking about Salmagard at all. Wherever she was, she was fine. She knew how to take care of herself.

He raised an eyebrow. "If not her, then what is it? What's wrong? These guys are insane—but they seem okay."

I sat up and turned around to lean on the counter, gazing out the window. The foot traffic out there had slowed down; it was getting dark. I didn't think I had to worry about the android clerk overhearing what I was about to say.

"He's going to kill us."

Sei choked, setting down his malt and thumping his chest with a fist. "What? How do you get that?"

"Just adding it up. He's trying too hard to put us at ease, setting a short deadline for a promise he knows he can't make good on. He said we'd have answers in the morning. That means we're not going to live that long. He didn't even ask for our names. He doesn't expect us to be in his life long enough for them to matter. He'll make his move tonight."

Sei didn't *want* to believe me, and I didn't blame him. But he wasn't stupid. He'd been in combat. He wasn't boxed in by the false sense of security that living in polite society tended to give people—he wouldn't close his eyes to danger just because he didn't like it. He sighed.

"We surprised him by waking up, didn't we?"

I nodded. "I'm not sure we were ever supposed to wake up. In fact—we definitely weren't."

"But he answered all your questions."

"The answers don't hold up. He admitted it himself—this is a modern place full of modern people. There's no reason to physically bring living humans here for reproductive purposes, not if there's no religious reason that they have to do it that way. They can keep their gene pool fresh with a chemistry set.

That was all just talk. He was stalling us, buying himself time. Telling us something we might not mind hearing. I mean, who doesn't want to get laid, right? Tell people things they like, and they don't ask questions."

"Buying time for what?" Sei asked, turning serious. We both looked out the window at the street.

"Time to figure out what to do about us. He's good. He knows how to adapt. He was winging it the whole time he was with us, and half of it had me convinced. And we can't get in front of this until we know who these people really are."

"You don't think we have a good chance?"

"I don't know what our chances are. I'm not saying our case is closed here. I've got a lot left to do, so I'd like to find a way out of this."

"Gotta get back to that girl."

I shook my head. "I don't think that's going to happen. If we do get off this planet alive, I think I'll stay away from her. I've done enough damage."

"I don't know your story." Sei rubbed tiredly at his eyes. "But if you really think we're in danger, we should worry about our love lives later."

"I do." I tried to focus.

Sei had a future. If he made it out of this, he actually had things to look forward to. I'd try to be considerate about that if I could.

"The people here definitely know something. They were all excited to see us, though," he said.

"But it wasn't the right kind of excited," I told him. "I'm not sure what that's about, but I don't like it. And he's lying about communications. He's got something. There's no way he doesn't."

"What do you think is going to happen? Are we in trouble right now?"

"No—if there's one thing he's said that I believe, it's that there isn't anywhere for us to go. He wouldn't leave us like this if there was. So that much is probably true."

"Sounds like you're just guessing."

"Maybe," I admitted. "I don't have the answer, but I have details that the answer has to include, and whatever Cyril has in mind, it does not involve us still being alive this time tomorrow. That's what everything's telling me."

"Are you always this cheery?"

"Only when I'm dying."

Sei raised any eyebrow.

"Look," I said. "He can put on the friendly act all he wants, and he can make it seem more genuine by telling us some things that we aren't expecting to hear. He can be self-deprecating and try to throw us off by not immediately caving—none of that matters. He can do what he wants. It's all misdirection. Ignore him and focus on the facts. He bought people. He bought people with purposes in mind other than freeing them. That's all you need to know about him."

"That's definitely what the Empress would say," Sei replied, nodding.

"She knows best," I said, stirring my malt.

"So? What's coming?"

I considered it. "Based on what I've seen so far, I think someone will show up here and take us home, just like he said. I think chances are good that they'll have a couple attractive daughters or something. I think they'll break their backs to make us happy. Until we're asleep, and then they'll get us back under control."

"If it's daughters, I'll have to be drunk first."

I snorted. "That's just an example of the sort of thing they *might* do. Maybe it'll just be good food or something, but people have been bribing each other since the dawn of time. It works. I feel like I have a read on Cyril's style. If they're smart, they won't hold back. They'll do whatever they can to lower our guard, and that would be one way."

I watched the android sweep. "That's what he's doing now by leaving us alone. They're cautious, or at least Cyril is. He's not sure who he's dealing with, and he doesn't want to take chances with us. I don't know if he's the bad guy or if all these people are rotten, but whatever they are, they aren't soldiers. At least, not all of them." I'd been watching; I'd seen only one man who had a noticeably ex-military air about him.

He might be a problem later.

"I'm not picking up on half of this—I know these people are weird, but of course they are. You couldn't have a crew like this and expect them to be normal. What's your plan?"

"I haven't got one. It's a bad situation."

"Man, it feels good to be able to talk again."

"Talk? I like having feeling in my hands." A little, at least.

"That too. I'm not trying to push you. I'm just trying to follow your lead here. Is it time for us to do something?"

"Yes," I said immediately. "I'm just not sure what."

"Do we play along and go to somebody's house?"

"Better not. We don't know that I'm right about that." There was only one pedestrian out there at the moment, and she wasn't headed for the shop. She got into a vehicle, which rolled away without a sound. "They could move sooner."

"Or not at all," Sei reminded me. "You don't have proof, do you?"

"Who're you going to trust?"

"I'm pretty sure you're New Unity. You want me to choose between a terrorist and a spiritual leader?"

"Should be easy."

"Yeah, I'll stick with you. I'm just saying."

"I know—we shouldn't hurt anyone unless we have to, and even then, not unless we know for sure. We still want to play by Evagardian law, even if we aren't in Evagardian space," I said. "Who knows how many of these people are actually complicit? But I've got my own suspicions about that."

"And they are?"

I got up. "That we don't have to go easy on them."

"Come by again soon, mister," the peppy android said from behind the counter.

"Take it easy," I told her, making for the back of the shop. Sei followed me through a door promising restrooms. "There ought to be a way out the back, right?"

"I don't know. I went to a theme park that had these kinds of buildings once, but they weren't this detailed. And I think that era was a little farther forward. I love this shirt."

"Yeah, it looks good on you," I told him.

I found a door, unlatched it, and pushed it open. We were in a narrow space between two buildings. It was fully dark now, and though there were lights on the street, the alley was in deep shadow.

"We can't blend out here—we have no shoes," Sei pointed out, easing the door shut behind us. "And they all know each other—they'll spot strangers straightaway."

"I know. I want to go back to the church. Something's wrong with these people, and I want to know what. I think we'll find it there." Whatever we were going to do, we had to do it soon.

"Why?"

"Because he didn't turn on the lights."

"What?"

"Cyril. Back when we first met him in the church. It was dark. He was going to turn on the lights, but he stopped when he saw it was us. At the time I was thinking about other things, but now I don't like it. There's something in there he didn't want us to see. He did everything he could to make it not seem like an issue, like he just happened to be doing it, but I'm not sure I buy it. Like I said—" I looked down at my hands. "We can't get out of this until we know what it is. Come on." I started down the alley.

"This is a hell of a planet," Sei said, looking up. "This weather is to die for."

"Yeah, that's another problem."

"What?"

"This planet. Terra imitators like this are priority—and while someone's obviously got some money to put something like this together, I don't believe they'd terraform for it. This is too perfect, too hospitable—I'm starting to think we *must* be on New Earth, which would mean he was lying about being in unregulated space. I mean, a planet like this wouldn't stay unregulated for long, would it? Everybody would want to come here—it's perfect."

"But then there'd be somewhere to go. If it's New Earth. Plenty of places to go—the whole planet's inhabited. There're, like, five billion people on New Earth."

"We could be on an island, or just someone's personal

preserve—it wouldn't have to be very big to be too big to escape on foot, or even by land. But I can't believe we're in
unregulated space—he just said that to get the advantage, to
keep us from acting like divas."

"Didn't really stop you," Sei pointed out, rubbing his hands
together and shivering.

"I'm making this up as I go," I said, pausing at the end of
the alley. "I'm trying to be convincing. Is it working?"

"I don't know. I think so."

"We'll go behind those houses."

"You sure you're up to it?"

"We can't risk whatever they'd give me to help."

"You think they'd drug you?" Sei asked.

"I don't know, but if they wanted to, walking in and letting
their doctor shoot me up wouldn't make it much of a challenge
for them."

"I see your point. Are they looking this way?"

"Just wait," I said, holding up my hand. "We'll get out of
the proper, stay out of the light. Then we can go around, get
back to the road, and follow it."

"How long before they know we're AWOL?"

I considered it. "I don't know. Cyril doesn't want this to get
loud, or he'd have come back with a bunch of guys five minutes
after he left."

"You've thought of everything."

"Probably not," I said, giving him a push. It took us a couple minutes to make our way out of the village. It was small,
but we had to be careful not to be seen. Did it matter if some
kid saw us? Probably not, but I didn't want to give Cyril anything to work with. He might not expect us to go back the
way we'd come.

The obvious route of escape would be to follow the road through the village and away. Going deeper into his territory would seem counterproductive. I couldn't read Cyril's mind; I could only predict how I would act in his place.

We'd find out if I was right soon enough.

It wasn't a long trip back to the church, and even in the dark it was simple enough to follow the road. The vehicles these people used didn't make a lot of noise, but they all had bright twin lights on the front, so we'd know if someone was coming.

I looked back at the town. There were plenty of lights on, and it was a charming sight against the black night. In another life, another reality, an isolated community like this—either on New Earth or out in unregulated space somewhere—would've been a nice place to visit.

And while I was wishing for things that weren't going to happen, maybe I could go back in time and fix everything else too.

It would've been great if we could've just believed what Cyril was trying to tell us. If the day's disastrous events had somehow delivered us to a safe place.

I would have loved for it to be true. But I knew it wasn't, and nothing could change that.

Cyril was a predator. He could fool Sei, and maybe he was fooling these people. But my instincts couldn't be deceived. Cyril was good, but he didn't know who he was dealing with— for all the good it would do me. I wasn't at my best, and he was holding most of the cards.

A bad situation was only getting worse.

Ahead, the church was dark, but I could see the steeple standing up against the night. I had nothing against temples or religion, but I doubted I'd ever be completely free of the negative associations with them that I'd formed on Nidaros.

And very faintly, we could see a little yellow out there, beyond the church, through the trees.

Cyril's house. Was he there now? It would have been good if we'd known where he was at the moment. But we didn't know. We had nothing to work with.

Sei paused and looked back at me.

"Tell me the truth," he said. "Are we getting out of here?"

I didn't have an answer for him.

We stole across the grass and let ourselves into the church. I felt my way to the panel Cyril had gone for, and activated the lights. Together, Sei and I considered the sanctuary.

My hands shook.

The Ganraen Royals were the longest-running joke in history. Contrary to what most of the galaxy believed, there was an incredibly competent government beneath the dozen or so deeply inbred families that reigned over the Commonwealth—but that government could only do so much.

For example: Princess Oriana, Prince Dalton's second cousin. Her conduct toward me when I was in that role gave me some very disturbing notions about what might have gone on between the two of them as children. Hardly a flattering impression with regard to the dignity and image of the family.

And there was the Squire, Earlus Manne, who spent untold billions on a fully zero-g planetside palace full of costumed comfort androids, diamond fixtures, and thousands upon thousands of gallons' worth of aquariums filled with priceless fish imported from Old Earth.

I remembered Queen Meeregald, with her outrageous body modifications and early death from her absolute belief that there was no chemical in the known universe that did not belong in her bloodstream.

As I stood in Cyril's church with the lights on, I reflected that I was starting to get tired of crazy people.

Did these people think that I was out here because I wanted to be? So all right, yes—maybe I had left home for selfish reasons, but they hadn't been bad reasons; they hadn't been wrong.

I'd made a lot of mistakes. I could never go back, and I never thought that I could. I couldn't *fix* it. *I* wasn't crazy.

I was just trying. I was trying *so hard*.

And there were people like this, and people like Willis and Freeber. They didn't know what they were doing. Cyril didn't understand. No one *understood*.

I was angry.

The sanctuary was flanked by eight massive sets of curtains, and behind each curtain was a grotesque painting the size of a small house.

Sei stared at them, fascinated.

One painting showed a stormy sea and a great tentacled creature of unfathomable size. There was a ship on the surface, tossed about helplessly, oblivious to what was beneath it.

Another showed what looked like a sun, but inside the sun was what appeared to be a monolithically large eye.

Sei gazed up at one that showed what could only be a black hole, with a tentacle appearing to emerge from the void.

Another near the rear of the church was a detailed portrait of a strange, relatively ugly man I didn't recognize.

None of those were the problem. The problem was the altar at the front of the sanctuary. It was large, circular, and made of stone. There were plenty of strange carvings in it, but the one that had my attention was the spiral groove in the center.

There was an altar just like it in one of the paintings, and in that image the groove was red.

I'd seen my share of dramas, and I didn't like where this was going.

This was what Cyril hadn't wanted us to see. These paintings and this altar. His explanation of his community's beliefs had struck me as detailed enough that it probably wasn't false—but it looked like he hadn't been telling the whole story.

Sei swallowed.

"I don't have anything against religion," he said, "but this seems kind of sketchy."

I collected myself, forcing my temper down. "Yeah. We can't stay."

"You really think that's what they have in mind for us?"

"I don't feel an urgent need to find out. Do you?"

He shook his head. "But how?"

"I'm going to just go ahead and make up my mind that we're in immediate danger. I don't care if it's true; we're going to move forward like it is. And I don't have much more sneaking around in me."

"You look awful," Sei said, looking troubled.

"Thanks. Doesn't matter if there's nowhere to go. I don't have the strength to get far on foot, and I don't think on foot's the way to go anyway. The road has to go somewhere. We'll steal one of their vehicles and take our chances."

"They have to be expecting that," Sei said, looking worriedly at the big doors leading to the outside.

"I'm not so sure. The vehicles only look old, but they're really just crawlers mocked up to look like they belong here. They're probably DNA and clearance keyed."

"Then they're no good to us."

"Not without a friend. These people might be crazy, but are they so zealous that they'll say no to two imperials?"

Sei considered it. "I'm game," he said, sighing.

The plan was far from airtight. If we were on property, there was a good chance that Cyril had some kind of security in place to keep the right people in and the wrong people out. If that was the case, we'd just have to wing it. Back in that little shop, I'd suspected what was coming. Now I was certain. The time for speculation had come and gone, and it was time for action.

If this was New Earth, then that road through town probably led to some other settlement. It might be a long way, but there had to be something. There would be law enforcement. Whose word would those people take? Ours or Cyril's? And that was provided we even made it out of here. Cyril seemed confident. I still wasn't completely sure why. The situation wasn't ideal, but it wasn't as if we didn't have plays to make, and surely he realized that.

His confidence bothered me. He knew something we didn't.

"Let's get moving," Sei said. He looked restless.

"We'll try Cyril's house first. He had that little building behind the place. He may have a vehicle in it. I think it's what those things are for."

"He's probably the worst hostage we could take," Sei said.

"I know. But we don't know that we need one, and I'm trying to plot a course that will keep us away from these people in numbers."

"I'm with you."

We hurried back to the doors, but Sei stopped me when I reached for the handle. He held up a hand, looking troubled.

"They're out there," he said quietly. I decided to take his word for it.

"We do have the lights on," I said, looking back at the sanctuary. Maybe that had drawn their attention. "We'll go out the back."

We retraced our steps down the aisle, making for the door near the steps leading to the altar. It was a preparation room with a small office. We moved through, entering a short corridor that led to another door.

Someone had seen the lights and come to investigate—that didn't mean we were in trouble. Just the opposite. It was a distraction. All we had to do was slip away unnoticed.

We pushed through the door and out into the night, crossing the narrow strip of open land between the sanctuary and the tree line. It was dark, and we were essentially blind, but I'd noticed during daylight that these patches of forest were extremely welcoming. There were no tangled roots to trip on—nothing but soft grass underfoot, and clean, picturesque trees.

I plunged in without hesitation, moving as fast as I dared. I was slowing Sei down, but there was nothing for it. I made for Cyril's house. We would see if he had a vehicle. If he did, we could try to take it. If he didn't, we'd make our way back to the village and take one there.

No—no, not without paying Cyril a visit first.

I hadn't seen anything firsthand, but he'd all but made it clear that he was running things around here. We didn't want him as a hostage, but we didn't want him as an adversary either.

We'd knock him out, tie him up, and leave him in a closet. Leaderless, his people would be less equipped to chase us down effectively, and we were going to need every advantage we could get.

Especially if we were on New Earth.

Even if we got out of here, Sei and I were still two imperials on a Commonwealth planet that was still technically at war. Even with the cease-fire in effect, and the detail that we weren't there by choice, we could still be in trouble.

Sei was a pilot. I was a spy. I was the spy who had murdered twenty million civilians and annihilated the center of government for the Ganraen system. If Commonwealth authorities caught up with us here and identified me, that would not be ideal.

We emerged from the trees, and hand lights came on suddenly, blinding us.

I tried to push Sei back.

"Go," I said, putting up my hand against the glare. "Just run. I've got this."

"No," he said, shrugging free and stepping in front of me. "I can take these guys."

There were five men, and a vehicle came rolling off the road, more getting out.

Sei started forward purposefully, then stopped, his eyes falling on the rifle in the hands of one of the men jogging down the hillside.

"Just kidding," he said, backpedaling toward me with his hands raised.

I wished he'd just run when I'd told him to—that one rifle was the only projectile weapon I saw, and it wasn't a smart rifle. It wouldn't do them any good against a target running in the woods.

I couldn't run, but Sei could. We could've divided their attention, gotten an advantage. Too late now.

Teeth grinding, I took a step back, but the man—the ex-military one, naturally—took aim at me, and I stopped.

How had *this* happened? A silent alarm at the church? Surveillance? If that was the case, how had we taken them by
surprise initially?

Because they hadn't been looking for us earlier. Now they
were on alert. But something wasn't right. How could they
know exactly where we would be? Sei and I were missing
something, something critical. We were two steps behind.

Cyril came running down from the road, leaving his vehicle's lights shining. He saw us and came to a halt, looking
relieved.

"Both of them? All right," he said, running a hand through
his hair. He stared at us frankly. "You two weren't supposed
to be awake for this. I'm sorry."

He didn't look or sound sorry.

"Very humane," I replied. "Why didn't you feed us a story
about sending us home and put us back in the sleepers?"

"Because you wouldn't have bought it," Cyril replied, shrugging. "You were too suspicious. And at least one of those
sleepers is faulty. That can kill you, you know. I wasn't going
to risk your lives."

"There's irony there," I pointed out.

"Pardon the cliché," Sei cut in, "but do you really think you
can get away with this? There's a record of sale. It doesn't
matter where we are or whom you're friends with. We can't
go missing with no answers. You should believe us when we
tell you that we're imperials. The Imperium *will* come for us."

"Let me worry about that," Cyril said, looking uncon-
cerned.

"I guess we'll have to," I said.

"Guys, you've put me in a very uncomfortable position. Can
we put this to bed like adults? You were both bought and paid

for, and brought here for a purpose. A higher purpose. The highest purpose. That's all there is to it."

Neither one of us had anything to say to that. His directness was refreshing, at least.

One of the men beside Cyril leaned in. "What do we do?" he asked.

Cyril let out a long sigh. "I think . . . I think we had best go on and move ahead. These two are a little too independent for my comfort, and the longer we keep them like this, the more risk we take on. We shouldn't underestimate them."

"How much are we moving up?" the man asked, motioning his guys forward. They took hold of Sei and me. I wasn't nearly strong enough to fight back, and there were two of them on me regardless. Sei was in an identical situation. Our chance to make a move was gone.

"All the way," Cyril replied. He turned and looked up the hill toward his house. "The procession's supposed to start at the mausoleum, but we'll just go from here."

"You're not coming?" The man seemed surprised.

"I'll be there shortly. I wasn't expecting to do this so early. Put the word out. It's the result that matters, not the show."

The man nodded and gestured to his crew, and Cyril began to climb back up the hill.

The men holding us pushed us toward the road.

At least we'd inconvenienced them. Maybe that was worth something.

It was completely dark now, and no one seemed to be in a hurry. That was good, because I was fading fast. My feet were sore from all the running around with no shoes, and I didn't have much strength left.

The guy with the rifle was out in front, looking thoughtful.

There was still a man guiding me firmly, and Sei was in the same situation. The other two were just behind us, watching.

I wondered what Cyril was really up to. Where was he going? What was he doing? Why was he hiding it from his own people?

It didn't matter; it was time for me to live in the moment. I looked at Sei.

"I wish you'd just run," I told him frankly.

"Well, I'm sorry. I didn't have a lot of time to decide," he said, glaring at me.

"Be quiet," said the guy in front of us, apparently the leader of this little band.

"Or you'll what? Kill us? Keep walking," Sei said to him.

"It's not that hard," I snapped. "Divide them."

"Excuse me? I'm a pilot, not a general," Sei shot back. "This is not my job. Small-unit infantry tactics are for the ground forces. I'm an Everwing pilot. What do you want from me?"

"I want you to think," I said, annoyed.

"I *thought* the thing to do was to stay with you. Defend you."

"You help me by going," I told him. "Obviously. They'd have to chase you or let you go. If you were out there, we still had a play. If they chased, maybe I could make something happen. What's wrong with you?"

The man leading me snorted.

"Well, I'm sorry for trying to do the right thing," Sei said, disgusted.

"The right thing is the smart thing, not what they do in dramas. We're both about to die because you had to play hero."

"You're an ass," Sei said.

22

"I *thought* the thing to do was to stay with you. Defend you."

Salmagard knew she wasn't going to get a better chance. She signaled Diana, who emerged from the shadows on the other side of the road, falling to a crouch and moving in silence.

"You help me by going," the Admiral said angrily. "Obviously. They'd have to chase you or let you go. If you were out there, we still had a play. If they chased, maybe I could make something happen. What's wrong with you?"

Perfect. Holding her breath, Salmagard crept forward.

"Well, I'm sorry for trying to do the right thing," Sei said, disgusted.

"The right thing is the smart thing, not what they do in dramas. We're both about to die because you wanted to play hero."

"You're an ass," Sei said.

Diana and Salmagard struck at the same instant, plunging hypos into the necks of the two men at the back of the group.

It didn't make a sound. They caught their victims as they fell, laying them out on the road and picking their way past to follow the others, who were oblivious.

"I don't think name-calling is constructive," the Admiral said.

"Oh my Empress, shut up," Sei snapped.

Salmagard nodded to Diana. Diana was strong enough that she didn't need to do anything in particular to secure a fast takedown. Salmagard was too light to leave anything to chance with a grown man; she had to compensate.

She leapt into the air, bringing down her elbow with everything she had on the back of the man pushing the Admiral. The blow struck him down as decisively as a bullet would have. Diana simply stepped in, grabbing Sei's captor from behind and putting him in a rigid headlock.

Salmagard leapt past the Admiral as the lead man turned, startled. She tackled him around the middle, carrying him to the ground with a crash. He tried to bring up his rifle, but Salmagard struck it aside. She grabbed a fistful of the man's shirt and hit him with a straight punch that put an abrupt end to his day.

The Admiral had fallen to one knee. "*That's* where Cyril was going. You guys," he said, face pale. He didn't sound good. "That was really bothering me."

And he looked worse than he had on Nidaros. Salmagard was there in an instant, injecting him with his antidote.

Diana dropped her unconscious victim and threw her arms around Sei.

"My knight in shining armor," the Admiral said weakly. "Where's your ship? The GRs? We have to get off this planet."

Salmagard was taken aback. "Planet? What planet?" She hauled him to his feet without waiting for an answer, looking to Diana. "Where do we go?"

"There was a big structure up there," the red-eyed woman replied, still squeezing Sei, who looked relieved, but also a little uncomfortable.

"The church?" he said. "No way. We can't go there."

"We aren't leaving?" The Admiral sounded puzzled. He pulled free of Salmagard, obviously feeble but still able to stand on his own. Barely. "What's going on?"

"We have to move," Salmagard told him, taking him by the hand.

"Well, not that way. Back—back the other way, to the house," the Admiral said, allowing himself to be pulled. There wasn't time to argue; they started moving. "This isn't a planet?"

"It's a ship," Diana called back to him. Lights appeared on the road behind them. Salmagard and Diana angled into the woods, but the Admiral was struggling to keep up.

"What?"

"It's not a ship," Salmagard explained tersely. "Just a habitat. There's a ship pulling it. That's where we've got to go, but it's on the other side of that settlement."

It seemed like the Admiral wanted to say something, but he held back.

They emerged from the trees, finding the house dark.

"I thought Cyril said he was coming up here," Sei said.

"He lied," the Admiral replied. "Just—just go there. Here." He pointed.

Diana bounded onto the porch and shouldered through the door. Salmagard followed with the Admiral.

"A ship." He sighed. "Explains a lot. I should've figured that out."

She gently helped him onto a sofa and hurried to the window. More lights were appearing in the night. Salmagard's heart sank.

"They're already here," she reported.

Diana groaned, shutting the door. "We should've gone for the ship first, then come for these two."

"If you'd come any later, we'd be on that altar," Sei pointed out. "But how'd you get here? What's going on? How did you find us? Where did you get those EVs?"

"Sales records at the Bazaar," Diana told him.

"I knew it," the Admiral murmured. Salmagard didn't want to leave him, but Cyril's people were surrounding the house. She had to make sure it was secure. She paused in the doorway. The Admiral looked awful, but she could see his face.

She'd seen that look before, back on Nidaros.

Salmagard made her way around the first floor of the house. Sei checked the upper floor, and Diana was keeping an eye on the situation developing outside.

"I count about two dozen," she said, letting the curtain fall back into place. "The lights on the road probably mean more."

"They won't make a move," Sei said as he returned. "Is it just you guys? Where are the GRs?"

Salmagard went to the Admiral, who was lying back on his sofa, his hand resting on his chest. He was wearing strange antique clothing, like the other people here.

"How are we getting out of here?" he asked.

She hesitated, heart heavy. "We have to call for help," she said, showing him the code crystal. She put it back in her pouch and sat down beside him. "But we need a com system to do that."

He took that in, and for a moment there was something like relief on his face. Then it was gone, and Salmagard wasn't sure she'd seen it at all.

"How did you get here? If we're moving, how did you catch up?"

"A . . ." She hesitated, trying to remember the words. "Fighter. Quite a fast one. But it can't get us out of here. It doesn't have the fuel, and it's not big enough."

He raised an eyebrow, reading between the lines. "I see," he replied, closing his eyes.

"I'm sorry," Salmagard said, feeling sick.

"Don't be. It's your duty. We're really on a ship?"

"It's just a dome. The ship's pulling it."

"How big is it?"

"A little over a kilometer in diameter."

"Sounds expensive. Where are we in relation to the edge?"

"Toward the aft."

"Does that do us any good?"

"No, we have to get to the ship. The tug."

"Where are your weapons?" the Admiral asked, frowning.

"They didn't want to . . . trust us with weapons," Salmagard told him.

"We can't risk puncturing the shell," Diana said. "And we can't fire on these people—they're victims."

"Victims?" Sei looked away from the window. "They were going to kill us. Sacrifice us to some imaginary space octopus."

"I think it's a squid," the Admiral said.

"No," Salmagard said, looking up. "Well, yes. Perhaps they were going to do that. But you're not the real sacrifice. You're a distraction."

"What?"

"For them. *They* are the sacrifice."

"I don't understand," the Admiral said, struggling to sit up. Salmagard helped him.

"Cyril is going to throw the entire habitat into Shangri La," Diana said. "Everyone on it is the sacrifice. They just don't know it. They think they're out here to do something, that they matter. But they're just bodies, a certain number for this ritual thing."

"Shangri La." Sei tilted his head. "That's a *black hole*."

"Yeah. Like the painting in the church," the Admiral said, grimacing. "Explains a lot. Are they doing anything out there?"

"No. They've got a nice perimeter, though. I don't think they know what they're up against," Diana said, peeking out. "I don't see any weapons."

"I doubt they've got any, especially if Cyril wasn't being straight with them," said the Admiral. Diana was watching him with open suspicion. Salmagard bristled, but the Admiral didn't seem to mind. "You obviously had help. I guess EI and probably IS both know I'm here?"

Salmagard swallowed. "Yes," she said.

"Good." He looked resigned. "I don't have to stress about it if it's already decided. Cyril won't let us stay here all night. What's the timetable for Shangri La? Is that immediate, or are we just worrying about Cyril?"

"Hard to say, but probably tight," Diana told him warily. "He accelerated as soon as he detected us coming. He might be planning to forget all about us and abandon ship to finish the job."

"I know just the moment he must've picked your ship up on his tow's scanner." The Admiral looked satisfied. "So that's what he was doing. You're right—he is planning to run. Did you see his file? Do you know who he is?"

"Yes," Salmagard replied, unable to hide the disgust in her voice.

"Would I like him?"

"I would hope not," she replied.

"I thought so. It's all falling into place. He's not a believer, is he?"

"No," Diana said. "He's a facilitator. The true believers set all of this up. They're out there in the wind, probably watching from the good seats."

"They aren't our problem." The Admiral shook his head, and even that looked pitiful.

Salmagard mimed the hypo with her hand. "Is it not helping?"

"It's not going to do me any good anytime soon," the Admiral said. "I have to get the levels up before my body responds. Takes hours. I'm not going to do you any good here. I'm deadweight."

Salmagard opened her mouth, then shut it and clenched her jaw. What could she do? Promise him that she would protect him? She would. She would protect him from Cyril.

Somehow, they were going to accomplish this rescue mission. There was no doubt in her mind of that.

But what then?

She felt a light squeeze. He'd found her hand.

"Relax," he said. "You saved me. I'll take it from here."

Staring at him, Salmagard touched his face, rubbing her thumb lightly over the stubble on his cheek. "You can't even move."

"Could be worse. Sei. How's it look out back?"

"They're out there, but not moving up on us yet," he called from the next room.

"If they don't have weapons, we win in close quarters. Nobody wants to be the first to die. They have to be careful about how they try to come in here. And I think you knocked out Cyril's favorite thug."

"The guy with the rifle?" Diana asked. The Admiral nodded minutely.

Sei came into the living room, tugging at his collar. "You think they'll just let us stay the night here? Or come in and talk?"

"I told you, I don't think so." The Admiral looked thoughtful. "Don't worry. With you here, we can't lose." He smiled at Salmagard. Under different circumstances, she wasn't sure how she might've reacted to that, but now there was only cloying nausea.

"We're getting out of here." The Admiral pushed himself to sit up straighter. "And this is how we do it. I think I've figured out what's going on, more or less." He turned to Salmagard. "Who are we signaling? Uniformed military, or GRs? Shangri La's in unregulated space, right? GRs, then?"

"Yes," Salmagard replied. And Collins had said that her men would be following as well.

"Of course," the Admiral said, looking annoyed. "Shangri La. I'm barely here. All right. You've got to use the tug ship's coms to broadcast our SOS so the GRs can find us so close to the black hole? Why can't you broadcast it from your fighter?"

"It's got no coms to speak of."

"The tug it is," the Admiral said.

"But we don't really have a good plan to do that," Diana said, peeking out the window. "There're more of them than I expected."

"You don't need a plan—you just have to break through," the Admiral said. "There's no other way. They don't have weapons. You three can just scatter from the house. If you end up in close quarters, you'll win. First you have to get past their perimeter," he told Salmagard. "They're not going to know what you're trying to do, and you'll have their attention— they're not going to worry about me. You're going to want to cause as much trouble as possible. Only go for the ship if you can shake them off first. Sei, you don't go at all. You have to get out there and just make a mess. You're buying us time. Diana, you can fake them out. Get past, make trouble, then angle for the ship. Make them think that's your objective, then break off. That's the soft moment—that's when Salmagard takes care of business. She's the one with the codes. Right?"

She nodded, swallowing.

"How's that sound? How's everyone's cardio?"

Sei and Diana exchanged a look.

"He's just like the commander," Sei said.

Diana scowled. "Don't remind me."

"I am an admiral," he said. "So I do outrank you. Sort of. Questions?"

Salmagard resisted the urge to look out the window.

"The longer we wait, the longer they have to get ready for us," the Admiral said.

"You're just going to stay here?" Diana said, raising an eyebrow.

"You said they were speeding up," he told her. "Cyril's getting ready to get clear—he's moving up his schedule. He doesn't care about us. He just needs to get the job done for the people that hired him to sacrifice these idiots. Don't worry about me."

"I wasn't," Diana said.

Salmagard thought her molars would grind into powder. The Admiral squeezed her hand again. It seemed to be all he had the strength to do.

"Waiting won't help our chances," he said. "We don't know how close we are to the point of no return. Once we get too close to Shangri La, even the GRs can't help us."

"He's right," Sei said. "It'd be nice to catch up, but if we don't know the timetable, this might be time we don't have. How fast *can* he get to Shangri La?"

"I'm not sure," Diana replied. "I don't know how fast the tug is . . . but we might not have much time." She looked to Salmagard, who nodded.

Salmagard turned to the Admiral, who surprised her by pulling her in for a kiss. Maybe there was a little strength in him after all. Salmagard did her best to return it, as if she could somehow communicate everything through this gesture alone—but he pushed her back almost immediately.

"I'm just being selfish," he said. "I'm sorry. For everything."

There was nothing to say to that. She felt she ought to say something, but there was nothing. Her head was as empty as her throat was tight.

Salmagard forced herself to let go of him and get up. She stepped back, her eyes still locked on his. Even if this worked, he was done for. Evagard would have him. He knew it.

There had to be a way to change that. The Admiral always had a plan, but he was only a man. Only human. He wasn't special. He didn't have a monopoly on strategy.

Salmagard could plan too. There had to be a way.

But first Cyril had to be stopped—or, failing that, they needed to set the beacon. There wasn't time to debate the

Admiral's plan. Diana and Salmagard had tentatively agreed on a course of action on the way, but they'd been approaching blind—once they were actually inside the habitat, it became clear their plan wouldn't work. They needed to adapt, and no one was better at that than the Admiral.

He wasn't trying to subtly tell her anything. He wasn't silently begging for her help. When she reached him on the road, it had been there, if only in that moment. She'd been his savior.

Now that was gone. He knew the truth, that she was bringing the Empire with her. That she was the instrument of his capture. But he showed no sign of distress, and not even resignation.

There had to be a way.

"We'll do it. I'll go out the front," Diana said, looking down at her hands.

"I'll take the back." Sei looked to Salmagard.

"I'll go that way," she said, pointing. "Go on my signal."

"What signal?"

"You'll know." Salmagard swallowed, looked at the Admiral, then turned her back on him and left the room.

She climbed the stairs to the second floor, looking in either direction.

She remembered when she had first set foot on the black surface of Nidaros. The swirling green mist, the towering spires.

She remembered the xenos there, and how it had all been so alien.

She'd been trained. She'd traveled. But nothing could have prepared her for the unknown, for the profound variety offered by the universe at large.

Alien.

That was how she felt now. This was all new to her. She thought about her family, and Alice Everly—about the life they had built for her, and the person they had shaped her to be. Or tried to shape her to be. Salmagard knew what their vision had been, and she knew what the result was. There wasn't much overlap.

There wasn't supposed to be room in an Evagardian high lady for things like hatred or rage. Or fear, or anything like it.

For a first daughter, there was never supposed to be a *need* for those things.

This was all the Admiral's fault.

Salmagard set her gaze on the window at the far end of the hallway and went down to one knee, positioning her feet. She activated her helmet, pressed her hands to the floor, and pushed off at a sprint. She leapt into the air, crossing her arms in front of her to break cleanly through the glass. Something so crude couldn't cut an EV.

She sailed out into the night air, the man directly below looking up in surprise at the figure in gray and the sparkling rain of glass shards.

Salmagard crashed into him, leaping free before he could hit the ground. She touched down and rolled, sprinting into the trees. Cyril's perimeter was pointless. He might as well not even have bothered.

There were shouting and footsteps behind her, and she could hear noise from the direction of the house.

Historically, threatening or challenging imperials never ended well for the people doing the threatening and the challenging. Even in the best of times, even when the Empress was at her most compassionate. Salmagard almost felt bad for these people.

Hand lights flashed behind her and to her right. Some of them were chasing her through the trees, and more were on the road using vehicles to try to get ahead. Maybe they wanted to cut her off.

Salmagard angled sharply, darting up the hill and onto the road itself. The nearest vehicle had to swerve, plunging down the embankment with a crash. She carried on across and into the trees on the other side, pouring on more speed.

The Admiral might not have any strength left, but Salmagard had plenty. She didn't need stims. Why would she, when she had all this fury and adrenaline to work with? How could synthetic chemicals compare?

It had been an enlightening day. Everything was different now. Things could never go back to the way they'd been before.

A figure loomed up out of the dark, and she didn't even slow—she just struck him down, letting her momentum carry her onward.

A part of her was glad firearms were no good here. Salmagard had never killed anyone outside a simulation, and she had no desire to—but with a weapon in her hand, here and now, she didn't know what would happen. Her training—the very best there was—was there, just under the surface. That was her purpose, after all. Countless months of training had made her a negotiator. More than half of that training had, in one way or another, pertained to combat.

And that was what she wanted.

But these people—they weren't the ones Salmagard really wanted. Whom *did* she want to get her hands on? Willis and Freeber? Yes. But no—they had been acting on orders from Idris. And Idris had been catering to his clientele. And his clientele was . . . what? Just people.

People with different values.

Salmagard was tired of values. No, that wasn't true. She was tired of galactics. She wanted the things she took for granted. She wanted a little imperial decency.

But even the Empire was no comfort now, not with what they were going to do to the Admiral. And she'd seen them at the Bazaar. The imperial tourists, the same people who would shake their heads and laugh about galactic savages with their primitive ways and less evolved sensibilities. Salmagard had seen them, looking on at the people trading humans as if it were a curiosity.

She knew there were bad imperials, and she knew there were good galactics. She knew it wasn't her place to judge good and bad. Only God could do that.

God, and the Empress.

But it didn't matter. She burst out of the trees, tearing across the grass. Speed came easily to Salmagard. She was used to being timed. Every drill, every VR training simulation—she was always timed. Every action was judged for efficiency and practicality. Every decision made, every shot fired—it all had to be accounted for.

Salmagard could see the lights of the settlement. There was noise and movement, but Salmagard wasn't interested in anything that wasn't in her way.

Under Cyril's synthetic night sky, she felt profoundly alone. These galactics weren't her people. Not if they thought people could be bought and sold.

At least, that was what she'd been brought up to believe. That was what Alice Everly believed. What her family believed. What all the great thinkers and writers believed.

But how was the Empire any different? They had used the

Admiral, perhaps used him up. Now that they were finished, his status as human seemed to have been revoked. He was no longer a subject or a citizen. Now he was just an inconvenience. Or, worse, an embarrassment.

It wasn't so different.

How could the Grand Duchess have made it any clearer? Her writings weren't ambiguous; they weren't difficult to understand. Any child could read and comprehend what the Duchess had to say. She believed in freedom of thought and the indisputable dignity of man, regardless of race or creed. These were the foundations of Evagardian life.

They were also only words.

In practice, imperials were no different from anyone else. Only now was Salmagard beginning to understand that. There was no natural law or higher power that prevented the wrong people from finding their way to positions of authority.

The Empress wasn't omniscient or omnipotent, no matter how much it might seem so at times. She wasn't really eternal. She was only a woman. If she was even real.

And for all anyone knew, the Empress of today had beliefs nothing at all like those of the woman who had unified Earth all those years ago.

Some Evagardians were Salmagard's people. Some weren't. How was she supposed to know the difference?

She didn't want to go home to that. That wasn't home at all.

Salmagard vaulted lightly over a short fence, avoiding the light and keeping close to the buildings, never slowing down. It was late in the habitat's cycle—everyone should've been asleep, but lights were on, and people were moving. The town was on alert.

She didn't care. Salmagard kept running.

A week before—no, a few hours before—nothing had been

more precious to her than her Empress and her home. The thought of never going back would have been unthinkable. Life apart from the Empire wasn't life; it was a disgrace. A living death.

Surely the Admiral had once felt the same way. Only a profound love for Evagard could have driven him to undertake the tasks that he had. To make the sacrifices that he so cavalierly accepted.

He had known after the destruction of the capital, even before he met Salmagard, that his bond with the Empire was broken. That he could never go home.

Salmagard had never disobeyed an order in her life. Not from her family, not from her mentor, not from the Service.

If she ever did, it wouldn't be a matter of wanting or not wanting to go home. She'd be no different from the Admiral. She would no longer have one.

Salmagard rounded a corner into an alley, only to be tackled from her immediate right. She threw her weight in midfall to ensure that her attacker got the worst of the impact. She shattered his collarbone with her elbow, but he wasn't alone. Salmagard leapt up, going after her nearest aggressor—there were only three, but she had to take them all down before their allies showed up to reinforce them.

She reversed course and landed a sharp kick to the knee of the man behind her. Salmagard gave him a hard shove into his friend, anticipating the grab from behind. She slipped aside and hit him hard in the kidney, then threw a punch to the temple that knocked him out cleanly. There was only one more obstacle still on his feet, and this one backed away, hands raised.

Salmagard kicked him savagely in the stomach, sending him

crashing to the ground. Even if he couldn't fight, he could still tell someone her position. But he couldn't talk if he couldn't breathe.

She got moving, trying to recall the layout of the town. There hadn't been much time to study it, but she remembered that the widest street led directly to the airlock.

But the widest street was hardly where Salmagard wanted to be. The alley was narrow, narrow enough for some acrobatics. If Diana and Sei were doing their jobs—and it sounded like they were—then taking the high ground could be useful.

There were massive containers on the ground, up against the buildings, and plenty of handholds to work with. Next to an imperial obstacle course, this was nothing.

Figures appeared at the mouth of the alley, cutting her off, but Salmagard wasn't going that way anymore. She bounded onto the nearest container, ran its length, and leapt to a mechanical protrusion, which was not as sturdy as it looked. It immediately came loose, threatening to drop her, but she was fast enough to catch the gutter. If she'd known a little more about these early-twentieth-century things, she might've known it wouldn't be able to support her weight. This was all a little too authentic. On Earth, many structures were made to look old-fashioned, but they were built to imperial standards, with proper materials. They wouldn't fall apart so easily. Had the structures of the past really been so flimsy?

She hauled herself up, clambering onto the shingles and leaping to the next roof, catching the edge and climbing.

Evagardian authorities had no detailed information on Cyril or his ship—only what they could get from Free Trade Peacekeeping Corps case files. An open investigation into Cyril's employers had led them to this scheme, which the Free Trade Commission apparently felt no need to involve itself with. What did they care about some mental invalids who couldn't even see that their little cult was nothing but a death trap? There was money to be made elsewhere, and though the Free Trade gene pool was less guarded than the imperial one, even Free Traders knew they were all better off if these people didn't reproduce.

The only good information that Salmagard and Diana had on the habitat and the ship pulling it was what they'd been able to get on scanners during their approach—and now that information existed only in their memories. There was nothing to consult, no one to ask. Salmagard didn't even have a combat scanner to rely on.

There was a mighty crash and a loud shout from somewhere down and to her left. Salmagard didn't know how closely they were sticking to the Admiral's plan, or if they were at all. But the key factor—forcing Cyril to divide his forces in pursuit—that much was working.

From the rooftops she had a new perspective on the town, but it wasn't helping her navigate—instead of doors and windows, all she saw was other rooftops.

She had to keep moving.

Salmagard couldn't imagine that anyone here could stop Diana, and Sei had a pilot's survival training. His combat training wasn't quite as extensive as that of a negotiator, but he was more than a match for anyone they might encounter here. Cyril's best guys were down, neutralized back on the road. They had been the ones escorting Sei and the Admiral.

This could work. There were nearly two hundred people in this little community, but ten percent of them were children.

Sixty percent of the remainder were women, none of whom had combat training. The same went for the men—veterans were not well represented here, and half of them were too old to be of use in a physical confrontation.

Some of the buildings had sloping roofs, forcing Salmagard to scramble up one side and slide down, but one such roof ended on a cross street, marking an abrupt end to her route.

Lights flashed, and a vehicle came around the corner at a truly irresponsible speed. Sei was piloting it, waving at her animatedly. Salmagard didn't hesitate. She leapt from the roof, landing on the rear of the cruiser, which was sliding wildly. She held on and jumped into the seat beside Sei, surprised that she'd survived the landing.

"Everyone could see you up there," the pilot admonished her, spinning the wheel, struggling to regain control of the vehicle. He got it straightened out and accelerated. "Your boyfriend's too cautious with all the fake-outs," he shouted over the wind, careening around another corner. "These people are sheep. We just have to be fast. Which way?"

"That way," Salmagard replied, pointing. She disengaged her helmet. A man ran into the road, then immediately changed his mind and dove out of the way. Sei laughed and followed Salmagard's guidance. Salmagard decided that, in a broad sense, she did not care for the approach that these fighter pilots took to operating vehicles.

There wasn't much wind inside the habitat, but in a fast vehicle there was plenty. Salmagard stood up, gripping the windshield.

It felt good. Her rage was manifesting as blood pressure and an odd sort of heat behind her eyes, pressing on her temples. Her EV's temperature control couldn't keep up.

The wind was so strong that it blew her hair free of the ribbon she'd used to tie it up. Her knuckles ached from her grip on the windshield.

Sei's vehicle slid into the main street, but he pulled it around to a hard stop, going through a full spin to do so.

There was a mob in the next street—but they weren't interested in Salmagard and Sei.

"Let's go," Salmagard said.

"That's got to be her," Sei replied, still staring at the crowd.

"We have to go."

"You go." Sei opened the door and got out, taking a few steps and looking back. He spread his arms helplessly. "I can't leave her," he said, and the look on his face told Salmagard he knew it was the wrong choice. Protocol. Training. They had worked so hard to teach Salmagard that these things were absolute, but they weren't. Out in the real world, they were nothing.

Salmagard didn't reply. She just dropped into the pilot's seat and pulled the door shut. She'd seen how Sei had operated the vehicle. More or less. There was no time to argue with him.

Sei hadn't been there; he hadn't seen how dangerous Diana was. Maybe he didn't know.

Or maybe she really did need help. Salmagard understood Sei's thinking, but she didn't respect it. What he was doing was strategically unsound, but under the circumstances there was nothing she could do about that.

If Sei wasn't going to stick to the mission, Salmagard would. This was her responsibility.

She had no authority over Sei. It wasn't that she didn't want to help Diana—because she did—but the best way to do that was to get the SOS out.

She seized the wheel and pushed down on the pedals, finding the correct one. The vehicle shot forward, and she turned the wheel desperately, thudding onto the curb and over the grass before rocketing into the street.

She knew where she was going. At the very end of the road was a single blue house. That was her destination. Salmagard pushed the vehicle harder, though it was protesting—she was probably doing something wrong. There had to be more to piloting it than turning the wheel and stomping on these antique controls, but she had no interest in doing it properly.

Another vehicle screeched into the road ahead of her. Salmagard couldn't avoid it. She struck the front of it at top speed, sending both vehicles spinning in a melded mess.

Glass shattered and metal wailed. The faux stars overhead spun in a blur, and Salmagard crashed to the ground five meters away and rolled.

New stars, black lines, and white spots scattered across her eyes as she came to rest on her back, fire spreading from her right arm, which was broken. Her head pounded.

There were running footsteps, and rough hands seized her. Salmagard felt herself being dragged upright, and her training couldn't ignore it. She thrust her leg between the nearest man's own and threw her weight into him, sending him toppling over.

She caught the arm of the other attacker and locked it, jerking him down and felling him with a head butt. Salmagard had never known physical pain like this. Nothing even remotely like it. It was inhuman.

A blade flashed, and she caught the woman's wrist, snapping it and seizing her hair, jerking her head down and slamming her knee into the woman's face. Shapes and figures moved around her, indistinct. Everything swam, and she was light-headed. But this wasn't something she had to think about. Even with only one functioning arm, she was still a negotiator. Fighting was automatic.

Something heavy struck her and she fell, catching herself with her injured arm and letting out a cry of pain.

She caught a foot before it could reach her face and she twisted the ankle hard, pushing to her feet and overbalancing the man.

Another one lunged in, and she knocked his arm aside and twisted it, forcing him to his knees. He struggled, but Salmagard raised her good arm, preparing to deliver a lethal strike to his exposed throat with the flat of her hand.

But she stopped.

Nothing was moving.

There were still half a dozen of them around her. Salmagard forced her eyes to focus, gasping for breath, hand still held high. The world blurred, then became clear. Her ears were ringing.

They were staring at her in horror. A woman was screaming. Another was weeping.

The ground was littered with groaning people. There was blood.

There was a clatter, and Salmagard saw another woman who had just dropped a knife. She backed away.

They were all backing away.

The man on his knees in front of her was old enough to be her father, and he was staring up at her. There was naked terror on his face.

She let him go and stepped back.

Salmagard straightened, looking around her. No one moved

forward. No one was approaching. There was no threat. Her broken arm hung limp, useless and painful. Her ankle felt wrong; she wobbled but didn't fall. There was a wave of dizziness, but it passed.

Still watching Cyril's people, she took another shaky step back.

It had gotten very quiet. There was no shouting, no sound of vehicles. No one made a sound.

Salmagard turned and staggered toward the blue house.

No one interfered. There were a couple of them ahead, but they all got out of her way. Salmagard stumbled up the walk to the door.

There was no handle, but there was a doorbell. It was just camouflage for the release. She hit it and the door slid aside, revealing the perfectly modern airlock that coupled the habitat with the ship towing it.

Salmagard stepped inside. The metal deck shuddered beneath her feet, and she felt a distinct change in the air pressure. The hatch closed behind her.

She crossed the airlock and leaned on the release.

Nothing happened.

The airlock was dead silent.

Behind her, a small world. On either side, metal, and the emptiness of space.

Ahead: absolutely nothing.

They'd locked her in. Salmagard wasn't a breaker; she couldn't beat this electronically. She didn't have breaching tools, and they'd be too dangerous to use in such close quarters regardless.

It had been obvious. Of course they would do this. Inside the habitat, the deception, the dreamworld—there were no rigid security measures there. But this—*this* was the real world. Any ship had this capability. Any hatch could be remotely sealed.

She sagged against the bulkhead, still trying to get her breath, still fighting down the nausea. Her loose hair was plastered to her face by sweat. Her breathing wasn't quite loud enough to drown out the sound of the recycler deactivating.

They were draining the air from the chamber.

23

THE door swung inward.

Cyril stood framed against the light in the hall, looking thoughtful.

I reached over and closed the folding console, leaning back in Cyril's chair. I was in his study on the second floor of the house, behind his desk. It was a beautiful little room, if authentic, extremely detailed nostalgia was what you were into. Paneled walls, paintings with period-appropriate lights attached. Real books on the shelves. The room smelled like leather and paper. There were lots of Evagardians who liked this stuff.

I wasn't one of them.

He leaned against the doorway, folding his arms and gazing at me. He'd loosened his necktie and rolled up his sleeves.

I turned the chair to face him, enjoying the plush leather. Cyril looked tired, and a little cross.

"Did they have chairs like this back then?" I asked, rubbing the leather of the armrest admiringly.

"I think so," he replied.

My eyes fell on the decanter at the edge of the desk.

"Do you mind?"

"Help yourself," he said.

I poured myself a drink and took a sip. It was whiskey, but it tasted like something you'd get in a dive bar on Oasis. But Oasis wasn't around anymore. I wasn't sure where you'd have to go now to get liquor this bad.

"Is this appropriate to the period?" I asked, frowning at the glass.

"I have no idea."

"It's awful."

"That's why it's still full. So everything you said just now was for my benefit."

I shrugged and threw back the rest of the glass. It burned.

"Once I knew this was a ship, it was obvious," I told him, putting the glass aside. "Your people think you know things? You're just a voyeur. If this is a synthetic habitat, then obviously you've got absolute surveillance. That's how you caught me and Sei so fast. The only reason we surprised you is because you weren't looking. And you noticed our friends' ship coming, so you bailed on us in town to look into it. I think I've more or less got it at this point."

Cyril nodded, chewing his lip. "And you pretended to be weak. You knew I was listening. You sent your friends out to wreak havoc on my town, all so you could come up here and get at my console."

"Come on. You're running the show. Of course you're going to have some kind of com at home—you're not going to commute to the ship every time you need to get something done.

I knew it had to be here, but if we started looking for it, you'd have brought your mob in here and stopped us."

"Then I guess your plan worked. What did you do?" He jerked his chin toward the console, disguised as the blotter on the desk.

"I called for help," I said, holding up Salmagard's data crystal. I'd taken it from her pouch when I kissed her. "Something tells me you weren't going to just let her hijack your ship."

"No, I can't let her do that. For some reason."

"I don't blame you."

"You think anyone's going to get here in time to help you?"

"Who can say? It's out of our hands."

"I have to say, this is an unconventional rescue. Two people? They didn't seem very well equipped or prepared either."

"It's complicated," I replied. "I don't know the whole story myself. But I'm right there with you. It's odd."

"I'm surprised you'd send your lady friend out like that."

I smiled. "You think you have anyone that can take her?"

"Military?"

"Obviously. Out there they might be at risk, but at least they're still answerable to themselves. If we just let you fly us into Shangri La, no one even gets a chance."

"You're going to Shangri La either way," Cyril said, waving a hand. "You all are. That is, assuming the ritual fails. Which I, as a largely rational person, can only assume it will."

I raised an eyebrow. "You're still planning to go through with it?"

"Of course. I always deliver what I promise. It's my job. Shangri La is just the backup plan."

"That's why you're still here. Why didn't you just go to the ship and ride it out?"

"When our friend," Cyril said, nodding to a painting depicting another of those squids, "fails to show up after I sacrifice you and your friends, *then* I'll step back and send the townsfolk on their way."

"You think he'll show, then?"

"I won't be around to see one way or the other; my job was to make it happen, not to watch."

"Fair enough. You come off a bit cynical for a spiritual leader."

"It's been a long couple of years. I don't like this kind of role-playing. It tires me out, if we're being honest. I usually get hired to con normal people. People like *this*—it's almost too easy. You'd think this would be relaxing, but it really isn't."

"I know exactly how you feel," I told him.

"You knew your people could never reach the ship," Cyril said, shaking his head. "Nicely done, I suppose."

"I doubt your people could stop them, but you could still lock them out. Which I'm sure you have."

"One hopes," he replied. "Who are you?"

"I think you should give it up."

"Why do you think that?"

"You can let my friends go; then you can take your ship and be gone before the imperials get here. It's the only way."

"By the time they get here I *will* be long gone," Cyril said confidently. "The only signal we've picked up must've been your friends. There's no one else close enough to matter."

"You're underestimating imperial technology," I warned. "And they aren't the only leverage I have."

"Now I'm really curious," Cyril said, brushing imaginary dust from his necktie.

"You're forgetting that you're alone with an Evagardian assassin. Just do what I tell you."

"Is that what you are? I'm actually inclined to believe you." He glanced at his old-fashioned chrono. "I know you were acting downstairs, for them as much as for me. Pretending to be so weak that you couldn't move, so I wouldn't be watching you when you came up here to look for my terminal. But you weren't making it all up. Something's wrong with you. You barely lifted that glass. I don't think you should be threatening anyone."

"Are you sure?"

"I think you're bluffing."

"You think I'm sitting here because I don't have the strength to stand." I put down the glass. "But don't I?"

I got up and leveled my finger at him.

"Walk away," I said.

Cyril wasn't impressed.

"I've seen that drama," he told me frankly. "And while I'm glad you've got some culture, we're already behind schedule." He produced a pistol and trained it on me.

I wavered, catching myself on the desk.

"I knew it," he said, shaking his head. He wiggled the gun, indicating for me to approach. "Let's go. Just relax—you'll be sedated when we bleed you. All of you will."

"That's considerate," I replied. "So this thing you do— helping people out, making things happen. The facilitator job." I made my way around the desk, pausing to lean against it. "How's the money?"

"I get by," he said, eyes flat.

"Do you need an apprenticeship or something to get into that?"

"It's an open market."

"Lots of people out there," I said, looking up. "They all need things."

"Just a matter of knowing how to get them." Cyril shrugged. "It's not an easy life. I can't really recommend it."

"How long have you been pretending to be the shepherd here?"

"Too long. Stop stalling. Let's go." He shrugged. "You won't feel a thing."

"That's reassuring," I said. "I thought you said we were all friends in this community."

"These people aren't evil," Cyril said, gesturing toward the window with the gun. "They just aren't very bright."

"What about the ones that hired you to oversee all this?" I asked.

"They're rich, so they aren't crazy. Just eccentric. Don't make me kill you; we need an even number of bodies for the ritual."

He knew perfectly well I was going to try something. After all, what did I have to lose?

But he didn't know that Salmagard had given me what I needed. I'd said that it took a long time to feel the effects, but I hadn't been telling the truth. Was I strong enough for a marathon? No. Was I strong enough for a fight? No. And I didn't *want* to fight.

But I was strong enough to take Cyril by surprise.

I lunged, knocking aside the pistol and hitting him with everything I had.

Which wasn't much. And Cyril wasn't like the zealots who populated his little community. He knew how to handle himself. Not as well as someone like Salmagard—but he had the advantage of good health, and you can't put a price tag on that.

Of course, even at full strength, my goal wouldn't have been to beat him up. What would that get me? We'd still have to deal with his flock; we'd still be stuck here. I'd gotten the SOS out; the mission had been accomplished. There was nothing left to do but buy time—and if I couldn't buy enough, the altar was waiting.

He caught me and swung me around, slamming me into the wall and hitting me hard in the stomach. Apparently he needed my blood for something, but the rest of me was fair game.

I wasn't really an assassin.

Yes, I had assassinated people—but that still wasn't my job. The Empire had real assassins, men and women whose only role was to kill people. That was a real thing.

But I wasn't one of those. Anyone can kill, but not just anyone can kill, then go onstage and sing and dance in perfect imitation of the man they'd just killed. There was no word for what I was. I was something special, something that fit in somewhere between all the other things.

That should've been a sign, long ago, that I was destined to be erased.

Many of my job skills fell under the rather broad umbrella of espionage, but as much as Deilani had loved calling me a spy, that wasn't exactly accurate either.

I hadn't been joking when I told Salmagard I could consider a career in acting.

Spy, actor, assassin—it didn't matter. At the end of the day, I was one of *those* people. The people who were, at least in theory, serving the interests of the Empress.

And one of those people who couldn't protect himself wasn't any good to anyone.

The Empire didn't care that I didn't like fighting, or that I'd never been any good at it. They'd made sure I wasn't helpless.

That was what made this so frustrating. I knew I could handle someone like Cyril, but my body wouldn't deliver. It couldn't.

I'd had nightmares like this.

Even if my muscles didn't want to work for me, I could still use my weight to my advantage. I wasn't much bigger than Cyril, but every little bit could help. I stayed aggressive, exposing myself to blows that I knew I could take.

We grappled, stumbling into the corridor, where I got the upper hand for a moment, landing the punch I'd been looking forward to ever since I met Cyril. He didn't even fall down. This was sad.

I was glad no one was seeing this. Cyril didn't have the expertise to fight effectively, and I didn't have the strength. Or the desire. In a strange way, we complemented each other.

I was reminded of the sporting fights from Cyril's assumed time period, where the combatants simply battered each other with their fists until one of them fell and didn't get up.

Savagery. Worse, this was pointless. The outcome didn't matter. But I didn't like Cyril very much, and I just wasn't the same person I'd once been. If this had to have a winner, it might as well be me.

I saw my chance and took it near the stairs. I hit him in the abdomen, then in the face with the last of my strength. I wanted to send him staggering back—I wanted him to trip and fall down the steps. Ideally, gravity would do what my body wouldn't, and put Cyril to sleep for a while.

Instead, my pitiful punch had none of the effect I'd hoped

for. He lost his balance, but compensated by grabbing me to keep from falling.

Both of us struck the railing with our full weight. There was a reason civilized people had stopped using wood to build things, in favor of metal and polymer. Wood just wasn't very sturdy.

The banister gave way with a crack, splinters flying.

We both went over into free fall, bypassing the stairs entirely to crash into the front hall some four meters down. It hurt even more than I'd expected it to.

Cyril and I lay in the wreckage, groaning. Above, his fancy light fixture burned my eyes with its harsh yellow glow and all its silly little refracting crystals.

I didn't know what he was thinking, but as I blacked out, I reflected that there had probably been a better way for me to play this.

I just wasn't at my best.

24

SALMAGARD'S hands were tied.

She was riding in the rear seat of a vehicle. There was a strong hand on her shoulder and a restraint across her body strapping her into the seat. She could smell some kind of perfume. She opened her eyes, and there was pain. Pain in her arm, pain in her head. The rest of her body too.

She focused on the big man beside her. He looked nervous, but determined. Seeing that she was awake, he tightened his grip on her.

The town passed on either side. A pillar with spinning red and blue colors flashed by, twirling silently in the night. It was surreal. Complete strangers. An alien antique vehicle.

The state of being a captive. None of it felt real.

There were other vehicles, and people were moving. They were all going in the same direction. Some appeared sleepy and confused, others distressed. A few were injured. Salmagard had been the one to injure some of them.

Many looked excited.

Her head was foggy. She had passed out from oxygen deprivation.

She remembered that the stars overhead weren't real. That she was in a carbon dome, a simple container being pulled through space. For all the loving detail it had been crafted with, this was nothing but a glorified air pocket.

Now the village lay behind them. They were on the winding road to the church, and there were more people walking along the side of the road with hand lights.

There were lights everywhere.

They pulled around the curve to see the church lit up so brightly that it hurt Salmagard's eyes.

People were lined up outside the door. They were all here. All of Cyril's flock.

The driver pulled onto the grass and stopped. The man beside Salmagard held on to her as the door opened, and more hands pulled her out. There were no fewer than three men guiding her.

People got out of the way as they approached the open doors. They looked at Salmagard as if she were a member of a different species. The interior of the church was even brighter. Salmagard had to squint to see the massive, outlandish paintings on the walls and the statue at the front. The pulpit. The altar.

Salmagard was Judeo-Christian. She was familiar with churches, but she'd never seen one this small, and never one this strange.

Diana and Sei were already at the front of the sanctuary, their hands bound, just like hers. Salmagard could feel a muting strip on her throat. Before all this, Salmagard had never thought of herself as having much to say—but she'd taken her voice for granted.

They marched her down the aisle to join the others.

Diana looked dazed and vacant; they'd probably already used chems on her to keep her weak and docile. She was bleeding from her head and looked generally battered. Sei wasn't much better off.

So they had been able to take down Diana in the end. Impressive. These people weren't strong, but they were resourceful.

Sei was looking questioningly at Salmagard. She gave a small shake of her head. She had failed, after all.

He swallowed, turning to the altar.

People were talking, but the sounds were hushed. It was a gentle murmur behind them, like a soft breeze. The church's interior did funny things to sound.

Minutes went by. The three of them gazed at the altar. There was nothing to do at this point but make their peace. It looked like that was what Sei was doing, but it couldn't have been any easier for him than it was for Salmagard.

Everyone in the Service was ready to die for the Empress or, if they were the sort that didn't believe in the Empress personally, for the Empire. For Evagardian society, the greatest and most enlightened way of life to come of all humanity. An achievement of staggering power and beauty. At least, that was the way the Imperium presented it.

But that wasn't what was going to happen here. They weren't dying for the Empress at all.

The talking quieted a little, but it didn't go away. The men hovering nearby didn't say anything, but nerves were thick in the air, and so was excitement.

Salmagard's mouth was dry, and she could feel her EV trying to slow her heartbeat. It was working. Everything was slowing down. She was crashing from the stim Price had given her, crashing from the beating her body had taken, crashing from the day she'd had. She didn't mind.

Anything to get away from her thoughts. She wanted a distraction, but even her broken arm wasn't enough.

There was a small commotion behind them, and Salmagard turned to look, but the men pushed back, keeping her facing the strange circular altar.

The noise level in the church rose somewhat, and she could hear people approaching.

The Admiral appeared beside her, his situation identical to her own. His hands were bound, and there was a muting strip on his throat as well. He looked like he'd taken a beating. But he'd been helpless; why had they done this?

Then she saw Cyril, who looked even worse than the Admiral. A makeshift bandage stood out white over his nose. One of his eyes was swelling shut.

Grimacing, he walked past them and up the steps.

Salmagard stared at the Admiral and realized he was standing under his own power. Something—something wasn't right.

He gave her a look, and she wasn't sure what to make of it. Was it a strange sort of smile?

Did he have something up his sleeve? Salmagard didn't understand. She tried desperately to put it together, but something was missing. She was in the dark.

Cyril took his place at the podium and leaned on it heavily. They could hear his ragged breathing clearly over the amplifier.

"Well," he said, and the church fell abruptly silent. "Friends, this has been an eventful evening. Some of you know what's going on; some of you don't. We've been honored by a visit from

the imperial authorities, despite the fact that we're not in Evagardian space and they have no grounds to accost us. I know
some of you are distressed by everything that's happened, but
I've just been told that though Joy's infirmary is very crowded
right now, there were no fatalities. I know this all must seem very
shocking, but I think that detail—in and of itself—sends us a
clear message."

That seemed to send a ripple through the congregation.

"Yes, imperials came here with hostile intent, but didn't manage to kill anyone? The same butchers that have cut such a
bloody swath through history. I don't know." Cyril shrugged
theatrically. "Sounds a bit off to me. You could be forgiven for
feeling like, you know, maybe someone's looking out for us."

There were cheers. Salmagard cringed. Cyril went on.

"We're not soldiers, friends. I truly can't tell you why the
imperials have taken such an interest in us. I suppose we could
find out by asking, but I don't think they'd tell us. And it
wouldn't be our way to compel them to speak. Does anyone
here want to torture someone? Show of hands."

No one moved.

Cyril nodded. "I'm with you. It doesn't matter what their
reasons are. Maybe their Empress doesn't like competition.
Doesn't matter. In a few minutes, it's not going to be an issue."

There was more cheering. Cyril waited patiently for it to
die down.

"Have a little mercy on the shepherd, won't you?" He smiled.
"They came at me in my own house. I haven't hit another person
since . . . since I was just a boy. I'd like to go see Joy myself,"
he added sheepishly. "But there's no time for that. We're moving things forward a bit, friends. Why? Because these people

are dangerous. I'm not arrogant enough to think we can keep them in this state. Trying to detain them until the appointed time would put you all at risk. They could escape or something could go wrong, and I'm not willing to chance even one fatality."

The cheering and applause were quieter this time. Salmagard was clenching the fingers of her good hand so tightly that they felt like they might snap. These people didn't even think to question Cyril. He had their absolute trust.

"And that's all there is to it," he said. "I'm going to get cleaned up. I know some of our primaries were sidelined during the confusion tonight, so understudies need to get dressed and step up. And Joy should be here—she should be able to put us at ease about the good health of our brothers and sisters who were injured—and then we're going to proceed after she puts our guests to sleep. So if you're participating, start getting ready now. If not, be patient. We begin in . . ."

Cyril trailed off, looking troubled.

The air behind him shimmered and a man in white armor materialized.

In an instant, chaos.

More men in white appeared. No one in the congregation knew what to do; every figure in white carried a rifle. A woman screamed, and Salmagard's heart leapt.

It was the GRs, just like in the dramas. They were everywhere, deactivating their camouflage to step out of the air like magic. They were forcing the congregation to their knees, taking control unbelievably fast—and all without firing a shot.

How were they here? How was this possible? No one had called for help. Salmagard didn't understand. Had they just gotten lucky? Had these men just happened to catch up just in time?

She turned to the Admiral in disbelief, but he was gazing at the stone altar.

It was a longing gaze.

Salmagard opened her mouth, but she couldn't speak. She moved toward him, and this time no one stopped her—but with her hands tied behind her back, what could she do? She'd entertained certain thoughts as she ran through the night earlier, but now that was all a jumble. The blood pounded in her ears, amplified by her forced silence.

The Admiral looked away from the altar long enough to meet her gaze. His eyes were open, but whatever he was seeing, it wasn't Salmagard. It was like she wasn't even there.

The man near the podium with Cyril spotted the Admiral and moved quickly, dragging Cyril along. He forced Cyril to the ground, bound his hands in a flash, and hurried down from the stage, touching his ear.

"I've got him," he said, shoving Salmagard roughly out of the way and leaning in on the Admiral, probably giving whoever was watching his feed a good look at his face. "It's him. There's no doubt."

Now the Admiral noticed Salmagard. He smiled.

She couldn't take her eyes off him. She tried to move forward, to get between the Admiral and the operative, but a female GR held her back.

"I copy," said the man in white.

Another man materialized, forcing a black veil over the Admiral's head. More of them moved forward, grabbing him and hauling him into the aisle.

He didn't resist.

Salmagard pulled free of the woman, but her hands were still tied. And even if they hadn't been, what then?

It was one thing to think it. It was something else with the GRs right in front of her—but they weren't GRs. Now that Salmagard was looking, she could see that. They were imperials, but they weren't Galactic Rescue. The armor and equipment were all wrong.

They looked more like some kind of strike team.

Salmagard wasn't kidding herself. She'd been trained to calculate the odds. Even with her hands free, even with the stars aligned in her favor, what could she do?

Nothing.

They were dragging the Admiral away swiftly, one of them keeping the muzzle of a pistol pressed to his neck. More of the armored men moved in to control him. They weren't taking any chances. They were treating him as if they expected him to be as dangerous as . . . someone like Diana.

But he was cooperating.

Salmagard knew there was no point, but she struggled with the ties around her wrists. She pulled with everything she had, even though the pain in her arm was almost enough to make her pass out. She couldn't even ask someone to free her; she couldn't speak. She couldn't make a sound.

No one was paying attention to her. Not even Sei or Diana. There was a medic with Diana, looking her over, and Sei hovered fearfully beside her.

Salmagard was completely alone in the crowded church. There was plenty of noise now, but she didn't hear any of it. As if she were standing in her very own dampening field.

The Evagardian agents had the Admiral halfway down the aisle. The others were corralling the congregation. A man made a grab for a rifle, and the armored man holding it just pushed him to the ground and held him down, tying his hands.

Cyril was in front of the altar, looking helpless and disbelieving. He knew he wasn't going anywhere. There was a man at his side, with one hand on his shoulder, and the other touching his helmet. He was talking to someone over the com.

Reporting that they had the ship and the Admiral under control.

Salmagard pulled harder, and the world went out of focus. The pain intensified, and she ignored it, but she had found her limit. She stumbled and fell to her knees.

The medic noticed her and scrambled over. "You're all right," he said, pressing a hypo of painkillers into her neck. "We know what you did here. You did good work. You're all right. You're going to be fine. We're here now. We've got you."

The men and women in white pulled the Admiral out of the sanctuary.

"You're safe," the medic said.

And the doors slammed shut.

Photo by S. Morris

Sean Danker has been writing novels since he was fifteen. He's a U.S. Air Force veteran, and he enjoys cooking, painting, and playing the piano.

CONNECT ONLINE

evagard.com
twitter.com/silverbaytimes